The Last Diner

Edited by Theresa Derwin

First Published in Great Britain in 2014 by

KnightWatch Press

ISBN: 978-1-909573-18-5

Published by KnightWatch Press.

This edition published 2014.

Conditions of sale

Cover art by Stephen Cooney

Cover Design by David R Shires

Contents

The Last Diner - APPETISER by Theresa Derwin_1

All You Can Eat by Stewart Hotston_____3

Inversion by Chris Amies_____19

The Treatment by Jay Wilburn_____37

Famished by Elaine Pascale_____57

Made from Locally Sourced Ingredients
by James Brogden_____71

Rocky Says Hi! by Lizz-Ayn Shaarawi_____93

The Critic by Richard Freeman_____107

Johnny G's All-Nite Diner by Jack Maddox_____115

The Last Supper by Steph Ellis_____131

Demons Drink Free by Shenoa Carroll-Bradd_____145

Small Sacrifices by Matthew Pegg_____157

McMurder, McBurger by Sarah Gibbel_____165

Having A Drink by T. T. Trestle_____177

Acquired Taste by William Holden_____197

The Fine Print by Rebecca Snow_____217

Big Night by Jason Norton_____231

Leftovers by Daniel Hale_____251

A Real Slice of Americana by Lisamarie Lamb_____267

A Good Bit of Crackling by Stewart Hotston_____283

Biographies_____299

To my Dave, my Thorin
Oakenshield, My Thor, I copvilate
you

The Last Diner - APPETISER
By Theresa Derwin

" So you're from Great Britain huh? Lived there once. Food was small."

Yep, whether you're a US resident, a Brit, or a food critic from Osaka, each town, city and country has its own culinary culture. In Britain it's Fish 'n' Chips or Pie 'n' Mash, America, pancakes and bacon with maple syrup, and in Osaka it's octopus. But wherever you've eaten, we've all been there; the restaurant or eating establishment that you remember forever because it gave you nightmares or food poisoning.

I used to be a Mystery Diner; you know what I mean? Where you go along to a café or restaurant, order at least three courses, pay the bill then make your report to the Powers that Be! Luckily for me I enjoyed most of my experiences, but it isn't always a memorable meal for the *right* reasons.

I know Chef Jamie Oliver says 'A liittle bit of dirt doesn't hurt' as he shakes mud off his garden-grown herbs before chucking them in a saucepan, but what if it was *more* than a little bit of dirt you were being fed? What if that mystery ingredient was a mystery because it couldn't be found in your local supermarket - on planet Earth that is?

In The Last Diner, I have collected together nineteen short stories set in or around eateries, where unnamed horrors lurk. From the insatiable appetite in 'All You Can Eat' by Stewart Hotston, to a totalitarian city ruler who wants the services of a famous baker in 'Inversion'. From a Diner cook who likes to give his customers the 'special treatment' and a case where curiosity, and the need for a late night burger, killed the cat, this is just the beginning of an anthology that will make you laugh, cringe, possibly vomit up your last meal and shudder.

From freegan restaurants, to burger joints, diners, five star establishments and the basement of a usurper's palace, the eateries presented her span the globe from the dingy to the deluxe. I hope you enjoy partaking of this refreshing collection, and I can certainly guarantee you one thing; you won't forget your meal at 'The Last Diner' in a hurry.

All You Can Eat
By Stewart Hotston

Warm tungsten light bathed Tinsel Town, shutting out the cold, dark early morning. The staff who worked there would often, on a quiet midweek night, stand at the sheet glass windows that fronted the restaurant and comfort themselves in the reflected illumination.

Tonight, a Wednesday in the coldest March in living memory, had started like so many others recently with the drunken but peckish crowd rolling out of the door at about midnight. As with most of London, the street on which Tinsel Town could be found was never completely settled as people worked all the hours capitalism could provide for them with a perpetual indifference to other, minor, regulatory systems like the sun or tiredness. Still, the quietest hours were between midnight and two when the drinking crowd had gone home but before the clubs had kicked out their myriad tribes of pierced, tattooed, alternatively minded accountants, teachers and lawyers. A profoundly average post office distribution centre sat around the corner which brought in a few night owls for coffee and scrambled egg before work started, but they never arrived before half two.

During these hours the three employees on shift that night, chosen from an ever churning roster of up to eight souls, would first wipe down the tables, reset the cutlery and eventually, after the paper napkins had been rearranged a second time, find themselves a seat, pour a cup of tea while trying to convince themselves that the presence of the other two was a sign they weren't alone. Some of the trios would chat, talking shit inspired by whatever the tabloid papers had to say; not all of what was said was ironic but there were enough degrees among the waiting staff to avoid the worst excesses of ignorance and resentment becoming fixations. Others would sit in silence, trying not to look at each other - the proximity of two other tired people enough to create the solidarity they sought. Occasionally the corporation, who had imported the idea of an all night American diner into northwest London after an off-site brainstorming session in the early hours in Vegas, would somehow conspire to employ a loner. They never stopped long. Regardless of the hours, the quiet times and the lack of other scrutiny, the restaurant's staff were a family as much as the modern world could make space for. Squint eyed silent types were repelled by the sense of acceptance that radiated from the very furniture as certainly as if their own mothers had decided to bring them a warm thermos and a change of socks while asking if they had made any new friends.

The three in that night were Morena, Fergus and Krishna. Krishna was a trained curry chef from Bangalore who had fallen out with his brother a week after arriving in Hackney to cook for him. He now fried eggs, bread and mushrooms instead. Morena thought he approached it with a kind of zen although Krishna pointed out he didn't believe in that shit for the same reason he didn't eat beef.

Fergus, ostensibly the manager by virtue of having to cash up and make sure the tips were handed out fairly, was holding an email printout. "'Eat all you can' it says," he said, summarising the instructions from the regional manager.

"We're not a bloody buffet," said Morena.

"We could do a buffet," said Krishna thoughtfully, dreams of korma and puri, bhaji and laddoo steaming in trays as people dipped their heads in raptures of gastronomic delight popping into his head.

"No," said Fergus firmly, his ginger hair gelled so tightly that it didn't wobble even as he shook his head.

"So how do we do that then?" asked Morena.

"Will we let them order and then order again?" said Krishna.

"They'll be allowed to order everything they believe they can eat in one go. Wasted food will have to be paid for in addition to everything they eat. Of course, everything they eat will just have one price."

"What?" said Morena.

"They order and pay one price. If they waste any food then we charge them an additional amount depending on how many whole dishes they waste."

"What if they have just one bite from each dish?" asked Krishna.

"Shut up," said Fergus.

"Well I'm not collecting extra money from people who waste our food," announced Morena with an expression that Fergus thought would have most people offering to pay just to avoid any trouble. He didn't mention it because, in the end, life is just too short to piss off a twenty-something girl with five older brothers.

"What if they finish everything and want more?" asked Krishna, unable to let it go until he'd thought through everything properly.

"Then they get to have more," said Fergus far more confidently than he actually felt. The last thing he wanted was to have some fat pleb come in and scoff all their stock for just £9.99. He looked again at the email; there was no expiry date or discretion to stop orcas settling in and ruining their takings.

"They'll come like zombies." said Fergus to the other two as he put the sign in the window advertising the deal, "they'll sense it through their failing pancreas, pancreatic...

what is the plural of pancreas?" The other two shook their heads and looked everywhere but at him. "It doesn't matter," he said, "the point is. The point is we'll have them crawling out of the sewers to come here at 3 am and eat our bacon, egg and sausages with toast and tea until they explode or we run out of food."

Morena shrugged, "as long as they tip."

"They won't tip," said Krishna sadly. "You British don't tip. Tipping is like admitting there might be value in what you've consumed and you never, ever admit that something you paid full price for was worth it."

"Thanks for the pep talk Alistair Cooke." said Fergus. "Now, why don't you get in the kitchen and warm the urn, the first of the living dead is outside."

Krishna started as he saw another Asian face in the window. It belonged to a shortish, balding man with a neat black goatee and a solid gut that, although not fat, had taken some serious eating to nurture and maintain. The man stepped back from the window where his face had been pressed like some insane ghoul and found the door.

"Hey, how are you?" he asked as he came in. There was no discernible accent and Krishna, who was hovering near enough to listen was immediately jealous of this Bangladeshi who could speak English like a native, who had the chance to be one of them with no questions asked.

Morena bounced up, "Hi." She twirled, her arm encompassing the sweep of the diner, "anywhere you want tonight."

"Great. Your sign says all you can eat?"

Morena stopped her fluttering and looked at Fergus who, in turn, rolled his eyes. "Er. Yes. Menu's on the table."

Their diner was wearing biker's clothes, the thick

black padded jacket open to the waist and a smart shirt was visible underneath. The jacket came off and Morena was impressed enough by the silver hourglass cuff links that she guessed he was a city type, just finished for the day and trying to get a meal in before the grind started all over again.

"Tough day?" she asked as she brought cutlery and an empty glass over.

"You have no idea," he said jovially.

"I'm Morena and I'll be your waitress today."

"Hi Morena, I'm Bobby. Can you bring me some bread while I'm looking at the menu? How does this deal work then?"

Morena explained about ordering whatever he wanted, "Just don't over do it because then we'll have to charge you for what you don't eat."

"Right," said Bobby. "Whatever, I'm just glad London has somewhere open at this time. New York, you can walk down the street at 4 in the morning and get pizza, Chinese, Korean, curry. Anything you want."

"You're from New York?"

"Lived there a while when the going was good," said Bobby. Morena thought hard about why the going might have been good once but not so now and distant news reports of financial crashes hovered like clouds on the edge of her memory.

"Investment Banker?" she asked.

He looked down at his shirt, "That obvious huh? Yeah, I like to say that I had two good years and then it all went to shit. Managed to escape the Fed and get back here. Originally from Stockport."

"Oh," said Morena, who had no idea about any of the cities north of St Albans. She had heard of Manchester, Leeds and Glasgow but couldn't tell you for sure which one was furthest east or if only one of them was in Scotland. She didn't regard this state of affairs as a problem that needed addressing.

"You? You must be from Brasil," said Bobby with an eye fixed appraisingly on her face.

She smiled, "Close enough." A slight sheen glistened across his forehead in the yellow light, "Is everything all right?"

"Just hungry," said Bobby matter-of-factly.

"I'll be right back," said Morena who remembered his request for some bread and butter. "Brown or white?"

"White." He read the menu quickly, placed it back between the salt and pepper shakers, then sat back as far as the rigid plastic chair would allow and tapped his fingers on the table.

Fergus was totting up the receipts from the homeward bound that had passed through prior to 2 am. He'd already done it once, but with only one customer there was nothing else for him to do. If it had been a woman he might have tried to find a segue into the situation but the diner's gaze lingered on Morena long enough for Fergus to know there was no point in him even opening his mouth.

Krishna was at action stations, griddle simmering, knife in hand. He was stood by the walk in fridge like an athlete under starter's orders. The others might not care about this deal but he was determined to cook such quantities of food that the little Bangladeshi would tell his friends. He could see by the man's clothes that he was someone of means; someone who had made something of themselves. He wondered if the man's mother was proud of him, if he sent money home or if she was already here in England.

Bobby looked up and down the menu. It wasn't that he didn't know what he wanted, rather he was having difficulty in knowing what to order first. He rubbed at his goatee. "I'll start with the chicken with two portions of fries, onion rings and a stack of three pancakes. They are proper corn flour pancakes yeah?"

Morena nodded, "we're a proper American diner in the heart of old England."

"Yeah. Right," said Bobby who was thinking of the size of American portions and remembering that the only large serving on London menus were the prices.

"How do you want your chicken - legs or breast?"

"A whole chicken," said Bobby without looking up from the menu.

"Um," said Morena and he looked up at her, "You will have to pay for what you don't eat."

"I'll then have some eggs, four, soft yolk or they're going right back. With the eggs I want more toast, number 34 twice, you know, the deep fried ribs with chilli flakes. Not BBQ sauce." His eyes lit up, "The king prawns; are they big?"

"I guess." said Morena uncertainly - she'd had no idea there were different sizes - surely the point of King prawns were that they were the largest.

"Twenty of them then, mayo on the side and half a lemon too." He looked around, "I'll need napkins."

"Anything else?" she asked, not quite sure what other food group he hadn't touched.

"Water please. Just tap water."

Morena noted the tap water down and showed the order to Fergus and Krishna who had gathered together to watch as Bobby's ordering had taken on epic proportions.

Krishna looked at the order; it would be a challenge to get everything out together. His heart beat a little faster as he started pulling out the pieces that would take the longest to prepare and cook. Fergus and Morena stood looking at the order sheet and then back up at the small man who had demanded a meal with enough calories to feed a family of six.

"I only have one question," said Fergus solemnly. "How the hell will all that food fit in such a small man?"

"It's not like he's some sort of grotesque American is it?" said Morena.

"You know the real fat ones are like the opposite of anorexics; they all say it's a lifestyle choice. Two sides of the same coin."

"That's horrible," said Morena. She left him gawping at Bobby to help Krishna. One day she wanted to be running her own kitchen and cooking fine dining. Tinsel Town was a crappy start but Krishna was an amazing chef. Since she'd been there he'd taught her to go from making burnt toast to cooking Hake three ways with a curried pea puree and celeriac and coriander foam. She kept trying to convince him to go on the television but he was too shy to do it even though the idea of winning would gleam in his eyes. Success was someone else's dream.

Bobby ate nine slices of bread before the first of his food was ready. Morena hardly noticed the first three - she would look over at the table to see his side plate was clean and Bobby gazing hungrily in her direction. After the sixth slice she found a spot where she could watch him from the corner of her eyes - it was like he sucked the food in, barely chewing before swallowing and taking bites that made her think of a horse eating sugar cubes.

The roast chicken, fries and onion rings came out first on a large steel tray. Bobby helped Morena unload the dishes and then, before she had stepped away, ripped the chicken apart with his bare hands. "Have you got those napkins?" he asked as he shoved the soft white flesh of a breast into his mouth.

He devoured the chicken and fries, stopping occasionally for a sip of water. Fergus, who positioned himself behind the till, was struck by the man's intensity. There didn't seem to be any order in which he tackled the food put in front of him. When the prawns were put down he was still chewing on the pancakes with maple syrup and butter; he simply ignored them until he had polished off the last of the stack.   However, he ate just two prawns before sucking the batter off the one remaining onion ring, dipping the strip in an egg yolk and feeding it in between his lips as if it were spaghetti. Fergus was relieved he ate with his mouth closed even if the speed with which he shovelled the food in meant there weren't many moments in which he was contemplatively chewing.

He mopped up the prawns, picked over one last scraggly rib and leaned back in his chair with a satisfied sigh. All three of them were in awe at the display of focussed and unrelenting appetite. Morena gave him a moment and sauntered over, "Do you want any pudding?" she asked smugly.

"I'm not really a dessert man," said Bobby ruefully, "But. I *could* eat." He looked askance at the 'all you can eat' sign. "So I think I'll have some more ribs, chicken wings, fried and with BBQ sauce this time. I'd also like some gammon with a couple of pineapple rings." He smiled conspiratorially, "they're the best bit!" She wrote it all down, her fingers working automatically while her mind processed the shock of what he was actually ordering. "Two fish finger sandwiches, the fish and chips. No mushy peas though. Oooh, hash browns, yeah I'll have some of them too."

Fergus stopped Morena on her way into the kitchen, fear and consternation competing for control of his face. "What the hell is he doing?!"

"He's eating all he can Fergus," said Morena.

"I fucking told you. Didn't I tell you? I told you," said Fergus.

"Where is he putting it?" asked Krishna.

"Uh, in his mouth," said Morena.

"I mean, where does such capacity come from? He is like Ganesh or a Preta," said Krishna earnestly, showing no sign that he'd recognised her sarcasm for what it was.

"I don't give a shit what mate of yours he's like," said Fergus. "This is it. No more after this."

"He won't eat dessert," said Morena, grinning even as she tried to sound consoling.

Bobby wasn't done. When he had sucked the last morsel of flesh from the last chicken wing and wiped the plate clean with their very last slice of bread he waved Morena over, picking the menu up as she approached. "I think I'll have a cheese and mushroom omelette. Better make it half a dozen eggs. Cheddar and American cheese please. Also, I'd like some mac and cheese on the side - although I want a full sized portion. I'd also like some more water."

Morena wrote down his order. "You've eaten all our bread," she said when she saw him rolling the surviving crumbs under his fingertips.

"You can run out and get some more right?" he said cheerfully.

Morena didn't answer. Instead she found Fergus, who was hovering at the entrance to the kitchen, and showed him the order.

"Holy shit," said Fergus. "The fat scrote is going to eat ten times the cost of his meal."

"If he stops *now* that is," said Krishna thoughtfully.

"He can't keep going," said Fergus desperately.

"And yet he does," said Morena. "He wants more bread."

"He's eaten all of it?" asked Fergus.

"We only had two loaves left," said Morena as if it were the most ordinary act she'd witnessed that night.

"Only two loaves?" Fergus' face gradually turned a bright and furious red. Morena picked up her bag to go buy more bread, leaving Krishna to start cooking the omelette.

Morena was gone for five minutes — to a small 24 hour off license a hundred metres up the street. She could hear the shouting before she reached the back door of the restaurant.

"Your sign says all you can eat man. You cannot be serious!"

"I've told you, you've had all you're going to get. There is no more."

"What is this? I can't believe you're stiffing me on this." Morena pushed her way into the kitchen to find Krishna peering through a crack in the swing door. She gave him a look.

"They're arguing in circles. The guest asked for another chicken."

"Wow," said Morena, genuinely impressed.

"Mr Fergus is saying that he has to pay and get out. He has banned him from ever coming here again."

"I've been waiting for a place like this my whole life," said Bobby. "You have no idea just how hungry I am." Morena felt a shiver run down her spine as he spoke.

"He is a spirit who committed some great act against his dharma in the past," said Krishna solemnly. He saw Morena looking at him blankly, "He died with very bad Karma and the man you see out there is walking this world never able to satisfy his hunger."

Morena peered through the gap in the doorway herself, "He doesn't like what Fergus is saying." When there was no response Morena looked around to see that Krishna was emptying out one of the stores.

"What are you doing?" she asked.

Krishna lifted a box of lettuces from the floor of the cupboard. "He will never be satisfied Morena. He will go from here hungry. There is nothing he cannot eat."

"Are you telling me he's some sort of psycho?" she asked with narrowed eyes.

"No. I do not think so." he shoved a six-pack of ketchup onto a work surface then stepped into the now empty closet. "He is no more evil than a roast chicken. He is hungrier than a beggar watching a rich man's feast. It is too late already." With this, he pulled the door to, and was gone from sight.

A roar came from the dining room, "I am hungry!" It sounded to Morena like a gorilla had taken up residence. She took one last look at the cupboard and stepped into the lounge. Bobby was sweating, his eyes open and bulging. He breathed quickly in shallow gasps. In front of him, his back to her, stood Fergus, hands up defensively. Bobby had a chair in his hands.

"Where is my dinner?!" shouted Bobby, seeming taller than when he had come in.

"Look," said Fergus. "I may have been hasty. You can come back but we won't be doing all you can eat in future." Management could go jump as far as he was concerned.

"You haven't done all you can eat now!" shouted Bobby.

"Mate," said Fergus, his tone as mollifying as he could make it. "You've got to see this from my point of view. I'm here to run a business. As it happens I love food too and I love feeding people - call it a vocation - but I can't let you bankrupt me or get me into trouble with head office just because you've got the appetite of a hippo."

"Whatever." said Bobby dismissively. A stream of half heard Bangladeshi curses issued like pellets from his mouth. Morena was about to approach and clear away the last of the dishes when Bobby suddenly had Fergus by both arms. She screamed.

"Fooking let me go you silly twat," said Fergus, his voice rising in panic.

"I'm hungry," said Bobby and his mouth opened. Morena bumped up against a table. She realised she had been backing away. She stood in silence as Bobby's mouth distended and his jaw dislocated itself; it was half a foot from top to bottom when Fergus began squirming but Bobby's grip held him completely firm.

"Help me Morena!" he shouted, "call the old bill!" Morena stood in unmoving silence, her mind frozen, as Bobby's mouth continued to lengthen. The teeth grew in size coming to resemble an open sewing box of needles and pins.

"Oh my god," she whispered when Bobby's maw smoothly enveloped a screaming, pleading Fergus and bit his head along with the top half of his torso off as easily as he'd sucked the flesh from the chicken wings earlier. Blood squirted from lips the size of marrows as his mouth closed and returned to its normal, human size. The legs tottered for a moment, as if unsure what was expected of them, then fell to the floor in a red slick of pale intestines, bone and flesh.

Bobby found the last of the BBQ sauce he'd been served and poured it over the steaming remains. With a sweep of one arm he lifted the bottom half of Fergus into the air and popped it into his cavernous maw. There was a crunch of bones breaking followed by a burp that shook the windows. Now Bobby looked at Morena, "I am hungry," he growled.

Morena pushed back against the table but it was screwed into the floor. Bobby looked cross with himself, almost disappointed as he approached. "You won't fill me up," he said absently.

"Don't eat me then," said Morena but Bobby wasn't listening; he was ready for his dinner. The first bite tore through her chest, taking off her head and one arm. He pulled a tibia from his mouth and used it to collect a mass of long black hair that was tangled around his teeth. "No finesse." he said. The rest of the waitress was dismembered limb by limb and eaten as he had tackled the ribs; he held the ends, turning them this way and that as he tore the flesh with his mouth. The blood was warm, wet. From his hiding place in the kitchen, Krishna could hear the smacking of lips and the sucking of fingers. He prayed and asked that he had done enough to find a better life the next time around.

The door to the closet opened to show Bobby's

bulbous eyes looking down at Krishna's crouching form. "I'm sorry."

"It is ok my lord," said the chef, "It is your way."

"The sign," said Bobby apologetically. "It promised me something I have long sought for. He bared his teeth in frustration." Krishna saw tusks in that face, the shadow of a trunk and heard the squeak of a mouse from under the vegetable cooler. "People should not make promises like that."

"How were we to know?" said Krishna gently.

Bobby looked at him with sorrow in his eyes, "I am supposed to be wise and knowledgeable Krishna. I am supposed to know these things, not get tricked every time I visit these godless people."

Krishna smiled, at least he was known by name. "There is more to eat once you are done." he said, waving at the food all around the kitchen.

"Thank you." said Bobby and, delicately, with great care, swallowed the man whole.

Inversion
By Chris Amies

The city of Malyzan nestles in rock at the head of a valley whose reddish stone gives the city its colour. Houses, granaries, schools and temples, all built close together and atop one another, cascade down to a red-brown river, and at the upper end of the city stands the Tower in Air, on top of its rocky pinnacle, reached only by a closely guarded stairway.

Azmand lived alone, his wife departed and his children grown to adulthood. In his little apartment there were often visitors and there was conversation and laughter and strong coffee and cakes; for Azmand made bread and cakes, and he and his friends loved all these things. Also they loved books, and Azmand could often be glimpsed on his balcony with a volume of poetry, consulting the lines to give him guidance for the coming day.

This morning as Azmand sat on his balcony the eastern sky was a delicate shade of pale pink and orange. The streets below were almost empty, very unlike his younger years when it would have been thronging with life even this early. These years there was a different atmosphere. Much was forbidden, much was dangerous to do or even think.

The only life he could see was a dark-clad figure swinging itself up from a ledge and climbing onto a rooftop. He smiled. As the figure drew closer, to the edge of the roof opposite, he could see a familiar face and dark eyes.

The dark figure ran to the corner of the building, hopped across, and in no time at all was lowering herself onto Azmand's balcony from his roof.

"And a very good morning to you, Afi," Azmand said.

"Hi," Afi said, grinning. "That was fun."

"I'd be careful if I were you," Azmand said. "People might mistake you for something you aren't."

"Oh, they always do that," Afi said, entering the apartment.

A moment later she emerged onto the balcony nibbling at a peach whose colours, Azmand noted, were those of the eastern sky at this precise moment.

"How are you this beautiful morning? And how is my daughter?" Azmand asked.

"I'm good and Dena's fine," Afi said. "Still asleep when I left. Sometimes I despair of her. Late nights, in the staircases and towers. She misses the sunrise." She wiped peach juice from her chin and came and stood by Azmand looking out at the block opposite and the sky above it.

"They don't bother me," she whispered. "The guards, I mean. They have other things to care about. And even if they look down from the Tower in Air it doesn't concern them. This is all a jail to them. Every bit of it."

Afi vanished into the bathroom and a while later Azmand could hear her splashing about.

True, Azmand thought. He has made this city into a prison.

Azmand did not like to even think the name.

Azmand knew two things about the new ruler.

The man had stolen the throne from Parand, the Silken Queen. Stolen it and slaughtered her and her generals and condemned a people to imprisonment in their own city.

And he ruled from a room of pain.

Afi issued from the bathroom wrapped in a towel and

began to dry herself vigorously. Azmand sat politely facing the other way, while the girl kept up conversation.

"What did your poet say this morning?" she asked.

How shall we capture

The lions in the desert?

Be sure when you go to take them

that they do not take you.

You can not eat a lion.

The reverse is not true.

There was a rustling behind Azmand as Afi dressed.

"How do you catch the lions in the desert? Trust your poet not to give us an answer," Afi mused. She came and sat next to Azmand on the couch, smelling of lemon water and youth and vigour.

"How indeed?" Azmand asked. "Will you stay for breakfast? I have made fresh rolls and the most delicious of cinnamon cakes, though I say so myself."

"Ah, always food," Afi said. "I would love to, thank you."

"It's my trade," Azmand said.

"Indeed it is," Afi replied. "I wonder that you aren't a fat man. Did you used to do a bit of climbing yourself in your youth, I wonder?"

"Nothing like you do," Azmand said.

"But as to the lions in the desert," Afi said, leaning slightly against him. "What if the cage were built so that it encompassed the desert entirely? What then? You have trapped the lions."

"A shame," Azmand said, "to turn the desert into a cage."

"True," Afi said. She smiled up at him. Azmand thought, *my daughter sees that lovely smile all the time.*

"But also," Afi went on, "what a shame to trap a lion.

"Malyzan used to be a crossroads of the world," she said. "People travelled here and sometimes stayed, and those who came brought ideas from all over. Now look at it."

***

When she had gone Azmand spread out his papers and ledgers and started to take stock of the week's business. He had not been at his desk for long when there came a hammering on his chamber door.

"Someone's in a hurry," he murmured. One of two things, he thought, or rather two versions of one thing: someone's in trouble, and they are on one side of the door, or the other. Until I open the door I really can't tell.

Azmand was not short, but when he opened the door he had to look upwards into the granite-hard faces of the two men on the doorstep. They were dressed in black robes and wore close-fitting grey caps.

"Good morning," he said.

"Are you Azmand?" one of them asked.

"I can make you a poultice for that sore throat," Azmand said.

"I have no sore throat," the man said. "Are you Azmand?"

"He answered our question," the other man said, "really."

"Many people can make poultices," the first man said. "My grandmother for example. Are you Azmand?"

"I am," Azmand said. "How is your grandmother, by the way? I may have known her if she was in that line of business."

"Do not attempt to make small talk," said the second man. "Come with us. You are required by our master, the ruler of Malyzan."

"I see," said Azmand.

"Come with us," the first guard said.

Azmand did.

***

With a guard each side, Azmand ascended the stone staircase to the Tower in Air. Closer to it, it was larger than he would have believed; *surely a trick*, he thought. It cannot hold up by natural means.

Then Azmand was dragged into the Tower and borne into the throne room.

The throne room was a low-roofed space carved out of rock. The floor was marked with lines of burnished brass; copper lamps gave light in the places where the low rectangular windows did not. There was a throne against the back wall. It was made of some kind of grey-white material, possibly ivory, Azmand thought. *Possibly* ivory. Quite likely not. Indeed as he looked more closely it became clear that a smaller animal than elephants had been used. It was upholstered in pale leather.

On the throne sat a figure dressed in grey. His face was sharp and fox-like, his hair red, and his green eyes stared at Azmand.

"Azmand!" the Usurper said, "I have set up the

chamber below my room of throne as a tavern where my generals and my ministers may dine. And because I am a benevolent master, I plan a banquet."

"You are most kind," Azmand said.

The Usurper frowned.

A bolt of pain shot through Azmand from arsehole to head, bouncing around in his brain for a while. When Azmand's eyeballs had stopped vibrating and his breath was back to normal, the Usurper said, "Do not be sarcastic. My dear mama told me that the correct response to sarcasm was a punch in the face, as sarcasm is an attempt to undermine your reality. I prefer to use my talent for pain. And you will address me as Your Grace."

And another flicker of agony danced through Azmand's wrists and fingers, reminding him of the time many years ago when an inattentive moment had led to him slicing into two fingers of his left hand with a vegetable-knife. There were a few seconds when he just stared at the blade embedded in his fingers, and then the world turned impressively bloody. The pain had come later.

"Azmand," the Usurper went on, "I wish you to work with my chef. You have a reputation for sweets and breads and cakes. It is even said that you work magic into your wares and I would try that."

"You could send your men down to buy some," Azmand said. "Your Grace."

"I prefer that you work for me," the Usurper said. "And do your best for me. Else I shall have your skin removed while you still live, and turned into a trampoline for your grandchildren to play on."

Another frown, and there was more pain, winkling itself between his vertebrae. Azmand was less moved by the childish if quite imaginative threat and more with the Usurper apparently knowing that he had grandchildren.

The man on the bone throne shifted and broke wind.

"You will go," the Usurper said, "and work with my chef. Go, Azmand."

***

Azmand was given a small room with smooth rock walls, a narrow bed and a window high up. Then the guards dragged him away from that and flung him through a doorway into a reeking, steaming hell that even so had a few nice smells going on. It was, he thought as he stood on spotless cinnamon-coloured tiles, the kind of hell where even the Devil is a cook. Huge steel pots stood on work surfaces and hung from the rafters. There were bags of spices and bundles of herbs.

"And who - may you be?" someone bellowed. Azmand turned towards the voice.

An impressive figure strode towards him, dressed in a white shirt and apron. She was about his height but far larger, blue-eyed, ruddy-faced. Her sandy hair was tied back under a white cap.

"My name is Azmand," Azmand said. "I'm a maker of bread and sweetmeats. I've been told to come and work with you."

"Really," the woman said. "Sweets. Can you peel potatoes?"

"Lead me to it," Azmand said. "I began as a kitchen boy. Many years ago."

The woman was mollified.

"I could do with some help," she admitted. "After all ... can't get the workers these days. But the ... the ruler's told you to come and help me, has he?"

"Well, yes," Azmand said. "Only this morning I was having breakfast with my daughter's girlfriend and reading poetry and looking forward to a day of getting the books in order and a bit of baking, and talking to my friends. And now I'm up here."

"Tell me about it," the woman said. "Oh, I'm Talitha."

She held out a large hand and Azmand shook it.

"Well then," she said. "Let's work together. Like I say, can't get the help these days. There's no life in them. As it happens there are spuds to peel. The generals will be here this evening. I'm surprised they eat really, there's not a lot of life to them either. We cook for the Us … the ruler as well. But he stays in the Room of Pain and everything we send up goes via his Taster first. You really don't want to meet the Taster. Although he'll be there for the banquet."

**

The same went for the guards who lumbered by in the afternoon when Talitha and Azmand had got down to some proper cooking and Azmand was preparing a batch of honey cakes. Three guards this time, swaying in and knocking pots. Talitha stood with her arms folded.

"We are inspecting," one of the guards said. "Keeping an eye on things, you know."

"And now you've inspected," Talitha said, "you can leave. I have work to do. I'm sure your master wouldn't like to hear you'd held this gentleman and myself up."

"Not held you up," another guard said. "Can do that with one hand. Even to you."

"I wouldn't try it," Talitha said.

**

In late afternoon there were more noises from the castle. Footsteps hurrying along the corridors outside. Exclamations and loud voices from time to time.

"They're back," Talitha said. "They'll need food and wine. At least they aren't allowed in here."

The dining hall was a wood-panelled room, whose decoration was a bizarre mix of styles. Greek jars stood around the walls, pictures of foreign scenes – Azmand recognised the Temple of Hoog with its sullen statues, and the sands of the Golden Chersonese. A forest glade hosted a proud-antlered deer, and a beach was home to a dark-eyed young woman in a purple and blue wrap. She reminded him of Dena.

There were also strange machines whose function Azmand could not tell, if they had functions at all. Executed in crude primary colours, they were styled in the manner of human faces – eyes, a nose, a mouth – as though a child had taken those essentials and drawn them before she had grasped the idea of curves. Above these machines at the far end of the hall a big square window showed only cornflower-blue sky.

In the centre of the hall were two long tables and stools before them. The tables were covered in plates and goblets – the Usurper's cohorts favoured an old-fashioned style.

And they, the cohorts, were seated and sitting watching them. Dressed in black, mostly.

"Aha," one of them roared. Azmand looked at him and then at the others. They were all very similar; he was sure that once he looked away he would not be able to remember their faces. They seemed to mostly be men but he wasn't sure of that.

"Not a lot of life," Talitha had said. Azmand thought of that while looking around the banqueting hall.

While their bodies were alive, and needing food and drink, it was their souls that were dead.

So their bodies were fed lamb, and rice, and bread, and spiced honey cakes, and wine, and while they ignored Talitha and Azmand and the three serving children that were all Talitha could muster, the ministers and generals talked and boasted and sang. But Azmand could not rid himself of the idea that he was providing food for dead people. Food went up to the ruler, carried by a child who said nothing, just took the pot and scurried away more like a rat or a spider than anything human.

***

After he and Talitha and the serving children had their supper in the kitchen, Azmand asked one of the guards,"Can I go home now?"

The guard stared down at him.

"You can not," he said.

"So when can I go?" Azmand asked. "After the banquet? That's in three days' time. I have business to attend to."

"You can not leave," the guard said.

"We'll see about that," Azmand said, trying to push past the guard. The guard seized him about the waist and threw him back into the kitchen.

"I demand to see His Grace," he said, drawing himself upright.

"No good," Talitha told him. "He sees you, you don't see him. Unless you want his grid of pain to get you."

Azmand dusted himself down and sat again. His head was spinning. *I can't leave?* He'd called the whole city a prison but now that creature on the bone throne was actually holding him prisoner.

"How long have you been here?" he asked.

"A year," Talitha said.

"A *year*? Do you have family on the outside?"

"No," the chef replied, "no husband, no kids; I moved here when the Queen was still in charge. It was a nice place then. But still. I had a life, like you do."

***

Azmand sat with a cup of wine and turned over everything he'd heard in his mind. Something drifted into focus.

"Talitha," he said. "What was it you said ... his grid of pain? He causes pain. He has some kind of magic."

"No," Talitha said. She'd had a lot more wine than him. "'s a grid. In the throne room. On the floor." Then she sat back. "I'm going t'bed. See you in th' morning."

***

In the morning Azmand woke up slowly.

Where am I? He wondered. Then it came back to him. The tiny cell, the high up window, the kitchens, the Usurper and his gift for pain.

He got up, found that he was still in his daytime clothes, and as he sat on the bed recalled first of all Talitha and then what she had said about the grid. That had to have been important because despite the lateness of the hour and the drink they'd had, it was clear in his mind.

He pondered. Then he went and found a guard.

"I must," he said, "see His Grace at once. It is most important."

"He sees you," the guard snarled. "You do not see him."

Yes, you told me that," Azmand said. "But it is vital. It concerns his safety. You wouldn't want him to think you weren't bothered, now would you? What does he do to guards who don't care about his safety?"

Azmand watched the guard processing this. Finally the grey giant nodded, and bid him follow.

***

"What is the meaning of this?" the Usurper screeched from the throne of bone. "I am told you have information."

"I heard your generals, Your Grace," Azmand said, "at the table last night, discussing murder. I believe they may be plotting to murder you. At the banquet."

"Interesting," the Usurper said. "You do not know which ones it was?"

"I do not know their names," said Azmand. "But they wore black."

"Fool," the Usurper said. "All wear black. Besides, I have the ability to do this."

And a blast of pain erupted in Azmand's rectum, followed by another in his head. Azmand was able to keep his eyes open and noted through the pain that the brass lines on the floor pulsed with a blue light. Very faint, such that it might have been the glow of the lamps; but Azmand was sure it wasn't. Then the pain stopped and the light with it.

"You will listen out tonight," the Usurper said. "And you will report to me in the morning."

"It shall be so," Azmand said. "Your Grace."

"Go," said the Usurper, sending a slash of agony across the backs of Azmand's knees. Azmand winced and left.

***

Next morning, after a similar day to the first, Azmand reported once more, but this time he said,"I heard them once again, talking of murder. But in fact they were discussing how to avoid you being murdered. They do have your protection at heart."

"Good," said the Usurper, and let Azmand go with the lightest caress of pain through his shoulder blades. Then as he was exiting the room there came a screaming bolt of agony through his head. Azmand turned, fell to his knees and through one half-open eye saw the blue glow in the grid fade.

***

"Ye're up to something, aren't you?" Talitha demanded. They were plucking fowls for the feast. "I know you. You haven't gone over to his side. I just hope you know what you're doing and you don't get us both killed."

"So do I," Azmand replied.

"Right," Talitha said. "Now we've got a lot to do. Let's get on with it."

Azmand turned his attention after a while to the honey cakes and almond delights that he had planned for the feast. The light in the room turned slowly reddish as the sun, unseen, approached the distant snowy peaks of the west.

***

Finally it was time. The generals and the ministers assembled. Each of them was frisked at the door. There were menials, small black-clad people who had been permitted, this once, to attend and be given scraps from the table.

When all were seated, the door swung open one final time and the Usurper stood framed in the doorway, lit in pale light. Accompanying him was a gaunt but much shorter man, dressed in clothes the pale grey of bone.

"The Taster," Talitha said.

The Taster looked at Azmand with pink, ratty eyes. Straight lank hair, straw-coloured, fell around the Taster's face and made him look yet more horrific. Azmand averted his gaze.

"So good to meet your Grace," Azmand said, hurrying forward. The strange pair shuffled in and took up seats at the head of the table.

When the soup had been tasted, and eaten, and the next course, baby fowls in wine and calves' brains in aspic, was on the table, Azmand started to relax. The Usurper was making inroads into the wine, and the generals' and ministers' boasts were becoming ever more comical.

"'Course," one of them yelled down the table. A big man with a yellow moustache dripping with red wine. "'Course I could have took this place over, like. 'Stead of you."

There was a momentary hush. A silence in which Azmand thought he heard something creaking and moving in the wind through the windows.

"What did you say?" the Usurper said with the politeness of one who knows that there is bugger all need to be polite but is just doing it for effect.

"Yes but," the moustachioed man said, "I would have made a right dog's cock of it if I had."

"Indeed," the Usurper said.

Azmand was seized by sudden terror.

"Have more wine, your Grace," he said, hastening forward. Then he was looking instead into the ashen, red-eyed face of the Taster.

The Taster hissed and Azmand was sure he saw a forked tongue flickering between the creature's lips.

"His Grace has had sufficient," the Taster hissed.

"Bollocks I have," his Grace suddenly said, seizing the wine-bottle and raising it to his lips. "You, Az-bollocks, where's the sweetmeats?"

"Coming, Your Grace," Azmand said.

He carried trays of honey cakes and rice bean cakes and sugared almond tarts to the table. The Taster took one of each and pronounced them good. The Usurper dug in.

"Me first," the Usurper said. "If there's any left, you have them."

"Now," the Usurper said, mouth rimmed with flecks of sugar, "is there anyone else who'd like to challenge me?"

Once again there was silence.

"Yes," said a voice. "I."

Twenty pairs of eyes looked up at the far wall, at the high square window as a dark figure was silhouetted in it. But only Azmand knew who that was.

His daughter looked around her and slid down the wall to the floor.

"Impossible," the Usurper slurred.

"Not at all," Dena said.

"How did you get in?" the ruler said. "You can't have ..."

"But we did," said Dena.

"We?"

A second figure came through the window. Afi, his daughter's lover.

"Guards," the ruler said. "Guards … "

"They won't help you," Dena said. "They are a little … inconvenienced."

"You killed them," the Usurper said.

"If it helps you to think that," Dena said, "then do so."

"No matter," said the Usurper. "I have ways."

And he frowned. More so when nothing happened.

"You don't feel … pain?" the Usurper said. "Who are you?"

"Oh," Dena said, "Just friends of the Silken Queen. She's not very happy, you know."

The Usurper gaped.

"Parand's dead," he said.

"As you wish," Afi said. "But many say it is not so."

The Usurper frowned again.

"It doesn't work," Talitha said. "Not in here."

"This does, though," Azmand said, pointing at the cakes.

"What?" the Usurper demanded.

"Feeling a bit ill, are you?" Azmand said. "Have something you need to get out?"

The ruler burped. Then again.

He was starting to look pale and stared at the Taster.

"It's poisoned," he said. "How could you miss that … it's poisoned, isn't it?"

"It's no poison," Azmand said. "Just a simple inversion. Didn't you say yourself, that I work magic into my wares? That's just what I've done.

"Normally, you eat your food. But now, your food eats you."

The Usurper coughed and spluttered. Blood sprayed from the Usurper's nose and mouth and he clawed at his clothes. A high-pitched keening noise came from him and he leaned over, supporting himself with one hand on the table and the other on the Taster, who flinched away. The Usurper's clothes were bulging and finally tore, great gouts of blood spurting from his chest and abdomen and bones cracking and snapping in two. The Usurper screamed thinly as the cakes ate their way up his spine. Blood and half-devoured entrails gouted onto the floor.

The Generals and the Ministers were yelling and swearing in horror. At the windows, more dark figures appeared, swarming down the walls on ropes, and unsheathed swords slung across their backs.

The Usurper sat bolt upright in his chair and something ate his eyes from behind, first one vanishing into a sugary mouth and then the other. He was still screaming despite not having much to scream with any more.

The Taster was immobile. Then in a momentary spasm, blood gouted from his mouth and he slid to the floor, making incoherent sounds.

"Nobody else needs to die," Afi was saying above the diminishing screams and the horrified shouts of the diners. "We will take back only your prisoners."

There was no objection. The bloody thing at the head

of the table slumped across its plate, knocking a goblet of wine onto the blood-slicked floor, and was still. Gradually, the ministers and generals succumbed to wine and tiredness, until they too slumped onto each other.

***

The Tower in Air was silent at last.

Outside, in the chill night of Malyzan, birds sang.

The Treatment
By Jay Wilburn

With Bailey, it began with urine. Most people started with spit. It was safer and quicker to use saliva, but Bailey began by pissing in the food. He only did it when a costumer was particularly rude, but when he decided they deserved "the treatment," he wanted to know they were eating food laced with piss. Everyone put saliva in their own food. It was a natural part of eating. Their bodies would never know the difference. Urine was alien to food and punished the rudeness properly.

So that's how he started. That is not how it ended. It was June 10th when it all unraveled.

On June 1st he was working the grill alone again.

"Just cook the shit in order, boy, how hard can that be?" Bubba hissed through the window.

He turned back around and went back to his football conversation with James Tomlin across the counter. Bailey knew for a fact that Bubba didn't care about football. As he leaned over the counter passionately supporting Tomlin's team, Bubba's arms made it look like the sleeves of his tee-shirt had to be custom made to bear his frame and shoulders.

"It's your system," Bailey called back as he leafed through the tickets. "If you want to change it, the middle of the shift is probably not a good time, Uncle Cousin."

Bubba turned to face Bailey blocking off the view of James with his broad chest. "Customers, boy ... behave better than your upbringing. Just read it and cook it."

"How much do I owe?" Tomlin asked as he stood up

with a squeak from the swivel stool. The radio on his belt hooked the back of the seat and he had to untangle himself.

"The cooking's no problem. Reading your handwriting …" Bailey spread out three slips on the silver base of the serving window and started dropping patties on the flat, metal grill with a series of hisses.

"Trouble reading has run in your family a while," Bubba muttered again through the window before he whirled back around into character. "Owe? Don't be ridiculous, J-Tom. You pay for your meals by keeping us safe."

"Usually that just comps me coffee," James said as he slid his wallet back in his pocket.

"Just don't say anything about the bodies in the back and we'll call it even," Bubba said as he lifted the plates down into the basin below the counter and wiped down the space between the salt shaker, and the napkin dispenser with the same grimy rag he had used all night.

"Order up," Bailey called as he rang the bell.

"Take this one for me, boy. I need to catch up on dishes."

"Are you kidding me? I'm the only cook."

"You could be done and back at the grill by now."

Bailey slid the hot plates up on his tender forearms and bumped his way through the swinging, kitchen door with his backside.

He stood over the table of prom kids as they took a while to try to figure out what they had ordered.

This place for prom dinner? Either your dates are easy or you are not planning on getting any, Bailey thought as they finally let him set their plates down on the table.

"Take it easy ladies," Bailey said as he hustled back to the kitchen to try to keep from burning everything on the unattended grill. "Real easy."

"Wait," one of the girls called.

Bailey turned around without walking back. "Yes, ma'am."

"My burger is medium rare … I want it medium," she said.

Bailey came back and lifted it as he looked down the front of her frilly, tight dress. He could smell her hairspray over the food.

"I'll take care of your meat right away, ma'am."

"And don't just reheat the same hockey puck," her date demanded as he smoothed down his wispy mustache and glanced down her dress too.

You should have taken her to the steakhouse in Tanner, Bailey thought.

Bailey smiled. "I wouldn't think of it, sir. This is a special day and everything should be perfect. I apologize."

As Bailey raced back toward the smell of smoke from the kitchen, wispy mustache shouted. "Give it the special treatment."

"You got it, boss."

***

Big Bubba's Short Orders was a greasy spoon with style and Big Bubba was Bailey's uncle, Bowler Cousins. Bailey liked to joke by introducing him as "my Uncle Cousin." Incest jokes went pretty far in the hill country near the highway.

Some folks would stop in on long trips through the mountains over to Tennessee toward Nashville or south down and out of the Great Smokey Mountain Ridge into Asheville where the southern hippies and hipsters lived and where punk rockers breast fed their babies in public. Others were heading north to explore a stretch of the river or to walk a piece of the Appalachian Trail. If folks were heading east, they were going home or they were lost. The unincorporated village of Korche (pronounced Cork by the locals) was too far from the coast or any other major town east for this to be the path to get there.

Korche was named after some place over the ocean like a lot of little towns across the South and the rest of America. Unlike those other places, the folks in Korche were not too keen on having their town's origin explained to them by outsiders. They didn't want to be told they were saying it wrong nor that there was already another town in the state named Cork. That's the sort of thing that could get spit in their food. Unless Bailey was working, in which case, it got them something else. What it got them depended on when exactly they stopped in during the summer that Bubba died.

Bailey moved on from urine early in June.

On June 4th, Bailey suggested, "If you'd hire at least one other person, this would go faster."

Bubba leaned into the serving window. His sweating forehead stuck to a couple of the tickets. "If you'd refrain from burning the food, I might be able to consider such a bold business move, CFO Bailey."

Bailey stacked the full plates as he had been told. "Maybe you could touch a spatula while I'm doing my second job, grill master Bubba. If the underside has turned to charcoal, then you waited too long."

"You surely know that from extensive experimentation," Bubba said as he stood aside and held open the swing door for his nephew.

"Stick a Korche in it," Bailey suggested.

Uncle Bubba said, "You know when we were kids, your Dad and I used to call it Crotch."

"You've mentioned it," Bailey said as he moved around to the table near the front door. "The kids over at Tanner High that haven't dropped out yet call it 'Butt Plug' now."

"Customers, boy," Bubba huffed as he walked back into the kitchen.

"Bailey Cousins, as I live and breathe," the man bellowed with his belly pressed on the edge of the table. "You know Deacon Russell and his wife Mrs. Bella and my lovely wife and first lady of Tanner PBC, Mrs. Sarah."

"Hello, everyone, and welcome to Short Orders," Bailey said as the plates burned his arms.

"We haven't seen you since your mother passed, son,"

Bailey pictured the inside of the stark sanctuary his mother used to drag him to visit. Tanner Primitive Baptist Church was the sort of place where guest pastors described Hell with the kind of precise detail that made Bailey believe they went there for vacations in the summer. It was the kind of church where someone got up to pray and then three words into it, everyone was in the floor shouting at God like they were ready to fight.

"No, sir, we stay real busy out here, Reverend." Bailey held the plates out for them.

"You should never be too busy for God."

"And yet here I am serving your food," Bailey smiled broadly.

Making them comfortable enough to eat every bite was part of the treatment.

Deacon Russell took his plate and his wife's. Bailey put out the others by process of elimination. He assumed the reverend had never eaten a salad in his life, so he gave that to Mrs. Sarah.

"Have you heard from your father recently, son?" the reverend asked.

"My father died."

"I'm so sorry," Mrs. Sarah said.

"Did he get shanked by one of those godless gang members?" the reverend asked.

"I think it was kidney and liver failure," Bailey answered.

The preacher at Tanner PBC said, "Tanner is the buckle of the Bible belt and it is our mission to rid God's country of the hillbilly sin poisoning the young people of Tanner. That poisonous meth cost you both your parents."

Bailey used to look around the Tanner Primitive congregation at people that crossed the highway to buy product from his dad before he got sent up or to have a poke at his mother afterward.

I guess the buckle is always right above the crotch waiting to be opened up, Bailey thought. He looked over at Deacon Russell and his wife eating their meals without looking up from the plates. Mr. Russell never came over the highway except to eat at Bubba's and to tell Bailey how sorry he was when Mrs. Cousins died.

"You need more drink, Deacon Russell?"

"I'm good, son, thank you."

Mrs. Sarah was still looking up at Bailey with her brow furrowed and the skin around her eyes all scrunched together.

"I never heard of anyone overdosing on meth and oxy like your mother did. It was quite a tragedy," the reverend noted.

"That's nice of you to say," Bailey said. "Can I offer you all each a slice of pie on the house?"

"That is very kind of you and cherry with extra whipped cream would be divine," the reverend said over a mouth of steak.

"Extra whipped cream?" Bailey said as he tilted his head. "That is a divine notion. I will treat you up right, sir."

If Tanner is the buckle, then Korche is plugging the corn hole and Big Bubba's Short Orders is serving food right in the middle of it, Bailey thought as he rounded the counter by the cash register.

Bailey came back into the kitchen. Bubba passed him carrying armloads of plates.

"Boy, you sure did a nice job of chatting up the customers to avoid the heavy lifting."

"I learned from the best."

"Careful, boy, you're making me blush."

Bailey flipped the items on the grill as he scanned through the tickets.

He pulled out four pieces of pie and spread them out on the counter on one side and below the serving window. He set the can of whipped cream beside three of them and then slid one across the counter to center it in front of him. He turned it carefully so that the crust over the bright, red cherries was positioned the way he needed it for this special treat.

Bailey pulled the apron around under the tie strings and unzipped slowly keeping his buckle clasped over his belt. He stared out at the reverend as he thought about girls on prom night.

He realized Mrs. Sarah was looking at him across

her husband's hunched back. She smiled back at him and waved. He waved at her with his left hand as he continued the treatment to the reverend's pie.

***

Short Orders was crowded on June 10th. People actually waited for tables along the space around the front door. The booths were full and the counter was packed. Locals walked inside, looked at the travelers yelling at their kids, and left to go try one of the restaurants over in Tanner.

The people passing along the highway didn't know there was another option.

Bubba called out to the counter crowd. "It is worth the wait folks. You'll love it so much that the rest of your vacation will be a disappointment."

A few people chuckled lightly under the den of noise through the restaurant.

He turned back on Bailey sweating in the food over the grill that was starving for space with items plopped down every few inches. "Boy, you have to move or we'll have a murder on our hands from these tourists."

He turned back before Bailey responded. "Let me fill you back up there. The tea is done cooking for sure."

Bubba leaned back and spoke over his shoulder. "Would it help if I offered a bonus?"

"Is the bonus room and board that I've all ready used?"

"It sure is."

"Then shutting the hell up and letting me cook would be a good–"

Bubba snapped. "I'm not even listening anymore, Butt Plug ... Ladies, I hope you enjoyed it. You folks come on over and take these seats here. I'm going to wipe it down and dry it off straight away."

After about the third to fourth round of seating, Bailey was taking pie to the table of a single woman that was taking up a four top. He had offered her one of the counter seats and she offered to leave sooner if he served her faster.

"Apple … just like you requested, ma'am. It's warm and fresh."

"Fresh out of the freezer and microwave, you mean?"

She was wearing tight jeans and a frumpy sweatshirt for a college east toward the coast. She had a book written in some other language. The title had a bunch of apostrophes in it.

As he set the pie down, Bailey tried to look down the collar, but the material kept scalloping up and blocking the view.

She picked up the fork and leaned back in the bench. "You lose something down there, champ?"

"What?"

She sliced the fork down into the pie and pushed the first bite across the saucer as Bailey watched. She stopped. She looked up at him and back down at the plate.

I forgot to smile, Bailey thought.

"I want to speak to the manager."

"There's just me and my uncle, ma'am, if there's a problem …"

She looked up at him again after he trailed off and pointed with the prongs of her fork. "Then get your uncle, champ."

***

"Are you kidding me, Bubba? You're going to believe this east coast cooze over your own kin?"

Bubba's meaty hand cracked against the side of Bailey's head. The back of his skull bounced off the door to the locker behind him with a hollow, metallic crash.

He was stunned as he reached up and held both sides of his head.

He still thought, *Why do we have a bank of lockers for two workers that live in the same house?*

Bubba stuck a thick finger in Bailey's face. "Don't bullshit me. I listened to lies from your worthless father as I watched his teeth fall out. I watched him hook your mother on it. I took you in and every day I can see the same … looks and … the same walk. I feel like I'm looking into a time machine. You have the same … stupid …"

"Bubba, it's not true. I didn't–"

Bubba raised the back of his hand up and the lockers crashed again as Bailey flinched and backed into them.

"That's my food, Bailey Cousins," Bubba was actually crying. His eyes looked alien and red.

"Bubba …"

"Your father nearly bankrupted this place stealing from me. He killed your mother from behind prison bars by poisoning her body and mind before he went up. This is my food, boy. This is all I am and you are going to put your … filth in it."

Bubba turned his back on Bailey and looked out the port window from the office area into the busy dining room.

This would be a good time to have a third worker, Bailey thought.

Bubba took a deep breath that made his back look broader. "You leave out the back and go back … to my house. Pack your junk and be gone by the time I get home."

"What?"

"You didn't mishear and I ain't repeating it for you. Saying things over never helped your father and I'm not going start with you."

God, I should have chopped the special ingredients up better and none of this would be happening, Bailey thought.

Bubba leaned against the frame on both sides of the swinging door next to the cash office and lowered his head. Smoke was wafting around the corner by the lockers from the grill.

"You can't put me out like this … not like this. I'm not like my father, Bubba."

"It hurts," Bubba clinched his eyes shut as tears leaked from the outside corners. He turned and leaned back against the office door as he bent over clutching his knees. If the swing door came open, it would crack him in the head.

"I didn't mean to hurt you. We can pretend like none of this happened. We'll go back out … and all of it's gone. My father, my mother, the college slut … all of it, Bubba. We can go back to normal … Bubba?"

Bubba stumbled forward and grabbed Bailey's shoulders with both hands. It was like being attacked by a drunk bear. They crashed into the lockers again and Bailey saw a flash of light and black dots from the impact. Bubba laid his head into Bailey's chest and groaned.

Bailey shook and he felt water around his eyes. He tried to reach up and wipe it away, but Bubba's meaty arms were pinning him.

Bubba raised his head up an inch from Bailey's mouth and spewed a wash of brownish paste across the boy's nose and lips. He tasted the salty, raw chunks on the end of his tongue.

Bailey gagged as he threw both his fists into Bubba's chest once and then again. Bubba staggered back into the office door cracking it down the middle with a loud snap. Bailey held the lockers and dropped to his knees spitting and retching. He crawled along the floor and then bobbled up to the sink. He turned on the water and cupped the wash to his face. He scraped his tongue with his finger nails. Bailey heaved twice feeling his muscles contract until his legs and back hurt. The water became blistering hot as he realized he had turned on the wrong side, but he kept bailing it over his lips as they were scalded bright red.

Bailey staggered back into the mop and bucket knocking them a couple clicks along the tile on the black wheels.

I just got the treatment, he thought as he fought a contraction in his abdomen.

He looked over and saw Bubba on his side across the silver kick base of the swing door. His uncle's skin was pale and grey. It stood out in sick contrast against the brown stains across his tee shirt and apron. The big man's eyes were unfocused. He was still breathing in shallow bursts that moved his lips back and forth across his teeth, but the gasps for air were spaced and irregular.

Time is muscle, Bailey thought. He heard that at his mother's funeral. It had something to do with a bad heart, but Bailey wasn't sure what.

He couldn't get past Bubba, so he ran around through the kitchen area. The meat on the grill was charcoal. Bailey paused and used a spatula to sweep the smoking food into the trash under the counter.

"What are you doing?" Bailey asked out loud. "Time is muscle."

I'm not going to ruin his food too, Bailey shook at the thought.

He ran out into the dining area behind the counter and in front of the dish sanitizer. He looked around at the faces as a few people looked up at him, looked down at their watches, and returned to their conversations. The door flapped back and forth a few times.

Bailey realized he was smiling.

What the hell am I doing?

"Customers, boy," he whispered.

He looked over still smiling as the girl in the frumpy sweatshirt glared at him.

I need to call for help. Drop this shit eating grin and tell one of the tourists to call on their cell phone, he thought.

"Is everything okay?" someone asked from the counter.

Bailey was still staring at the girl who started all of this.

"Everything's normal in the great land of Korche," Bailey shouted. "You all will be treated right in short order."

She stood up and began to storm out of the restaurant.

"You need to pay or we're reporting your tag to the authorities."

She turned on Bailey. "Excuse me?"

"Walking out on a check in this state can have a warrant placed on you through your tag. It will follow you east even if you drive all the way to the ocean ... ma'am."

Customers were staring now. Only half the tables were full. The other half were piled with dishes.

"I should call the cops on you."

"I'll call him for you," Bailey offered. "We call him J-Tom. He comes in for free meals all the time. He went to school with my late father and my uncle. My Uncle Cousin is still back there laughing about you trying to get me fired to dodge a check to hold on to mommy's money for weed. He's laughing so hard he's on the floor now."

Her eyes filled with liquid and reddened around the edges. Bailey smiled wider.

She pulled out money and slapped it on the counter. Bailey opened the register and made exact change. When she tried to take it, he held on to it so her fingers were touching his. She just looked down at something on the floor.

"Would you like a piece of pie to go ... on the house? For all the misunderstanding?"

She let go of the money and walked out the door.

"Thank you for the generous tip, ma'am," Bailey called. "Come again."

He watched her round the corner outside.

If I run out the back now, I could grab her before she got away. I could hide her car tomorrow. No one even knows she stopped here. Everyone that saw her is going somewhere else. I can see what's under that sweatshirt finally.

Bailey turned and walked through the swinging door to the kitchen.

***

"So where is he?"

Bailey refilled the mug from the caffeinated canter. "Resting ... he'd probably like to see you. He won't say it out loud, of course."

"Man needs his pride."

"I get that," Bailey agreed as he glanced over the serving window counter at the grill.

"It was his heart?"

"Yeah, it's probably not hurting him much now, but he's in no shape to serve."

"You're a good kid running the place for him, son."

Bailey went back through the swinging door and began flipping items on the grill.

"I'm trying to behave above my upbringing."

James Tomlin looked up from his paper and stared at Bailey for a long moment. Bailey had to look down to plate the food.

"We all are, son ... you ..."

James dropped his eyes back to the paper as Bailey set the out the plate.

"More ice?"

"Yes, please, thank you, Bailey."

James took a large crisp bite through the burger and lettuce. He looked down at the burger and up at Bailey as the boy set his full, water glass next to the coffee mug.

"Holy shit, this is good. Even the tomato is good. Don't tell Bubba I said this, but this is the best burger I've ever bitten into ... what are you doing to it?"

Bailey smiled wider. "It's just beef burnt on a grill, Mr.

J-Tom. It's all in the seasoning ... I started experimenting soaking the tomatoes after I slice them too."

"Keep it up and I'll have to start paying."

"Bubba won't hear of it ... just keep ignoring the bodies in the back."

"You know he's proud of you, Bailey," officer Tomlin said. "He says so all the time. As far as your upbringing ... your folks would be proud of who you are now ... I know it."

Bailey stood with his hand on the swing door a moment longer and then walked back into the kitchen.

***

Bailey washed out his armpits in the sink with scalding water. He toweled off with an old apron and tossed it aside by the open, office door. The cash boxes were open and empty. The ledgers were still on the small desk where they had sat since the day Bubba died. Some of the pages were empty.

He walked around the unused lockers and over a bag of trash he meant to take out a couple days ago.

By August 11th, Bailey had been living at Big Bubba's Short Orders all day and night for a while. He took Bubba's truck into Tanner to get supplies from the grocery store two mornings a week. He woke up early to prep, wash dishes, and put a spit shine on the dining area.

He had put out scented candles.

He looked around the stains on the tile in the kitchen. It needed more than mopping. It smelled like dirty mop water.

He was dodging vender calls and had stopped turning in the sales taxes. He had stopped keeping the books.

Bailey reached in the cooler and pulled out the wad of pages from the accounts ledger. He set them on the prep counter, which clearly need to be scoured.

He unfolded them and began massaging the muscle.

Bailey had watched a documentary of a master sushi chef. The guy made octopus soft and delectable by rubbing through and breaking up the fibers until it was soft and pliable.

He was sure he could make it work.

This all happened because I was sloppy with the special ingredients and got caught.

Bailey used the heel of his hand to press into the tough center of the cold heart. He worked his thumbs around the surface over the edges. He imagined the scar tissue inside breaking up and smoothing out of the organ.

"It's like an aged steak, Bubba," Bailey muttered. "You'll be proud of what I make out of this mess."

When his hands got tired again, he left the heart to warm. It was finally going into the specials tonight.

"I'll even add a little to the collards and green beans to season it like pork ... I'll cut it up real fine."

He took the paring knife and began slicing through the shoulder cut he had left out to thaw yesterday. He sliced the flesh away from the large knob of bone. He took out a wooden mallet and began pounding the cut out flat. He had some spinach, goat cheese, and baking twine for something he wanted to try.

"If it works out, I'll need more shoulders."

Someone pounded on the front glass. Bailey looked through the serving window and waved them off with the mallet in his fist. The man pounded again and held up a piece of paper Bailey couldn't see.

He snatched an apron off the floor that he didn't remember dropping and draped it over the bits of muscle and flesh.

Bailey called through the glass. "We don't open until 10:30."

"Health Inspector ... I need to talk to you now, please."

Bailey reached up and turned the deadbolt with his purple hand.

The man walked in and introduced himself. Bailey wasn't hearing the words. All he could think about was the bag of trash in the kitchen.

Get it together, boy

"What can I do for you?"

"We got a complaint earlier this summer about food tampering," he explained. "We need to follow up."

I should have gone out and killed her that night. Most of her would be gone by now.

"Where's your partner?"

The man laughed. "There are eight of us for the entire state. I almost gave up on finding this place."

"Well," Bailey said, "come on back in the kitchen. That's where I keep the bodies."

They walked around the counter. Bailey reached into the rack in front of the sanitizer. He pulled out a knife caked in tendrils of thick red. It was longer and thicker than the paring knife.

"The place looks over due for a cleaning," the man suggested as he wrote on the clipboard.

"My uncle is in the freezer right now. We should discuss this with him."

"What happened back here? Why is the kitchen ... like this?"

The man had his wrist over his nose.

Bailey adjusted the knife in his fist before he gave the inspector his answer. He drove the blade up into the man's lower back where he thought the kidneys or liver might be under the jacket.

I'll find out for sure in a minute.

The man heaved and choked as he dropped the clipboard. He tried to stagger for the door while Bailey held the knife in his back.

They turned around and Bailey pushed him forward into the knobs on the grill. The man bent at the waist. Bailey shoved the inspector's chest and face down on the metal surface below the edge of the serving window. He held the man's neck with his forearm.

Bailey felt the heat rising off the metal in the air around his wrist and elbow, on both sides of the man's face. The inspector was screaming and struggling, but the grill wasn't hot enough to sizzle yet. But he could smell the scent of flesh cooking.

Bailey pumped the knife in and out of the bloody jacket in a sawing motion.

This is going to take a while, he thought.

Famished
By Elaine Pascale

If curiosity killed the cat, then altruism killed Graham "Gray" Donovan.

Or was the true culprit his raging hunger?

Gray had left the second shift at the Hope Center for Boys acutely aware of his famished state. This was not the midnight mouth boredom that he routinely fought and won. This was a stomach rumbling, headachey, fatigued and desperate craving. At 38, Gray knew he needed to monitor his diet. He had a stressful job finding homes and jobs for the unwanted and unappreciative. He was not an exerciser. And he had watched his mother die, relatively young, from heart complications. His father, while still alive, had had to endure surgeries in order to keep the vessel pumping, and his quality of life had been greatly reduced.

Gray also knew that he would not be able to talk himself out of the hunger: it was as authentic as a heart attack. And, Buk'a Burg'a's neon sign was beckoning, announcing *Drive-Thru Open 24 hours*.

Buk'a Burg'a was an old friend to Gray. He had first been introduced to their culinary delights at the tender age of three. His mom had been working an evening shift and Gray had turned up his nose to the casserole she had left for him and his father. His dad, tired after a long, hot day working construction, had surrendered easily. Gray could remember how cool the wind pouring through the open window of the car had felt compared to the hot upholstery of his seat. He recalled how the air had smelled as father and son closed in on the small brick restaurant. It had smelled of salt and grease, of spicy condiments, of guilty pleasures. He had only smelt that kind of anticipated guilt once again: prior to his bachelor party a dozen years before.

The french fries had been warm and crisp on his tongue, the burger pillowed by rolls ten times softer than the day old bread his mother brought home. The dessert had come in a little frozen cup: a miniature ice cream cake with (delight of delights) a small wooden spoon. His father had even let him try both an orange drink and a milkshake: a luxury they could scarcely afford.

Since that time, Gray had engaged in a love/hate relationship with the food chain. He hated the temptation of the place; he hated that everything about Buk'a Burg'a that tasted good was deadly. However, he loved the open door policy the restaurant had for hiring his charges and giving them a sense of self-esteem and an opportunity to work.

Realizing there was no turning back from the promise he had made to himself of a giant burger and fries, he turned into the empty parking lot and proceeded to the drive-thru. The restaurant itself had been closed for at least an hour but the grill worked through the night. Gray waited, his car making distressing noises to compete with his stomach, and listened for a voice to come through the darkened speaker box.

When no voice came, Gray called, "Hello?"

He was answered with faint feedback and some sounds of static.

Gray worked under the assumption that he had just been asked for his order. "I'd like a Big Burg'a and a large fries." Again, he was met with a cacophony. "Phillip Glass could have worked wonders with that one," Gray tried to joke in order to lessen his bubbling impatience. He understood that this was officially the graveyard shift, but he really expected people to have a little more pride in their work. The nonsensical sounds raged on through the speaker. Gray figured that he had been told the price, which would only echo what he had been able to deduce from the menu on the glowing billboard in front of his car.

"Could you—," he almost asked for the drive-thru attendant to repeat the order, but decided that feedback was the one type of feeding he was done with for the evening. Besides, his orders were usually correct when he went through the drive-thru; they had computers to assist the workers, and to ensure accuracy.

Yet, he wasn't quite done with the attempted communications: "Can I add a milkshake to that?" Guilt. He was not sure of the source—there was no longer anyone at home to monitor his food intake.

This time, there was no response but Gray knew he could add the item at the window. This certainly was not rush hour and he would be inconveniencing no one except for the employee who wanted to return to his iPod or his nap.

He navigated his car around the building to the window where the cashier was stationed. A young boy, barely legal to be working at this hour, stood facing the glass. He looked out at Gray as if surprised to find him awaiting an order. Gray wondered if maybe his voice hadn't gone through the intercom at all.

The boy remained staring. Gray noticed that he wore no headset or other communications equipment. Gray pulled money from his wallet and waved it in front of the window which needed to be activated from inside the restaurant.

"Uhhm…hello?" Gray smiled and snapped the twenty. "My order?"

A moment of clarity crept into the boy's eyes. He leaned toward the window, triggering a sensor and causing it to open.

Gray handed the boy the money and waited for his change and his food. The hunger still ravaged through him yet there was consolation in knowing that satisfaction was just moments away. Even now, the boy did not move. He simply stared at Gray in a way that was indecipherable. Had he placed the boy at this station and the look was one of recognition? There were too many shades of meaning behind those eyes for that interpretation. The more Gray involved himself in the staring contest, the more he realized that the boy looked scared.

"Can I help you?" Gray asked, fully aware of the irony of the customer posing that question.

The boy shook his head and swallowed: a large, gulping movement that looked as if he were on the receiving end of a particularly full beer bong. He passed Gray's change to him through the window. After Gray pocketed the money, he realized that the boy was still leaning through the window even though his hands were now empty.

Gray tried once more, "Long night, huh?"

Still, the boy said nothing. His face was pale against the backdrop of halogen. He gulped again, his mouth opening and closing a few times but no sound escaped. It was no longer a mystery why the intercom transaction had been botched.

Without removing himself from the window, the boy reached behind, seeking Gray's order. His hand fumbled and fought with the counter while Gray watched this strange game of Blind Man's Bluff. It was impossible to tell from the boy's poker face when he made contact with the bag, but it was eventually passed through the window.

The turned-down top felt sweaty, but Gray was in no position to be picky. In fact, he felt that there was nothing in the world that could come between him and his hunger.

He nodded an un-responded-to thank you and proceeded to drive away. The look on the boy's face was disconcerting. He had seemed to want to tell Gray something, yet, every time the chance was presented, he had remained silent. Another wave of guilt washed over Gray. He attributed it to the fact that he had spent the past decade helping teenage boys. It was clear that this boy needed something, but Gray was unable to help. If there had been something he could do, the boy would have asked…right?

Before pulling back onto the main road, Gray glanced into the rearview and thought he saw the boy still hanging halfway out of the drive-thru.

"Hunger and darkness do a number on the mind." Gray shook his head to clear it. Ignoring all thoughts of caution while driving, he dug into the bag for immediate gratification. He was faced with an unexpected delay as his hand found something metallic instead of the burger he anticipated.

"What the…?" he swerved onto the shoulder in order to peer into the bag. There was a small piece of steel that resembled a place card. It had the number 12 embossed on one side. The other was speckled with a brownish crust. As Gray lifted the item for a closer view in the strong moonlight, he noticed that the "crust" had hair stuck to it, as well as a small piece of skin.

Gray covered his mouth, anticipating vomit. It was a stroke of good fortune to have an empty stomach, and, consequently, a clean car. The smell of metal, mixed with something sour, replaced his hopes of salty fries.

Somewhere, his mind registered that he hadn't even asked for the milkshake.

"I should go back…"

He reluctantly turned the metal piece over in his hands but the stains appeared to be isolated to a single side.

"I should go back…"

Surprisingly, Gray remained aware of his hunger. *Selfishly* aware if the descriptor had been left up to his ex-wife to assign.

"I should go back. I should give this back and get my bag. There's nothing wrong with getting what I paid for. There's nothing wrong with complaining about finding… this…" he discovered that he was still presenting defenses to the woman who had walked out five years prior. "The drive-thru is open all night; I can get my food and be home by midnight. I'll need new food, clean food. What's the crime in that?"

If curiosity killed the cat, then a sense of consumer righteousness killed Graham Donovan.

Gray turned his car around, repeating meaningless mantras: "What's the worst that can happen? That catatonic boy messes things up on me again? I will check the bag before I drive away. What could possibly go wrong? No harm in this. Just make sure to check the bag." He wasn't sure if his present unease could be attributed to the deserted nighttime streets, the inexplicable object that was still in his left hand, the unnerving boy, or all of the above.

He tried not to imagine the source of what could only be blood on the marker. Maybe an unsanitary worker had had to kill a very large bug. A bug with hair and skin. Or maybe a mouse. There were definitely people cruel enough to beat a mouse to death; the parents of his clients had often done far worse than that.

This time, the Buk'a Burg'a sign was annoying, not beckoning, as he pulled up to the order box and waited to be asked for his order.

Nothing.

After a minute, Gray backed his car and approached the box again, questioning if he had driven over the trigger on the first approach.

Nothing.

He was becoming largely impatient, simply wanting his night to end so he could go home and remember what it felt like to have a full stomach. He decided to throw protocol aside and drive up to the cashier's window. He planned to order two sandwiches this time.

As he pulled around the building to come up on the window side, Gray saw that the boy was still leaning out. The sliding doors, ignoring their orders to remain open when blocked, were opening and closing on his inert body.

"My God," Gray gasped and finally his stomach was ignored. He pulled up beside the boy, lowering his car window so he could reach through.

"Hey…hey, buddy." He touched the boy's hand which was dangling over the small ledge. It was cold and lifeless. The boy's mouth was open and blood was dripping from his nose and ears.

"Hey," Gray tried again, "Hey, we need to get you some help."

He pulled his car to the entrance side of Buk'a Burg'a, knowing the door would be locked. He pounded hard, desperate to attract the notice of the grill crew or whoever it was that was supposed to keep the food supply alive at this ungodly hour. His adrenaline must have surged past his hunger as, without warning, his fist punched through the glass in the door. Actually, it was adrenaline backed by the metal piece, still clutched between now bloody fingers. Gray reached through the hole he had made and disengaged the lock.

"Hey! We need help here." The restaurant was oddly quiet. He expected the commotion of timers and fryers and workers. He felt alone but he didn't have time to assess that feeling as he made his way to the drive-thru cubicle.

Which was, oddly, empty.

"Hello?" Gray called again while reaching for his cell phone. He noticed that the scent of food smelled old, as if the odor had been constructed some time ago. It was the smell of a kitchen after dishes had been done and put away. It was the smell that had greeted him, along with his ex-wife's anger, when he used to come home late.

His cell phone slipped from his hand and Gray realized that the cuts from the glass door had been more significant than he had suspected. He grabbed some napkins from the counter and wrapped them around his throbbing hand. The thin paper stuck to his hand and soaked through immediately. "Great, now two of us need help." Yet, there were still no employees in sight, no one to ask how they could help him or if he'd like an extra-large instead of a large. No one to check on the sound of broken glass. No one at all.

Gray studied the wall in front of him while dialing 9-1-1. The faint green tiles were tattooed with pictures of former employees of the month. His phone was silent, but the lack of service (this entire night had been about lack of service) did not register as quickly as recognition of a few of the boys. There was Brian James, who had been considered a successful placement until he failed to return to the residential one night following work. There was Terrence Daly whose foster mother had reported him missing. There was Eric Lynch, who had left a note behind, in his locker at Buk'a Burg'a, saying that he had gone to search for his birth mother. The agency could find no trace of him later. He had simply disappeared. Brian, Terrence and Eric had all disappeared. The most recent photo was of the boy who had hung through the drive-thru window, but was no longer there.

Disappeared.

Gray shook his phone in an insane attempt to receive a connection. Maybe the machines interfered, or maybe an establishment that routinely hired teens intentionally tampered with connections to keep their employees from chatting away dollars.

Or maybe, the reason was even more devious.

Gray tried to remain rational. He shook his head as he had shaken the phone, hoping to reconnect the wires in his brain that had apparently been fried from hunger. This was Buk'a Burg'a, where he had experienced his first burger. This was where he had shared classmates' birthday parties, where he had brought dates. This very parking lot was where he had tried his first and last cigarette. This restaurant is where he had come after swimming, after playing ball, after clubbing, after work. This was where he may eventually indoctrinate his own children to the wonders of fast food. This was no haunted house. The boy in the window had most likely experienced some sort of seizure. That was common amongst teenagers with their sudden growth spurts, hormone fluctuations, and drug abuse. The workers were probably getting him to help right now. In the rush and panic, they had forgotten to turn off the lights.

The disappearing boys were simply a coincidence. Coincidences happen.

He may have successfully convinced himself of the normalcy of his surroundings had it not been for the rats.

What was most remarkable was that Gray had not noticed them before. What was even more remarkable was that they were walking, single-file, toward a set of stairs leading to a basement. Their organization, their silence, and their marked purpose did not bode well. Or, at least, these characteristics did not bode any better than the bloody metal marker, the missing boys, and the lack of food to be found in the establishment.

If curiosity killed the cat, then Gray's determination to follow through on the injured boy killed him.

He began to follow the trail of rodents, repeating his mantra, "After I find out what happened to the boy, I'll just check the bag and get out of here. I'll give the...the thing back, if anyone's around, ask for my food and get out of here. And, this time, I'll check the bag."

There was, in fact, a method to this rambling madness. On some level, Gray was aware that there had been no drive-thru mistake. He had been meant to find the marker so that one more employee of the month would not be assumed missing.

The marker was now covered with his own blood as well as someone else's. Gray was feeling dizzy from fatigue and hunger. He was beyond hunger, he was famished.

The rats were descending the stairs, still in single-file, so that Gray was able to pass them as he hurried down. He could hear voices, murmuring, whispering...praying.

At least he had found people.

The basement was dark except for the light of a few large candles. The patterns of wax betrayed their re-use. There was the scent of incense covering some larger, untraceable smell. The rats that had joined were taking some sort of communion on the floor. It looked as if they were gobbling scraps of raw burger. And, like the rest of Buk'a Burg'a, the basement was empty.

Gray's attention was drawn to the open door leading to the back of the restaurant. There seemed to be a small concrete enclosure that was not visible from the drive-thru path. After each individual rat took his meat, he then took his place in the line leading to the exit. The rats intuitively knew that this was where the secrets ended. The voices, now chanting, were louder.

He steeled his nerves and made his way to the door. There were people in polyester uniforms covered by heavy, black robes. The hoods only partially concealed the Buk'a Burg'a visors beneath. What was surprising was how many people were actually present, yet he had been unaware of them as he walked about upstairs. And they had been unaware of him. The rats, now filled with a fatty "host" were in a circle, observing the ceremony.

Bags were being passed, conveyer style, to the trash compactor, which churned hungrily. The machine sounded as famished as Gray felt. He watched as bag after bag after bag was passed along. They were the smaller bags that get passed through the drive-thru window; smaller bags, that, when checked, contained a small order of french fries, or a single cheeseburger, or a slice of pie. The contents of these bags were crunched and clanked and clattered. The straining, squealing noises coming from the machine belied any images of soft food. The employees seemed relieved as each bag was accepted and digested. Gray never knew that taking out the trash could be so spiritual. He was so captivated by the ritual that he almost forgot why he was there—to get help for the boy.

"Uhhm," he cleared his throat.

The person closest to the trash compactor glanced at Gray then took another bag from the person beside him. He put ketchup and salt packets in the bag along with napkins: readying an order as if he stood before the drive-thru window and not the garbage bin. The bag was wet, the white paper soaked with some pinkish substance. It fell into the trash with a thump denoting a weight heavier than the standard food order.

"Uhhm," Gray tried again, "I was checking…there was a boy…I can't find him now…was he hurt?"

Another bag was passed down the line and tossed into the machine before anyone paid any attention to Gray. This bag showed resistance and the meditative spell was broken.

In a few moments, Gray would wish that he had taken the stairs up to the exit before they had noticed him. By then, it would be too late.

While one employee worked to disengage the jammed bag, the others grabbed Gray. He struggled and complained but it was as if he didn't count: he was just another slab of meat that needed to be turned and dressed and sold. The workers had a job to do, a production protocol to follow, and interlopers were not allowed. Fighting them off was difficult with the injured hand and he was greatly outnumbered.

When the trash compactor released the troublesome object, it slipped from the employee's fingers and slid across the floor.

"Unclean" intoned a young man who held Gray's arm. At first, Gray thought he was the object being described until another employee pointed to the bag and said, "Not acceptable."

Gray watched as a metal marker, exactly like the one

he was still holding only with the number 3 on it, was slid beneath the bag. The teen who had dropped it began to flail his arms wildly. Foam appeared at the corners of his mouth, which was opening and closing soundlessly, just like the boy in the drive-thru window. His movements had caused his hood to fall back and Gray could see how young this boy was; about the same age as the one who had passed him the bag containing the metal marker. A group of workers began to approach the boy, each holding a jar containing a different condiment. When the boy saw what was in their hands, he fell still. With methodical precision, he was covered with pickles, onions, ketchup, mustard, and special sauce. It was more with resolve than with resignation that the boy allowed the hooded employees to take his arms and legs and lift him above their heads.

Gray tried to struggle against the ones who held him but their grasp was too tight. Before he could register what was happening, the boy was tossed into the trash compactor. He went easily, as if jumping into a pool on a hot day, but the compactor did not digest as easily. There was great deal of churning, grinding, and splattering. At one point, the boy rose up, pushed to the side by the biting jaws. That is, half of him rose up: the other half had become a gnawed mess. One employee had to take a large metal stick and stir the concoction so that the sacrifice could be completely consumed.

"Clean" the employee murmured and the others hummed in agreement. The rats seemed to hum, too.

As the employees dragged Gray closer to the compactor, he saw the rats ripping open the bag on the floor. A hand rolled out and was immediately swarmed upon.

The pickle dispenser was ready, but Gray was not. He shrugged and twisted so that the dressings fell from his clothes. He tried to dodge the squirt bottles of sauce and spice. He kicked and twitched and bit the shoulders closest to his mouth. He was hungry enough to bite hard and scared enough to fight for his life.

Mustard stung his eyes and his wounded hand. Mayonnaise globbed around his nostrils, making breathing extremely difficult. His feet slid beneath him on the puddles of food and blood, but the employees held tightly.

The compactor was silent and waiting. Gray knew what had happened to the boy in the drive-thru window. He knew what would happen to him.

"Why?" he managed to ask, but this was not a movie. The villain would not provide a lengthy dissertation of his evil plan, thereby allowing the hero more time for escape. In real life, heroes died because of their hunger all of the time.

The walk to the compactor was not long, but Gray did not go easily.

If curiosity killed the cat, a trash compactor killed Graham Donovan.

Made from Locally Sourced Ingredients
By James Brogden

Something flashed through the Land Rover's high beams and hit the front bumper with a heavy thump. Jeff let out a whoop.

"Got the bugger!"

In the passenger seat, Iain didn't reply. He simply reached into the back to gather his torch and a wide-bladed shovel as Jeff steered to a stop, killing the engine but leaving the lights on. They illuminated a stretch of hedgerow, and the empty lane ahead. Sudden and absolute silence enveloped them – the kind that only existed in unmarked country lanes at four in the morning. The engine ticked as it cooled.

"Felt like a big 'un, too!" added Jeff optimistically.

"Just get the cool-box, yeah?"

They climbed out. Jeff opened the back of the Land Rover and struggled with a large picnic cooler while Iain swept the ground with his torch back in the direction they'd come.

"See anything?"

Iain grunted a no. "I think you might have only clipped it."

"No way, man. I hit that fucker dead on." Jeff dumped the cooler on the road and took his own torch around to the front to inspect the damage. Iain heard him muttering angrily.

"You know that big bunny catcher I had put on?"

Iain was only half listening, still unable to find their kill in the long roadside grass. "Hmm?"

"Yeah, well whatever it was, it weren't no fucking bunny. Look at what the bastard's done."

Iain's torch stopped. "Found it."

He could only see one of its hind limbs poking out of the grass – the rest was an indistinct furry mass – but that was enough for him to tell that it was at least the size of a badger, if not bigger, and that it was still alive. The limb was twitching, long claws flexing against the asphalt as it tried to push itself to safety. Mercifully, it wasn't making any noise. He hated it when they squealed.

Jeff quit complaining about the condition of his ride and came back to see.

"How can it still be alive?" he wondered. "How hard we hit it – no way. What the fuck is it, anyway?"

Iain stepped forward with the shovel raised, and aimed at where he thought the animal's head must be. "Sorry about this, mate," he said to it under his breath, and brought the shovel down hard. There was a flat, wet crunch and the twitching stopped.

"It's dead, is what it is," he told Jeff. "Let's get it on ice."

They carried over the cooler, along with a second shovel, and between them managed to scrape and lift the carcass into it, chucking a couple of freezer blocks on top before clamping down the lid. Then they sparked up, leaning on their shovel handles and smoking into the night.

"Seriously, mate," said Jeff after a while. His face was round and pale in the headlights, like an earthbound moon. "I mean what the actual? It's not like any kind of badger I've ever seen. The teeth for one thing."

Iain took a last drag on his cigarette and flicked the glowing butt into the darkness. "You know, you think about this kind of thing too much," he answered, and got back in the Land Rover. Jeff stood a moment longer, finishing his fag and staring at the long smear of blood which they'd left on the road, black in the red tail-lights. He shuddered, climbed back behind the wheel and drove them away.

After they were safely gone, something considerably larger than the thing stuffed in their cooler crept out of the hedgerow and carefully licked every trace of blood from the asphalt. It sniffed at the burning fag end, then at the trampled grass, and then finally at the smell of tire rubber which was still warm on the road.

Cautiously, it began to follow.

***

Alexander Rouse, proprietor and head chef of 'Savannah', the capital's premiere (and indeed only) freegan restaurant, narrowed his eyes in suspicion as Iain and Jeff opened the cooler. They glanced at each other nervously. They'd done unsavoury jobs for dangerous men before, and Rouse was right up there with the more barking of them. He was short and stocky, the story being that he'd once been a butcher, which accounted not just for the muscles acquired from a background of chopping carcasses apart, but also the particular speciality of his establishment. It took something of a psychopath to make a success out of even a normal restaurant, never mind one that used road kill in the cuisine.

"How fresh is it?" he asked.

"Don't you want to know what it is?" said Jeff.

Rouse turned the kind of gaze on him which gave the impression that he was assessing what kinds of joints could be cut from him.

"What are you, fucking David Attenborough? It's whatever I want to call it on the menu. The customers won't be able to tell the difference. All I need to know is how fresh it is so I don't poison any of them."

"It's fine. Roaded it ourselves this morning," said Iain, impatient for this to be done. The thing was giving him the creeps, even dead and lying in a box.

"Fair enough, then." Rouse counted out their finders' fee from a fat roll of twenties. They dumped the carcass on one of his stainless steel work surfaces, pocketed the cash, and disappeared.

Rouse spent a while turning it to and fro, trying to get a sense of its anatomy; where the joints might be, the cutlets, the fillets – and more importantly, what the hell he was going to call it.

"You," he decided, "are a badger. You're going to be on the sett menu, my friend." Chuckling at his own joke, he picked up his skinning knife and went to work.

**

As the taxi pulled up outside Savannah, Lilla squeezed Patrick's hand in excitement.

"I can't believe you actually managed to get us a table here!" she beamed. "The waiting list must have been horrendous."

"Oh, not so much," he shrugged. "Only about six months or so."

She laughed, then realised that he wasn't joking, and her hand went to her mouth in shock. "My god, you're serious! But…" she did a quick bit of mental arithmetic "…we'd only been going out for a month by then."

He smiled; perfect teeth in a clean-cut face. "I like to

plan ahead. Come on." He got out, went around to her side and opened the door for her. Perfect manners to go with the teeth. She'd never have predicted that they would still be together after only a few dates, and wasn't sure how much life this particular fling had in it; to be honest, his forward planning scared her a little, but she supposed it was the sort of thing that made one a success in the City. Let him plan as far ahead as he liked. For the moment she was simply going to enjoy a night out on the arm of a handsome and embarrassingly wealthy young man at one of London's most exclusive restaurants.

At first sight, it wasn't all that impressive. It seemed to have been built out of distressed clapboard and reclaimed timber, with its name hammered together out of cut-up pieces of old road signs, like a ransom note. If not for the huge windows it would have looked like a farm shed dropped into the middle of the street.

Inside, once their reservations and coats had been checked, they found the same artfully contrived facsimile of urban decay. Bare walls, exposed I-beams, and no two tables or chairs alike. She loved it, and said so.

"The Sunday Times called it the Grand Temple of Freeganism," said Patrick, holding out her chair. "The philosophy of subverting modern consumerist culture by embracing found and foraged food. Or some such nonsense."

"Which of course explains the outrageous prices," she commented, picking up a menu. "And the fact that you could buy several small African countries with the jewellery being worn in this place."

"You," he murmured, leaning forward, "look completely gorgeous."

"That," she responded, "was the correct response. You have been trained well, haven't you?"

"Not at all. This is natural, untutored smarm."

She laughed. "Oh shut up and tell me what I should be ordering. I can't make head or tail of this menu."

"Funny, since that's probably what's on it."

"Lovely."

The menu, though short on courses, was long on information, providing explanations of how, why, where and when the ingredients of each dish had been sourced. The vegetables were grown organically in local allotments; the herbs foraged from patches of waste-ground; the trout caught from under the shadow of Big Ben despite the Thames having being declared biologically dead mere decades ago.

"And they really do serve up road-kill," she read, shaking her head.

"Think about it, though," said Patrick. "Take a deer or a pheasant, say, that's been living wild. It's not going to have been force-fed all the chemicals and antibiotics that factory-produced cows and chickens have. It's going to be leaner and probably healthier, never mind that it died from a car instead of a bullet. Then there are the things you just don't get to taste normally. I think I'm going to go for the *blaireau au sang*."

"What's that?"

"Badger casseroled in red wine with armagnac and a glass of pig's blood. It's an old French peasant's dish, apparently."

"Well your old French peasant can keep it," she humphed. "It sounds disgusting."

"Possibly. But since it's also illegal to hunt badgers, one has to ask oneself: when am I ever going to get the chance again?"

"Let's just say it's not high on one's bucket list. I'll have the fish, thanks."

Their food, when it arrived, was everything that the pretentious restaurant critics had praised. Their 'plates' were compressed discs of reindeer moss, eaten like poppadoms along with their main course, while their cutlery was made from peeled oak twigs carved at one end and raw at the other for them to chew as primitive toothbrushes. The starter – a terrine of venison, Trafalgar pigeon and foraged wild quince on a bed of toasted nettle and bittercress salad – was the roller coaster ride her tastebuds had been promised, and her line-caught trout was meltingly wonderful, more inhaled than eaten. Patrick even managed to convince her to try a mouthful of his badger casserole. It was rich, heavily aromatic, and the meat was much less gamey or tough than she'd imagined for a wild animal.

"Interesting, isn't it?" he grinned.

"It's not what I was expecting at all."

"Does it taste like chicken?"

"Why would it taste like chicken?"

"Surely you've heard that theory," he said, surprised.

"What theory?"

"You know, that if you're eating something unusual for the first time it always seems to taste like chicken."

"Is that the kind of thing you boys learn from watching Dave TV all the time?"

From a quick glance around, the *blaireau au sang* seemed to be quite popular with the other diners, and she found herself almost regretting her choice. But soon there was a new culinary adventure to distract her as the dessert arrived – praline shortbread wafers made with hazelnuts from the trees on Hampstead Heath, in an elderberry and rose-hip coulis – and its strangeness was pushed to the back of her mind.

***

Danny, the kitchen assistant (or galley slave, as liked to call himself, but never within earshot of that psycho Rouse), unhitched the locking bar on the big wheelie-bin in the back alley, flipped up the lid, and dumped in the sack of scraps which he'd collected. He did this automatically, without looking, and so didn't notice the thing whose head he dumped it on.

He heard it, though.

As he shut the lid, there came a tumbled sound of shredding and thrashing from inside, as if something large was tearing the bag apart to get to its contents.

Danny was no stranger to rats - nobody who worked in the restaurant trade in any city could be – but this sounded like a huge bugger. He couldn't work out how it had gotten in. Savannah, due to the kinds of ingredients it used, got more than the usual attention from Environmental Health, who had made Rouse get these special wheelie-bins with the lockable lids, and nothing that didn't have a thumb should have been able to open one. It could have been a junky, he supposed, but what kind of junky would be so desperate as to hide in a dumpster for scraps?

Either way, he didn't want to know. Hopefully whatever – or whoever – it was would eat their fill and sod off. Danny wasn't going to report it. It was the kind of thing that got places like Savannah closed, and Rouse was the kind of Chef who wouldn't just shoot the messenger – he'd skin him, wear his arse for a hat and eat his liver with some fava beans and a nice chianti. In a pinch, Danny could always blame one of the Romanian cleaners.

The thing in the dumpster thrashed again, so hard that the bin actually rocked on its wheels.

Danny the galley slave shuddered and went back in to volunteer for washing-up duty.

***

Afterwards, Lilla and Patrick went for a walk by the river, finding a secluded spot where they could watch the city lights on the water twisting like broken neon eels. They were oddly beautiful.

"It's weird," she said. "To think that what I ate for dinner came from just over there this morning."

"I think it's weird that you think that's weird," he replied.

She frowned. "Explain."

"For thousands of years we – humans, that is – have eaten food that we've caught and grown ourselves. It's only in the last fifty or so that we've had this whole supermarket system going on. How sick must we be as a society that we can't see where our food comes from?"

"You say such sweet, romantic things," she cooed, fluttering her eyelashes at him.

"I'm sorry, I'll try that again. That's a smashing blouse you're wearing, my dear."

"Oh shut up," she laughed, and swatted him.

And he disappeared.

That was her first impression, anyway; that her playful shove had somehow pushed him out of the world completely. The thing that came out of the bushes moved so silently and so fast that it bore him to the ground a dozen yards away before her brain had time to register the attack for what it was. Then there was just a tangle of flailing limbs in the darkness, Patrick screaming "GetitoffmejesusfuckingchristGETITOFFMEEEE!!!" and the creature's own peculiar cry – a stuttering, indrawn mewling snarl. The thing (there was fur, she could see that much, and legs which seemed to bend in all the wrong directions as it scrabbled to maintain a grip on him), had its claws on his face, forcing his jaws apart, and its snout was right in his mouth, snuffling at him, *smelling* him from the inside out, while he bucked and yelled and she just stood there paralysed, watching, doing nothing. Why wasn't she *doing* anything?

Then it reached up with its hindpaws and tore his belly open, and she did something then. She screamed.

So did Patrick. Screamed and howled and begged and prayed and wept as it laid him open in the night air. Soon he stopped, but she carried on loud enough for the pair of them as she saw his intestines gleaming, just like the river had gleamed while they had been walking and talking a million years ago, and now she could smell them: the burnt-metal tang of his blood, the shit in his bowels, and – dear God as if that weren't enough – the meal he had lately eaten.

The creature dipped its head into the ruin and began to eat Patrick's dinner from out of his own dying stomach.

At this, her screaming turned to retching and she stumbled away, bringing up her own meal as she went. It wasn't very far before all she could do was crawl, and the wet noises behind her continued as the creature finished with Patrick and moved on to what she'd left on the ground.

She didn't get very far. Its stink caught her first, making her whirl around out of some instinct to at least face the threat, just as its weight crashed into her, crushing the breath from her lungs. Its claws gripped her forehead and chin, forcing her mouth open, and its black eyes bored into her, obsidian and pitiless. She was nothing to it, she understood – just something to feed an appetite. Its muzzle pressed right between her teeth, slick with Patrick's death and its own drool, tusks against her lips, and she gagged, but her stomach had nothing left to give. The creature took several long, deep breaths of her.

Then it was gone, as quickly as it had appeared, and there was nothing but the broken serpents of light on the black river.

***

Through a fog of shock there were strobing emergency lights, faces, an ambulance, a hospital. People waved small torches in her eyes and asked her what her name was, did she know what had happened, was there anyone they could call - but they were on the other side of the fog and couldn't touch her. This was just as well, because there was something else on the other side of the fog which she didn't want to know about.

When it cleared a little, she found herself in a hospital bed in a curtained-off resus room surrounded by strange machines and the bustling noise of an Accident-and-Emergency department.

The curtain was drawn back by a male nurse carrying a tray of swabs, dressings, and a bowl of water. Seeing that Lilla was aware of him, he produced a tired but warm smile. "Hello, miss. Back with us, are you?"

Words clambered over each other in Lilla's throat. "I'm. In hospital," she managed.

"That's right. Just a few scratches, that's all. There's a police officer outside who wants to ask some questions, but I told her she could just wait. We'll have you cleaned up right as rain soon enough. My name's Sam."

Sam the nurse set the tray down on the bedside table and began cleaning her forehead. She sat patiently, like a child, and let it happen, watching the water become redder and redder. It reminded her of something on the other side of the fog.

"Patrick!" she said in sudden alarm. "Oh my God! Patrick!" How could she have forgotten? "Where is he? Is he alright?"

"The fellow who came in with you?"

She nodded. "We were... we'd had a meal. We were going for a walk. By the river. Then a. A thing. It. Oh god..." she murmured woozily and flopped back against the pillow, fogged again. "He's dead, isn't he?" she whispered, as if by doing so she could avoid drawing attention to it and thereby make it untrue.

The nurse gently placed a steri-strip across one of the larger cuts on her forehead. "Do you want to see him?" he asked.

No! thought Lilla. *Are you insane?* But nodded.

"Right, well let's get you cleaned up properly first. Do you have a name I can give?"

"Olivia," she answered faintly. "Olivia Martin."

After some enquiries, Sam took her to a room and showed her a human shape under a sheet, but it wasn't Patrick. It couldn't be. It had his face and hair and the mole above his right eyebrow – it was in fact an excellent copy – but it simply couldn't be him. She knew he was dead, but that knowledge was out there beyond the fog, where it couldn't hurt her.

She was left alone for a moment, but Sam was back all too quickly.

"Miss Martin," he said, still kind, but with a business-like edge to his voice. "Sorry about this but we're going to be needing this room now. Can you give me a minute?"

"I'll, yes, I think so. What's happening?"

But Sam was bustling around the room, laying out trays of equipment and checking the machines while a porter came in and began to wheel away the bed in which not-Patrick lay.

"Where's he taking him?" she asked, startled.

"If you'll take a seat in reception I promise I'll get back to you about your man as soon as I can," Sam assured her. "Somebody's coming in hurt and they really need this room, sorry."

Lilla backed gingerly out of the room, not wanting to be in anybody's way, and as she did so she saw an emergency bed hurrying towards her, surrounded by a crowd of doctors and paramedics all talking medical gibberish to each other at the same time, and followed by a stricken-faced young man who was very smartly dressed except for the blood all over him. The patient was an older man entwined with tubes and wires, and his torso was heavily wadded with dressings which had already turned crimson.

Both men looked vaguely familiar – even despite the oxygen mask strapped over the face of one – and it took a moment for her to place them. The restaurant. They'd been several tables over; she remembered because Patrick had said he'd recognised the older fellow from a deal he'd worked on last year and wasn't it a small world? They'd laughed at the coincidence.

Lilla stepped aside as the bed rolled past, and knew that the huge, awful wound which lay beneath those dressings was no coincidence. She stopped the blood-covered partner as he staggered at the rear of the procession.

"It attacked you too, didn't it?" she said.

He turned wet, muddled eyes in her direction, but she doubted that he was seeing her very clearly. His mind was in the fog.

"It was so fast," he replied vaguely. "It didn't even look at me. Just went straight for Will." Then his throat started working, and she knew that she had to be quick and cruel because he was on the verge of losing it altogether, just like she had.

"What did you have for dinner?" she demanded.

He frowned with confusion, and almost seeing her properly. "What? Why?"

"At the restaurant. What did you *eat*?"

"I had the risotto. Will had the casserole. What does it matter?" He pushed past her and followed the paramedics.

Not a coincidence in the slightest. She felt herself becoming wobbly again, the fog pressing in on all sides, but shook it off angrily and went to look for that police officer.

***

Lilla found her seated in the waiting area, scribbling in a notebook.

"Excuse me, officer? You wanted to see me?"

The WPC looked up, taking in Lilla's haggard appearance - the blood, the taped-up wounds – then realised who she was and stood hurriedly.

"Yes! Yes I do! They told me you were being…"

Lilla cut her off. She couldn't be sidetracked. If she lost momentum the fog would get her again. "Officer, my name is Olivia Martin. My boyfriend and I were attacked earlier tonight."

"So I understand. Can you tell me exactly what happened?" Her pen was poised over the notebook, ready to record the nightmare in neat, safe handwriting. For some reason it made Lilla angry.

"That's not going to help," she said. "You need to get on your radio and tell someone to go back to the restaurant where we had dinner, because I think other people are in danger of getting hurt."

"I'm sorry, Miss Martin, I don't quite follow."

"Those men who just came in," Lilla pointed back along the corridor, "were attacked by the same thing. Only it wasn't after us, not as such. It was after what we ate. That's why it didn't kill me – because I threw it back up."

"Threw what back up?"

"The badger casserole."

The WPC's mouth twitched at the corners, ever so slightly, and this just made Lilla's mood worse.

"I know how it sounds…" she began angrily.

"No, Miss, it's fine, honestly." She plainly thought that Lilla wasn't playing with a full set of tiddlywinks. "I'm sorry, I'm just trying to make sense of this."

"Sense? *Sense?* Exactly what way of seeing my boyfriend get killed do you think would make sense to me, officer? You need to find everyone else who had that casserole and you need to do it now or more people are going to die!" She was shouting now, which was not wise. The officer stepped back apace sharply, the patronising smile switched off, and Lilla saw her hand move fractionally towards her belt, which carried such reassuring items as handcuffs, pepper spray, and a truncheon.

Lilla forced herself to calm down and backed away, hands in the air, placatory. "I'm sorry. I'm sorry. Look, I just think I'll go and have a nice, quiet sit down. How about that?"

"I think that would be a very good idea," said the WPC, still wary.

Lilla spent the next quarter of an hour doing anything but having a nice, quiet sit down. She knew that if she relaxed the fog would get her – or even worse, she'd have to think about that shape under the sheet. She knew that her parents were probably on their way, but all they would make her do was rest, calm down, and think. Every time the outer doors of the A&E department slid open she expected it to be another ambulance carrying a victim of the same thing that had attacked her. Could it really have targeted them because of what they had eaten? The idea seemed absurd. But if it were true, exactly what had they eaten to attract something that vicious?

Dear God, what had the chef at Savannah fed them?

***

The restaurant was dark and closed when the taxi dropped her off for the second time that night. She'd been in A&E longer than she'd thought; it was past midnight.

This was a mistake, she told herself. There was obviously nobody left. She cupped her hands against the window and peered inside: chairs stacked on tables and a closed sign hanging neatly in the door. No mangled corpses. No monsters.

Just a faint light far across the other side of the room, coming from the door to the kitchens.

The front door was locked, but with a little exploring she found a side alley which looked like it led to the delivery area. The problem was that there was no light down there;

anything could be waiting for her. The only thing giving her enough courage to come this far had been her guess that the creature hadn't killed her before because she didn't have what it wanted, and the assumption that this still held true.

This was a *big* mistake. But she did it anyway.

The alley turned out to be harmless, and she came out into the yard behind the restaurant, cramped and stinking with boxes, bottles, and wheelie bins. The restaurant's back door was open, spilling light and the agonised moans of a man into the yard.

She crept closer to the sound, until she reached an angle where she could just about see into the kitchen. Saucepans and a shrapnel of broken plates littered the floor. She must have made some kind of noise without realising it, because a ragged voice called out.

"Hello? Is anybody there? Please, for God's sake, please help me!"

She edged further in, trying to see in every direction at once.

Alex Rouse, proprietor and head chef, was wedged in the corner of two cupboards, sitting in a spreading pool of his own blood. One hand clutched a carving knife, its blade black with the blood of the creature which had attacked him; the other hand was clutched to his stomach, and for a moment she wondered why he was holding links of sausages to himself. Then she realised, and shrank back against the door. He raised the hand with the knife, pleading.

"Hospital…" he gasped.

There was so much blood. She couldn't go near him.

"I lost my phone earlier tonight," she apologised. "Where's your landline?"

"Fuckin' hell," he groaned. "Mobile. In my coat. Back of the door."

She found his coat on a hook and fumbled through the pockets for his phone, then, when he told her its PIN, fumbled at the phone itself, her fingers shaking with adrenalin. The first app she got was the last one he'd used: the photo album. She stared with increasing anger and disbelief at picture after picture of the road-kill that Rouse had butchered. Only by a massive stretch of the imagination could that thing be described as a badger. She waved the screen at him.

"What is this?" she demanded.

"What is *what?*" he retorted, and then screamed at the pain this caused him. "My guts hanging out and you want to talk ingredients? Just call a fucking ambulance."

"*What did you give us?!*"

He laughed, and screamed again. "I gave you exactly what you paid for! Something gross to gossip about with your rich girly-girlfriends and your high-society arseholes. "Ooh, you'll never guess what I ate!" I could shit on a plate and you'd pay to eat it if some dickhead in a magazine told you it was trendy, as if any of you would have a fucking clue in the first place. I don't know what it is. I don't think anybody does. All I know is something else likes the taste of it a fucking lot, and if you don't call that ambulance soon we are both dead when it comes back."

"What do you mean, *when it comes back?*"

He waggled the knife. "I hurt it. I don't know how much. Maybe scared it off. Maybe not."

She began to dial.

"Fucking finally," he muttered, and his head fell back exhaustedly.

Something shifted in the darkened restaurant behind them. It sounded like chair legs scraping against the floor, as if a whole banqueting table of people had suddenly got to their feet at once.

"No…" Rouse moaned.

The connecting door to the restaurant slammed open and the thing which had attacked her leapt over the kitchen work top, scattering trays, dishes and utensils. It was like the thing in the photos only much, much bigger. At least the size of a wild boar – and there was something porcine about the tusks curving out of its muzzle, even though its body was long and low like a weasel. It stared at her for a moment, as if to confirm that she had no chance of stopping it, while Rouse screamed and tried to back away through the cupboards. Then it leapt down and buried its face in his midriff, finishing the job it had started on him as he kicked and shrieked.

Lilla ran – out of the kitchen, through the yard, along the alley and out into the street, completely forgetting about the phone and thinking only of flagging down a car for help.

The driver of the white van which hit her could hardly be blamed. He wasn't speeding, or talking on his phone, and did his best to miss her in a great panicked swerve, but still managed to clip the top of her right thigh with his front bumper and send her spinning like a dancer onto the pavement, where she struck her head and blacked out. What he did then was entirely blame-worthy, however. He stopped a hundred yards down the road and glanced in the rearview mirror to see if there were any witnesses. The area was mainly industrial units, completely deserted at this time of night. He agonised for a moment. He already had six points on his licence and a thing like this would mean losing it for sure - along with his job, mortgage, house, and marriage, in that order. Hating himself, he made a quick, anonymous 999 call, and drove away.

***

The rannul limped out of the alleyway, after sniffing to make sure that it was safe. It had done its best to satisfy the primal instinct which told it to clear up after the remains of its dead pup, and the long night had left it near exhaustion. Across the road, in a patch of waste-ground between two warehouses, it smelled a gap in the world back to its nest in the Middens. But it had to be careful; the human female was lying over there.

It double-checked, and then ran across the empty road. When it was parallel with Lilla, lying half on the pavement and half in the weeds of the vacant lot, it stopped. Human was not the best meat – it usually reeked with pollution – but times were hard and it had been away from the nest for a long time. The rest of the rannul's pups would be hungry when it returned.

It took its road-kill by an ankle and dragged it away into the Middens.

The pups, it turned out, wouldn't touch the woman's flesh. They toyed with it and mewled and complained at its stink, until the rannul snarled its frustration at them and flung the human away, not wanting to kill it and pollute the nest with its blood.

***

When Lilla awoke, every part of her body hurt. Cautiously, she checked herself; scratches, bites and abrasions galore, but nothing serious other than a walloping great bruise on her hip which spread up her side and all the way down that leg.

It took some time for her to take in the details of where she was. When she did, she clamped her eyes shut and wrapped her arms around her knees, willing it to go away. This must be what insanity looked like. No sky should be that colour, the same bruise as her skin. No tree should move like that, clawing at the ground and screaming from a hundred tortured knot holes. Even so, she could still hear – the cries of animals which might have been birds, if there were such things as birds here.

She was in the land on the other side of the fog.

She wanted to be insane. She might wake up in a padded cell wearing a straitjacket and pumped full of anti-psychotic drugs, but at least this wouldn't have to be real.

But pray as she might, it didn't go away.

Eventually hunger drove her to her feet, flinching from the grass which writhed between her fingers. The message from her body was simple: eat or die. She'd survived being hit by a car and attacked by a creature from an alien reality, twice, and she was by no means ready to let something so pathetic as hunger kill her just yet.

Lilla tore strips from her clothing and bandaged up the worst of her wounds. She found a long stick which would serve as both a prop for her injured leg and maybe a spear, and collected enough small stones to fill her pockets, then set off to investigate those bird-like sounds and see if Patrick's theory was true.

She wondered how much of this new world tasted like chicken.

Rocky Says Hi!
By Lizz-Ayn Shaarawi

Sissy examined the mushroom cap and frowned. She tossed the fungi onto the pile on the counter top as she called over her shoulder, "Bob Ed!"

Pots and pans clanged as a large form filled the kitchen's entrance. Bob Ed's enormous frame squeezed through the doorway. "What are you hollering about now?"

Sissy pointed to the mushrooms. "These morels. Where'd you find these?"

"Over toward Butcher's Hill. I thought you liked 'em." He wiped his bloody hands on his worn apron that had been white many, many washes ago.

Sissy pulled the mushroom cap back and exposed the underside. "This is a false morel, suge. Look at this. See how the cap's attached at the top of the stalk? Real morels have a honeycombed cap and one hollow room right here."

Bob Ed peered closely at the mushroom. "Ah, hell. I was just trying to do something nice for you." He hung his head.

Sissy wrapped her small arms around his girth and gave him a hug. "I know, suge. You just got to be careful is all. We don't want to make no one sick."

"All right. I'll try to remember." Bob Ed started back toward the kitchen. "I got that deer what was hit by Trader's Junction. He's carving up real nice."

"That's good. We can make a stew." Sissy smiled as Bob Ed ducked back into the room. The sound of tires on gravel drew Sissy's attention to the front window. Her smile faded.

A sleek, dark hybrid sedan skidded to a halt in front of the dilapidated building. The car doors flew open and a young hipster couple stepped from the vehicle. The man clicked the key fob and the alarm chirped. The woman, Tamsin, chided him. "Really, Rufus. I don't think anyone is going to steal our car."

Rufus sneered. "You never know what these hillbillies think. For all I know they'll try to..." He spotted a shadow by the café's front window.

"They'll try to what?" Tamsin asked as she stepped over what could only be described as a hubcap sculpture.

"Tamsin, they're watching us." Rufus spoke barely above a whisper. She followed his gaze to the front window where Sissy stood. Rufus smiled and nodded to her. Sissy glared but nodded back.

A sharp elbow jab caused Rufus to yelp and jump. He glared at Tamsin. "Let's go ahead and get this over with." She said.

Rufus plastered on his best fake smile and strode to the door.

A small copper bell chimed above the door as it opened. Rufus and Tamsin wandered in and scanned the room. The wooden counter was clean but rubbed shiny from years of scrubbing. A couple of cracked formica topped tables dotted the room accompanied by wobbly chairs. However, it was the display covering the wall behind the lunch counter that made them stop and stare in awe.

Bleached skulls, from small mice to large deer, hung from the walls. Every inch of space held a token or memento of bone. Rufus held his phone up and took pictures. Tamsin swallowed dryly, uncomfortable with the display. "That's some collection you have there."

"Bob Ed cleans the meat from them. I just boil off the bones."

Rufus turned a charming smile towards Sissy. "You use every bit of the animal?"

"You could say that." Sissy stared down her nose at him, his charisma sliding off of her like Teflon.

As if an unspoken tag out just occurred, Rufus stepped back and Tamsin took his place at the counter. "What my husband means to say is we admire you ethics when dealing with your food supplies."

Bob Ed's figure darkened the kitchen door. "You alright, Sissy?"

It was Tamsin's chance to turn on the charm. "Is this your husband?"

Bob Ed looked to Sissy. Without taking her eyes from Tamsin, Sissy growled, "That's between us and Jesus." Bob Ed nodded.

And tag.

Rufus headed over to Bob Ed who eyed him with suspicion. "I like the skulls. Really gives the place a unique spin. I appreciate things that are different."

Bob Ed beamed. He pointed to a deer skull, the antlers still attached. "This here is - Beau, we found him out by route nine." Next came an elk skull. "And this one's Charlie. He was sick with worms so we couldn't eat him. Sissy let me keep the skull and we used the meat for bait." Bob Ed turned his back to the city folk.

"You don't waste anything do you?" Rufus asked.

"No, sir. Lest we try not to." Bob Ed whirled around.

Tamsin screech but recovered herself. Perched on Bob Ed's thick thumb and forefinger was a small raccoon skull. The movement of his fingers clicked it open and closed.

"Say 'hey' to the nice people, Rocky." The jaw clacked menacingly. Bob Ed spoke out of the side of his mouth in a high pitched voice "Hey, y'all."

Tamsin's smile turned rictus. "Cute. I like it."

"Y'all gonna buy some food or what?" Sissy stepped between Bob Ed and Rufus.

Rufus's grin stretched to a shark-like leer. "Oh, yes. We'd like to buy."

Sissy's brow furrowed in confusion. "I don't like your tone, mister.

"You see, Rufus is the premier restaurateur on the East Coast -" Tamsin began.

"But I plan on conquering the entire country... for starters." Rufus's leer widened to the point that Sissy, for a brief moment, thought his cheeks might split and devour her whole like a snake, though a copperhead would appear less sinister than this fella. "And to do that, I have to be on the cutting edge of cuisine. The latest and greatest dining experience and it must happen before anyone else discovers it. Downhome cooking. Unspoiled ingredients. Taking from the land only what it gives, be it wild vegetables from the woods or meat cut down unexpectedly in its prime."

"And that's us?" Sissy ventured.

"Precisely." Tamsin took over. "How do you supply your restaurant?"

Bob Ed thundered up to the counter. "You listen here, our food's clean. Ain't nobody got sick from eating here."

"You're missing my point."

"The hell we are." Sissy countered. "You can't just come up in here and start talking about our 'food supply' and 'supply ethics'. Y'all trying to get us closed down?"

"We want to buy your restaurant." Rufus and Tamsin threw their hands out like they were game show hosts showing off the grand prize.

Sissy and Bob Ed stared at them, wary.

As the city folk realized that Sissy and Bob Ed were far from enthused, they changed tactics once again. "It will *still* be your restaurant."

"In fact, we'd like you to come to New York and cook for us."

Sissy walked out from behind the counter. Rufus and Tamsin braced themselves to be bathed in gratitude. Sissy passed them and opened the front door.

"Get the hell out." Sissy rolled her head from side to side.

"Aw, hell. You got her neck going." Bob Ed took a step back.

And Tag.

Tamsin strode over to Sissy. She slammed the door closed and grabbed Sissy by the hair. Bob Ed charged but stopped short as Rufus pulled a semi-automatic handgun from his waistband and pointed it at the big man's face. "Slow down there, Slim." Bob Ed backed up but the veins on his neck throbbed and his jaw clenched so tight that it was surprising his teeth didn't break.

"Y'all about to get in a whole mess of trouble."

Tamsin rolled her eyes. "Sit down, Bubba. Let's be civil."

"It's Bob Ed."

"We don't really care. But what we do care about is launching the first Hillbilly themed restaurant in Williamsburg."

"Who you calling 'hillbilly'?" Bob Ed asked.

"If the sweaty John Deere baseball cap fits…" Tamsin gave him an exaggerated once over.

"This is what's going to happen," Rufus said. "We expect a sample menu, we'd like to visit your foraging grounds —"

"The what?" Bob Ed shook his head.

"Where you get the food from. I'd like to take some pictures to bring back to the investors."

"Well, shoot. That's the woods back there and the occasional road kill out route nine or so. We used to go over down by Dixiville on that there main highway but it make the tourists squeamish and Sheriff Taylor asked us to stop."

Sissy stepped up. "Bob Ed does the cooking. I'll take you to the 'supplies'." She glanced down at Tamsin's cute kitten pumps that probably cost more than Sissy and Bob Ed's trailer. "You might want to change those shoes." She gave Bob Ed a reassuring smile. "Suge, you whip up one of them venison steaks with a *nice* mushroom gravy, some 'taters with wild onions, and wilt up some collards with pepper sauce." Sissy reached behind the counter and pulled out a machete. Tamsin yelped and ducked behind Rufus who swung the gun wildly. "If y'all want to make it through the forest any time soon, we're gonna have to cut a bit."

Tamsin crept out from behind Rufus as he slowly lowered his gun. He cleared his throat. "Okay. Let's see where the magic happens."

Dust stirred as the wooden door to the slaughter room opened, but the room itself was clean save for the large deer dangling from a hook in the middle of the room. Part of the torso had been cut away. "That's where the truck hit it, the meat's no good" Bob Ed explained. The phone's camera clicked away.

"This is perfect. Just perfect." Rufus glanced over at Sissy. "Let's see the woods."

Bob Ed nodded to Sissy and headed back to the kitchen. He paused in the doorway to give Rufus a hard stare. "You hurt one hair on her head and I'll kill you dead."

"Don't worry, you're both worth much more to me alive than dead." Rufus assured him.

The gun dangled from Rufus's hand, catching glints of sunlight, as he and Tamsin, now in brightly colored rain boots, followed Sissy as she led them through the wild woods. As they went, she pointed out sorrel, chicory, white mustard, and purslane. Wild asparagus grew in tufts on a hillside. Brambles of blackcaps scraped their arms and pulled at their clothes as they picked handful after handful and gobbled them on the spot. The electronic *snick* of the phone's camera sounded obscene in the otherwise unspoiled woods, but the couple didn't seem to notice.

As the forest became denser, Sissy was forced to use her machete more and more. She had just tackled a particularly thick tangle of bushes when she stopped abruptly and pointed. "Garlic scapes." Rufus squinted and searched the area. Sissy crept back, circling behind the couple. Rufus spotted the green curls of the scapes and broke into a grin. "Lovely. Absolutely lovely." He ambled over to the plants and aimed his phone.

Little flicks of red caught Tamsin's attention. She

slowed to admire a wild raspberry bush. Sissy hovered behind her. Tamsin reached out for a particularly juicy looking berry. Sissy closed in, her hand reaching towards the unsuspecting urban dweller. Pebbles rolled and rattled as Tasmin took another step. Sissy's arm whipped out, lighting fast.

"Careful, now." Sissy grabbed the back of Tamsin's blouse and yanked her back. Tamsin glanced down and found that she was teetering on the edge of a large precipice. Spindly bushes grew out and up from the drop, camouflaging it. Trembling, she stumbled back from the edge. "Some city fella done fell to his death here round about six months ago." Sissy informed them. "Y'all got to keep an eye out. Lots of sink holes and drop offs."

"Perhaps we should head back." Tamsin shot a frightened glance to Rufus. He nodded. "Might as well, we've seen what we came for."

Mosquitos buzzed and hummed around their faces as they trudged back towards the restaurant. "So how are y'all planning on bring all this back to New York?" Sissy asked.

Rufus dodged deer droppings. "We'll use reclaimed wood for the walls, transfer the skulls over—"

"Bob Ed ain't gonna like that. He's very close to them skulls." Sissy said.

Tamsin snorted. "Can't he just get more? It's not like you don't have road kill everywhere."

"It's not just road kill. Bob Ed is very particular about his meat. It has to be fresh. It can't be spoiled or infested with bugs or worms. We might not have much, but we're proud people and we do right."

"Well, I'm sorry if I offended you." Tamsin replied.

"No, you aren't but if it makes you feel better to say

it, it's fine by me." Sissy stormed ahead, around a curve in the trail.

Rufus grabbed Tamsin's arm. "Can you at least try to be civil?"

"They're hicks. Why do we even need to negotiate with them? Just steal it. Like they'll ever go to New York and find out."

"It has to be authentic. That's why my last two ventures failed. They weren't honest. They weren't real."

"Or maybe they were just bad ideas? Poor location choices? Fickle diners?"

Rufus shook his head. "This one has to work."

Tamsin's eyes narrowed. "I'm not going back to waiting tables. There's no way I'm putting up with that crap again."

"This will be the one. I promise." Rufus put a reassuring arm around her shoulders. Tamsin frowned but nodded.

They rounded the corner of the trail. Sissy was nowhere in sight.

"Goddamn it!" Tamsin hit Rufus's chest. "I knew it! We're going to die out here, lost in the middle of hillbilly central because you can't think of your own concept for a restaurant that won't burst into flames and bankrupt everyone even remotely connected to it!"

Rufus grabbed her arms and shook her. "And you've been such a big help, haven't you? How much did this shirt cost? A couple of hundred? A thousand?"

"I should have nice things!"

"You can have nice things. I've never said you couldn't! I just don't understand why a five hundred dollar shirt is so much better than the exact same thing for eighty."

"I have to promote a look. I need to show I have taste."

"Don't talk to me about taste. When we met, you were slinging hash at shitty truck stop."

"It was a theme restaurant!"

"Some theme. How does the tip song go again?" Rufus stomped one foot and clapped his hands in time. "We're so glad you came in, we're really glad—"

"Shut up! Shut up!" The crack of her palm against his cheek echoed through the forest. They both froze. A twig snapped.

"Can't leave y'all alone for two minutes, can I?" Sissy drawled. "Come on now, we're almost there."

"Where were you?" Tamsin wailed.

Sissy gave her an incredulous look. "I had to pee. Why, you wanna watch?"

***

The copper bell chimed as Sissy led the couple back into the diner. Bob Ed popped his head out of the kitchen. "Go on and sit. I'm just finishing up in here."

Rufus and Tamsin took their seats at the counter. Rufus plopped down with an exhausted sigh. Tamsin, shaky and trembling from her great outdoors experience, nearly fell onto the seat.

Bob Ed set two mismatched plates in front of them. The deer meat, brown and succulent, was lightly covered in steaming brown gravy flecked with mushrooms. Ivory peaked whipped potatoes speckled green with diced wild onions towered over a lake of dark, rich collards infused with jalapeno-spiked vinegar. "Y'all want some 'shine to go with that?"

"I'm afraid I'll have to pass, I'm driving." Rufus chuckled.

"Oh, I'm game." Tamsin said. "Load it up."

Sissy set a Mason jar in front of her with a half inch of clear liquid in the bottle. Tamsin took a sip. Fueled by liquid courage, her bitch façade slid neatly back into place. She studied the Mason jar. "My God, but you love your stereotypes, don't you?" Tamsin chuckled.

"You'll be laughing out of the other side of your face once you get all that in your belly." Sissy replied.

"I'm a big girl, I think I can handle it."

"Suit yourself."

Rufus examined the plate. His nose crinkled as he sniffed each portion before lifting his knife and fork. As each small bite, chewed thoroughly, disappeared down his gullet, his glee grew.

Tamsin picked at the food but emptied the Mason jar. She gave them a wry smile. "You didn't poison us or anything, did you?"

Bob Ed's face darkened. "I told you, ain't nobody got sick from eating here and I don't plan on making y'all the first."

"Calm down, big man. She was just joking."

"Weren't funny." Bob Ed grumbled.

"I'll try harder next time." Tamsin slurred.

"That was delicious." Rufus wiped his mouth with the napkin and rose from his seat. "We'll have our lawyers pull up the contracts and have them FedExed to you in a couple of days."

Tamsin rose to follow, wobbled a bit, and clung to the counter. "Wow, that booze really hit me all of a sudden."

Her knees buckled and she dropped to the floor. "Rufus…" She managed to squeak in a small voice.

Rufus tried to pull Tamsin to her feet, he stared accusingly at the other couple. "Don't look at us. She's the one that can't hold her liquor."

"Just lay her down in the back seat, she'll be fine by the time you reach Jacksonville."

Bob Ed gave Sissy a look. "Don't you think it's best if they took Hopper's Pass?"

"Well, I suppose it would be faster this time of year. But you watch them curves with her being as skunked as she is."

Bob Ed came out from around the counter. Rufus reached for his gun but Bob Ed rolled his eyes and pushed Rufus out of the way. He hoisted Tamsin over his shoulder as if she weighed nothing and carried her out the front door.

Rufus cleared his throat. "So you'll hear from us."

"Can't wait." Sissy spat as she lit a Newport and leaned back against the wall.

Bob Ed passed Rufus on his way in. "Y'all drive safe, now."

Sissy stood in the window and watched the hybrid silently slip from the gravel parking lot. Bob Ed stood behind her and wrapped his arms around her waist, nearly enveloping her. She leaned back into him.

"Dammit, they just keep coming, don't they?" Sissy said as she blew a large plume of smoke out of her mouth.

"And we'll get rid of them every time." Bob Ed said.

She jerked and stared up at him. "Oh, hell. You didn't use the poison mushrooms, did you?"

"No ma'am. I was careful." He assured her.

She sighed and burrowed deeper into his embrace. "What are we going to do now, Bob Ed?"

"Don't you worry none, hon. I got it taken care of."

Sissy noticed a small blank spot on the skull wall. "Bob Ed, where's Rocky?"

"Boiling in back."

"What he'd get up to this time?"

"Chewed through the brake line of that fancy car they got."

"Well, at least he didn't bite them to death like the last one."

"That was too messy, even for the slaughter room. Don't want no forensics lying around like on CSI."

"Don't forget to put him back before Sheriff Taylor comes."

"I won't." Bob Ed kissed the top of her head. She patted his arm.

"I saw some garlic scapes out by the death drop. Might head out in a bit."

"Those'll cook up nice with a bit of rabbit."

"I'll set the traps on my way."

Sissy reached for her machete. Bob Ed kissed the top of her head before he ducked back into the kitchen.

The Critic
By Richard Freeman

It had been a good meal, but not an excellent one. Good, but not good enough to stop him from tearing the establishment apart. The service was good, the restaurant was spotlessly clean, the ambience was fine, but he had a reputation to keep up; he couldn't let his readers think he was getting soft.

Mori Hideki, you see, was a restaurant critic and the most feared restaurant critic in Osaka. His column in the *Osaka Observer* could make or break an eatery and he had broken far more than he had made. A meal needed to be transcendental before he gave it a favourable review. Even then, he did it begrudgingly. The fact was Mori Hideki enjoyed giving bad reviews. He enjoyed the little power trips it gave him and he enjoyed finding new and horrible ways to pick a restaurant and its food apart.

It was a good life being a restaurant critic, reviews aside; he usually ate very well (though he seldom let his readers know that). His meals and the accompanying drinks were free. He had the admiration of his peers and readers and fear of the entire restaurant community of not only Osaka but the whole of Nippon. He also got to travel the world and report back the finest eateries on the globe. He had visited Jean-Claude Vrinat's peerless *Taillevent* in Paris, Heston Blumenthal's legendary '*Fat Duck*' in the village of Brey, Berkshire, England and Thomas Keller's *Per Se* on Columbus Circle New York.

It was a life most could only dream of and yet Hideki was only ever happy if he was criticizing someone else's culinary efforts. At the moment as he was mentally composing his review and he strolled through Dōtonbori, the finest restaurant area in the city.

As he wandered back towards the JR Osaka Loop Line to take a train back to the offices of the *Observer* a smell hit his nostrils. Hideki was a foodie and his nostrils were more bloodhound than man when it came to the smells of cooking. Smell is linked intimately to memory and the scent now wafting under his nose sank deep into his psyche and transported him back 30 years to his mother's kitchen in Takatsuki. It was exactly like the smell of her home cooking. He smelled *Takoyaki* the octopus dumplings, exactly as she had cooked them. *Kushikatsu* the cheese and vegetables deep-fried in dough. These were not the smells of street vendors or restaurants, but his mother's kitchen smells.

Hideki had not eaten food like that in years. He had considered it fare only fit for bumpkins whilst his palate had turned to other delights. Now he felt his mouth begin to water, even on a full stomach. He turned and followed his nose.

The scent led him through a maze of little back streets he never even knew existed. As a critic writing for such a big paper as the *Observer* the small establishments that filled the back alleys of Dōtonbori usually fell under his radar. Finally he came to it; a tiny back street restaurant whose sign proclaimed it to be 'The Blue Dragon'.

The front looked grubby. The windows had not been cleaned in years and prevented a clear look into the interior. The painted sign, a coiling sapphire dragon, had faded with age. The front door looked peeling and old. *Oh but the smell!* He pushed the door open and entered.

The wall of alluring smells hit him and he began to salivate again. The place was busy, every table packed full of happy diners enjoying their food. A portly, smiling man with thinning hair approached. He was dressed in an apron and had his shirtsleeves rolled up.

"May help you? Table for one is it?

"No, not today but I'd like to book a place for next week?"

"Certainly sir, answered the man producing a pen and paper from his pocket, and your name?"

"Mori Hideki"

The man looked more than a little startled and took a step back looking Hideki up and down for a moment.

"The Mori Hideki, of the *Osaka Observer?*"

Hideki grinned and nodded. He enjoyed his reputation and liked to see restaurant owners sweat and squirm under his gaze. But this fellow seemed to gain his composure quickly and offered a broad smile.

"Never would have expected that such a great man would set foot in my humble establishment" he bowed low and seemed more pleased than apprehensive.

"Shall we say next Thursday? I can have the review in the *Observer* on Saturday."

" You do me a great honor Mori san."

"Till next week then, I will anticipate an excellent meal. Don't disappoint me."

"We try never to disappoint at The Blue Dragon."

"I'm glad to hear it my good man."

The owner bowed again and Hideki turned and walked back onto the street. He mused, as he walked back towards the station. The Blue Dragon was so different to the grand, five star restaurants he usually reviewed. It would be a pleasant change for his readers.

That afternoon he tore apart the restaurant he had eaten in. Even though the meal had been fairly enjoyable his review made it sound as if he had been eating excrement from inside an open grave. He was particularly pleased with the piece.

As the day drew on Hideki found his anticipation of the meal at The Blue Dragon returning. Could his enjoyment of actually eating be returning?

***

The portly owner greeted Hideki warmly upon his arrival.

"I have prepared a special room for you so that the other diners will not disturb you"

"How thoughtful of you"

Hideki grinned inwardly. He enjoyed being thought of as better than the masses.

His host led him past tables full of other diners to a door. It led to a smaller room with a table laid out ready for his guest. Hideki sat.

"I will bring the menu Hideki san. Would you care for a drink?"

"Kirin Fukkoku beer"

"Certainly", he scurried off as Hideki made himself comfortable. The host, whose name Hideki had not even enquired of yet was back within moments holding a glass of beer and a menu.

Hideki perused the list for a moment and let nostalgia choose for him.

"*Takoyaki* to begin followed by black cod with miso sauce and pumpkin moci with ice cream to follow."

"An excellent choice," the owner enthused.

Hideki mused on his choice as he sipped the beer. It

was far more standard fare than his normal repasts. But he could write a piece on simple foods and nostalgic dishes from his humble past. Yes that was a great spin, getting back to your roots.

The octopus dumplings were exquisite. The soft moistness of the dumpling contrasting with the chewiness of the tentacles. The cod flesh fell apart like an exotic flower opening and melted in his mouth. The sweet stickiness of the mochi rice paste mingled with the pumpkin and the cool persimmon flavored ice cream. Before long he was pushing the last dish away and smacking his lips.

"Was everything to your liking Hideki san?"

His host had reappeared.

"It was wonderful. The finest meal I have ever eaten!"

"That is wonderful, and would you like anything else?"

It was then Hideki realized that he was still quite hungry.

"Can I see the menu again?"

The host complied.

Hideki ordered a second meal; *Kushikatsu*, followed by salmon in wild cherry and Adzuki Beans with sugar all swilled down with beer and rice wine. Again the meal was delicious but again he still felt hungry, ravenous in fact. As always the food was on the house so Hideki ordered more.

Dish followed dish, tempura ice cream, yakisoba, chicken thighs in plum sauce, horse mackerel, wild boar stew, sukiyaki, deep fried pork cutlets, miso soup, hayashi rice, korokke, the list went on.

Suddenly Hideki stopped. The chopsticks tumbled from his grasp. He realized that he had eaten enough for half a dozen men. But he was hungry, more hungry than he had ever been in his life. It was a deep, gnawing hunger as if he hadn't eaten in days.

"Is every thing to your liking?"

He looked up to see the restaurant owner grinning at him.

"I'm sill hungry" Hideki whined.

"And so you will always be."

"*What*, I don't understand?"

"Hideki," the host explained, almost gleefully, "you live off other people's hard work whilst never lifting a finger yourself. You scandalize good, honest folk out of spite, and the feeling of power it gives you. You eat the finest food in Nippon and your thanks to those who sweat over it is to throw it back in their faces in the shallow, whinging, spineless little reviews you write. Do you realize how little you are? Do you realize how inconsequential what you do is? You take and take and give nothing in return. Your overweening arrogance and cowardly peevishness has put hundreds of people out of work. Mr. and Mrs. Yasunaga killed themselves last year after what you wrote about them. Did you know that? They had run their restaurant in this city for forty years! Well now it's time for revenge. You will never enjoy another meal Hideki and you will forever more be hungry."

The man held up a polished dish to show the critic his own reflection. He recoiled in horror. His visage had changed beyond recognition. Gone was the chubby face and fine hair. What looked back at him was a mockery. Gray skin barely stretched over a skull like face. The eyes were little more than tiny balls of orange light in two deep, black sockets, the nose was no more than a pair of slits and the mouth hung open, it's long black tongue dangling over jagged, rotting teeth. Drool slavered from his tongue and mouth, coating his shirt. He raised a hand. It was a wizened thing ending in broken, filth caked nails.

"Hideki san, you are damned and I bid you welcome to a hell of your own making."

"What am I?" He managed to croak the words from the twisted mouth.

"Well beside a cruel, petty, overpaid, vane, talentless hack, you are now a *jikininki.*"

"A w-what?"

"A jikininki, a hungry ghost. In life jikininki were greedy, selfish people. Now you are fated to be a jikininki for evermore. A cadaverous ghoul cursed with an insastiable hunger. Never again will that hunger be sated. Never will you know peace. You will eat and eat and yet be starving forever, starving to death, a death that will never come."

The man clapped his hands and several neatly dress waiters began to clear away the empty dishes whilst other brought more overflowing with food.

Hideki pushed his face forwards into a plate of sushi and began to eat knowing he would never know the feeling of a full stomach again.

Johnny G's All-Nite Diner
By Jack Maddox

They drove south from the apartment and all the blood. It was the middle of the night, and once they were out of the city the sky was endless, pinpricked with stars. The desert was a cold, blasted purple in the moonlight. To Sheila it looked like the surface of some alien planet. She told Keith that and he laughed, revealing his meth-stained teeth.

"Ain't no aliens out there," he said. "They're sittin' in this car right now."

Sheila agreed. She felt like an alien herself, always had. Something in this desolate place called to her very bones, made her feel like she was being pulled into the landscape by some weird gravity.

There were trees out there in the sand. They were black and twisted, and pointed at the dusty black Challenger like accusing fingers as it whipped by.

"Keith, maybe you oughta slow down," Sheila said, brushing his shoulder with her fingertips. Keith wrenched his arm away and pressed down harder on the gas.

"We got no time to slow down," he growled. "We gotta throw off the pursuit, else we ain't never gonna get to Mexico."

"We ain't gonna get to Mexico if you get pulled over for speeding," she said, and even Keith knew she had a point, and besides, it was going to be a real laugh if they ran out of gas and tried paying at some station with the cash they had in the trunk, with it being splattered with that guy Morgan's blood.

Sheila couldn't stop seeing what had happened in Morgan's apartment. Morgan had been pleading with Keith, on his knees and insisting the lab had burned when the Feds stormed it but he was going to build another one, a better one, please God he wasn't trying to fuck anybody over. What Morgan hadn't counted on was that Keith was good at one thing, and that was fucking people over before they could even think about doing it to him.

Morgan had made one sad dash for the door, and the bullet took him in the back of the head, blood and brains flying in clumps, all over the walls, all over the cash. Keith took all the money with them, including Morgan's share. He wasn't going to be using it anymore anyway, Keith had said when they pulled away in the Challenger; not unless he was buying ice-cream cones down in Hell.

Sheila didn't care much about Morgan being dead. It was getting caught that scared her. It scared her worse knowing that if it came down to choosing between her and Mexico, Keith would choose Mexico. He didn't seem to need her as much as she needed him. So she turned up the radio so she wouldn't have to think, then head-banged to Rob Zombie's "House of 1000 Corpses." A sixteen-year-old in ripped stockings, combat boots, and makeup that made her look like an escapee from a haunted house. She dressed that way because Keith liked it, had pierced her nose and eyebrows and both nipples because he thought it was hot.

She liked making him happy.

Keith's eyes flicked over her, and he nodded in approval. She settled down after a while and watched the miles click by on the odometer.

※ ※ ※

She'd met Keith in high school. He was a senior, she was a freshman. The only reason he was a senior was because he had a little network of fellow students doing his homework for him. He was smart about it, too, recopied everything in his own handwriting and made sure to answer one or two questions wrong, so he didn't stand out. The teachers knew he was doing it, but they didn't care. It meant one less problem student at the end of the year.

Sheila had been getting books out of her locker when Keith spun her around and planted a kiss right on her lips. She was too surprised to close her mouth, and he tasted like the joint he'd smoked in the boys' locker room. When she tried pushing him away he bent her wrists back until they hurt and said, "You don't stop until I tell you to stop, sweetheart."

Their relationship had followed that short, simple statement for the next two years, and Sheila never stopped before Keith told her to. Not the first time he made her snort a line, not all those nights in the back seat of his Challenger, not all those nights he lost her to his buddies in their weekly poker game.

The only time she almost stopped was when she was lying on a folding table in the back of some abandoned warehouse. He'd beaten her so bad she had trouble staying awake, angry about some backwoods deal gone wrong and taking it out on her. The guy Keith had called Dr. Death, was doing what Keith had paid him to do, and Sheila felt every sharp metal tool he used to reset her bones because Dr. Death didn't bring anything for the pain, and she almost screamed.

Before she could, Keith had leaned down and whispered in her ear, "You can go ahead and scream if you want to, babe. It's not like anybody cares."

So she let Dr. Death finish, and even through all the stitching she didn't scream. Not once.

***

It was four in the morning when they saw the diner.

It sat on the side of the road, and looked so old it might've been sinking into the desert, a long white building with a gravel parking lot dominated by a huge buzzing neon sign. Half the letters were burnt out, but Sheila could still read them by the moon; JOHNNY G.'S ALL-NITE DINER, OPEN 24 HRS. Beneath that, in smaller letters, *good eats, good company.*

Sheila thought nothing of it, but then Keith spun into the parking lot hard enough to throw her into the passenger door. She rapped her forehead a good one on the window, too, and yelped, "What the fuck, Keith?!"

He ignored her, screeched to a halt, and stretched his long, tattooed arms. "Feelin' hungry, babe?"

"You want to eat? What happened to throwin' off the pursuit?"

"A man can't drive on an empty stomach. 'Sides, when we gonna get a chance to eat before we hit the border? I want some real old-fashioned American steak and eggs before I get stuck eating wetback shit for the rest of my life."

Sheila looked around, eyes wide. There were a dozen other cars strewn around the parking lot, which was strange enough for this early in the morning. But the selection was odd. Several pickup trucks, a tricked-out Ford Roadster, and something that looked like a gangster car from some old black-and-white movie. Too many people in one place. "What if somebody heard about us? What if they see the license plate?"

Keith smiled and took something from under the driver's seat. It was the snubnose revolver that had killed Morgan. Sheila hadn't thought the thing would fire, not with the electrical tape wrapped around the grip and the rust on the barrel, but it had done the job well enough.

"If anybody gives us any trouble, I'll deal with it," Keith said, and he stroked the gun like it was Sheila's thigh. "I'm a stone-cold killer."

***

A little bell over the door jingled when Keith and Sheila stepped into Johnny G's All-Nite Diner. They might have stepped into a time warp and ended up in the Fifties. A long counter with stools down one side, a row of booths down the other. A checkered tile floor, and a huge jukebox in one corner. It was currently pumping out "Helter Skelter," the lights and dials inside flashing like an acid trip.

"I like it," Keith muttered, more to himself than to Sheila. "It's like Denny's for assholes."

They slid into the nearest booth. A waitress appeared almost instantly, bearing a note pad and two menus. "What'll it be?" she asked, a smile lighting up her weather-beaten face. Her name tag said she was AILEEN, and told Sheila to ASK ME ABOUT OUR WORLD-FAMOUS PANCAKES!

"Coffee," Keith said, eyeing the woman's tits. "Two of 'em. Black as night."

Aileen wrote the order down and said, "You folks might want to try the blueberry pancakes. Johnny's whipping up a fresh batch right now!"

She sashayed off to get their coffee. Keith rolled his eyes.

Sheila peeked around at the other people in the

diner. There were thirteen of them, she counted. Most sat by themselves, except for a tall man with a pencil-thin mustache and his girlfriend, who wore too much lipstick and a polka-dot dress. They sat at the counter, holding hands. Keith never held her hand.

A fat man sat sweating by the jukebox, his eyes darting here and there while he shoveled home fries into his mouth. A leash was wound around the hand that wasn't working his fork, leading down to a mangy dog with one chewed ear and fur that was mottled black and white and brown. The dog was asleep, its ribs moving up and down as it breathed.

A man in a long grey riding coat sat at the counter, flirting with the waitress when she was close enough. His hair was combed tight against his skull, and he sported an impressive handlebar mustache. He caught Sheila's eye and gave her a wink and a little salute. When he did, she saw the letters JWB tattooed across his first three fingers in blue ink.

"Got's to take me a long and satisfying piss," Keith announced, sliding out of the booth. He stretched, his back and neck popping, and said, "Get me a big fat cheeseburger when that cunt waitress comes back. And a vanilla shake. Got that, babe?"

"Yeah, I got it," Sheila said, even though she forgot his order almost as soon as he said it. She was looking down at the salt shaker, staring at its crystalline contents in the hope that it would make her forget everything that had happened that night. But she'd remember what Keith wanted when Aileen came back to take their order. She took Keith's order. Aileen took her order. It all balanced out.

She was good at taking orders.

***

Keith hadn't been gone thirty seconds before the man in the grey coat plopped down in the booth opposite Sheila, as if it were his seat and Keith had been keeping it warm for him. He flashed her a white grin and said, "Good evening, little lady. Been on the road long?"

Sheila, who'd been thinking about Mexico, about how she didn't know anybody down there and couldn't speak one lick of Spanish, blinked in surprise and said, "No, not too long. Um, Mister, that's my --"

"You just have that traveling look about you," the man said. "In my trade you get to know looks after a while. Some folks look like they've got a long way to go in those deep, dark woods. And if you're not careful you might end up in a witch's gingerbread house, getting pushed into the oven."

"My momma used to read me stories like that," Sheila said, finding herself entranced by the man's Southern accent, the way he flourished his hands a little when he talked.

"A fine old tradition, telling stories," the man said. He drummed his fingers on the table, and Sheila's eyes were drawn to the JWB inked across his knuckles. "Sometimes it's all we have to do in here...at least until someone new comes along. Telling stories is my forte, really. Used to be an actor. Only got famous for one performance, though."

"Was it something I would've seen?"

"Nah. *Julius Caesar.* I was Brutus. Where are you headed?"

"Down to Mexico." She bit her lip, feeling like she shouldn't be talking to JWB, no matter how charming he was. "My boyfriend has a job down there, so..." She trailed off, unsure of how to continue.

Aileen came back then, walking with that funny way of hers, hips swinging side to side like a ship sitting in a cove. "Wilkes," she said with a wry smile, "you bothering the customers again?"

"Last I checked, I was only a patron of your boss's establishment for the past two hundred years or so, lady," Wilkes said in an amiable tone, before his tattooed hand snaked out and smacked the waitress on the ass with a sharp CRACK. Sheila flinched, thinking of the gunshot in Morgan's apartment, the back of his head coming apart.

Aileen just laughed and said, "Normally that would cost you a fiver, mister big bad son of the South, but lucky for you I'm on duty." To Sheila, she said, "Don't let this sweet talker charm you out of ordering, sweet thing. What'll it be?"

She ordered Keith's cheeseburger and shake, and a stack of blueberry pancakes for herself. Aileen dropped her a surprisingly lecherous wink and went back to the kitchen.

As she shouldered her way in, the white kitchen door swung wide, revealing the massively fat man working the grill, attending to five or six hissing, spitting skillets. He wore grease-splattered whites, a paper cap cocked on his balding head. Sweat beaded his upper lip. Sheila tried not to think about the man sweating into Keith's food.

Before the door shut again on that little corner of food-service Hell, the fat man turned his head aside, quick enough it seemed he knew Sheila was watching him. The left side of his face was smeared with greasepaint, like a clown's makeup.

It took everything in Sheila not to scream.

***

Wilkes kept rambling on about his life as an actor, and Sheila nodded and smiled in all the right places, but she wanted nothing more than to grab Keith and run. He was taking so ever fucking long in the bathroom, and she was more scared with every passing minute.

"So..." she said to Wilkes just to make conversation. "Are you the guy who owns this place? Johnny?"

"No, no, no," Wilkes said. "He was here first. Built the place and then we all kind of wandered in. Folks come and go, but this here is pretty much the regular crew." He threw one arm out, gesturing to the crowd at the other end of the diner. "God's special little children. Ha!"

He leaned in too close to her and said, "We all try to run. Some make it farther than others. How far have you and your boy-toy run, my dear?"

"Don't know what you're talking about," Sheila said, shrinking into her jacket a little. Her hands were shaking.

"I can smell it on you," he said, closing his eyes. "Cordite tends to cling to the clothes. Small caliber, unless I miss my guess."

She said nothing. What was there to say, anyway? Pretty soon Wilkes would pry it out of her, and he'd tell the waitress, and the waitress would call the cops, but they wouldn't get there in time to keep Keith from killing her.

"Who's packing the shootin' iron? You or your boyfriend?"

Before Sheila could speak, Keith snarled: "Well, this looks fucking cozy."

He'd washed his face and hands in the bathroom, and now his skin burned an angry red. Or maybe it just always looked that way, and she just now noticed it.

He towered over Wilkes, a young bull in a Ramones T-shirt and shredded jeans, his arms pumped with muscle, his bloodshot eyes glaring.

"Keith, baby, I--"

"Shut up, bitch," he said, and she did. He pointed at Wilkes. "Trying to cop a feel off my girl when my back's turned, is that right?"

"Nothing of the sort," Wilkes replied, and there was no tremor in his voice.

He stood.

Keith outweighed him by at least forty pounds and stood five inches taller, but the man with the handlebar mustache didn't even flinch. "We were just enjoying a lovely conversation, the girl and I. You have to keep a close eye on this one, my friend. She might just take another man's heart."

"She doesn't do shit without my telling her," Keith said, pointing one black-nailed finger right at Wilkes's nose. "So you'd better fuck off, pal, before I take *your* heart."

Wilkes smiled. "Not in this life, friend. Or any other."

Keith snorted, and Sheila only realized what was going to happen when his hand came out from behind his back.

He pressed the snubnose to Wilkes's forehead and pulled the trigger.

***

The gunshot was loud in that little diner. Sheila shrieked as Wilkes's head snapped back, painting the window behind him with blood and brains. His body thumped down into the booth's other seat. His feet twitched once, twice, then stilled.

Keith swung the revolver around and aimed at the other patrons, holding the gun sideways because he saw it done that way in a movie once. "EVERYBODY DOWN!" He screamed. "DOWN ON THE FLOOR! I ALREADY KILLED SOMEBODY TONIGHT, SO DON'T FUCK WITH ME! DOWN!"

Nobody moved. The lady in the polka-dot dress took a dainty bite from a slice of strawberry pie she and her man were sharing. Aileen scribbled something on her notepad. Even the dog in the corner didn't wake.

Keith's gun arm wilted a little, and when he told everyone to get down again his voice had a strangled quality, like he'd swallowed a live frog with plenty of fight left in it. And still nobody dropped.

"Go empty the cash register, babe," he said without turning.

"Okay," Sheila said. She got up, glad to be away from the smell of Wilkes's fried hair and the bits of his skull scattered across the table. She jumped the counter and opened the register, an old-fashioned affair with an actual bell that chimed when the drawer slid out.

Keith still had the gun up, and either ignored the looks of amusement the other diners were giving him, or hadn't noticed in the first place. "All right, here's how this works. My girlfriend's going to take all the money from the till, and we're going to leave."

"Keith?"

"I see anybody poke their head out the door, I'll blow your fucking brains out, every last one of you. I'll kill you so bad your own mother won't recognize you."

"Baby?"

"You just keep on eating your fucking fries and forget we were here, understand?"

"Babe?"

Keith turned to her and screeched, *"WHAT?!"*

She flinched, but still went ahead and said, "There's no money."

He blinked once, then vaulted over the counter, shoving Sheila aside.

The drawer was empty.

He shoved the register off the counter with a crash, kicking and screaming, *"Where's the fucking cash?"*

The woman in the polka dot dress giggled and said, "Johnny G. doesn't charge us, sweetheart. We're all friends here. Except you, of course."

Keith's lips drew back in a wordless rictus of rage, and he leveled the snubnose right at the woman. She didn't look concerned. Neither did the man with the pencil-thin mustache, who reached into his belt and drew a .357 Magnum with a barrel wider than a man's thumb.

"Mine's bigger than yours," he told Keith with a grin.

Someone behind him laughed.

Keith turned, and saw Wilkes sitting up, half his head blasted off, his one remaining eye shining with good humor.

"Go ahead and put your piece down," he said. "The counter will do. I think we both know you're going nowhere."

Keith did as he was told, dropping his gun on the Formica, and sat down on one of the counter stools like all the air had run out of him.

Sheila was still behind the counter, pressing herself hard against the wall, her eyes opened wide. She saw everything at once, it seemed: Wilkes scooping up the pieces of his head and putting them back together with deft fingers, the diners edging forward, the dog down in his corner finally looking up with interest.

"I'm sure you've noticed that this particular diner serves a very specific clientele," Wilkes said, his face now whole and unmarked. "You don't recognize any of us, I see. Probably never cracked a history book open in your life, right, Keith? Well, suffice it to say we're all part of a little club. And we don't allow people like you in."

He drew so fast his arm was just a blur in the air. His pistol was just a little Derringer, but sounded loud enough when he put a bullet into Keith's kneecap. Keith hit the tile floor, screaming, cords standing out on his neck as he clutched his knee. Blood splattered around him in a little shower.

"Only need one shot," Wilkes said.

The other diners sprang forward, yanking Keith up by the hair and slamming him down on the counter. The men held him down, while Aileen and the polka-dot woman ripped his shirt open.

"As Johnny G. would tell you, if he wasn't so busy fixing our dinner," Wilkes said over the cries and curses, "meat's damn expensive these days. Also, when you get past a certain point in your own personal reality, you find that only certain kinds of meat will do."

The fat man burst out of the kitchen, his face painted in full clown makeup now, a bleeding grin scrawled across the lower half of his face. He held a cleaver in one hand, a meat skewer in the other. Both looked obscenely sharp.

Sheila was trying to scream, but her throat had locked up and all she produced was a dry click. They seemed to have forgotten her, anyhow.

"Place your bets, folks!" the fat man roared. "How long does this good boy last?"

"Well, that all depends, Johnny," the polka-dot woman's boyfriend drawled. "You going to take your time, or just be done with it?"

"Not for me to say," Johnny G. said.

"I give him two hours," Wilkes said. "He looks pretty fit, other than a little wear around the edges from the smokes and liquor."

"Forty-five minutes!" Aileen cried.

The man in the corner looked down at his dog, and something, some kind of message, seemed to pass between them. "Hour fifteen," he stuttered.

Keith had stopped crying and now just looked at them with eyes opened enough for all the whites to show. He looked like a deer waiting to die after being struck by a speeding car.

Wilkes turned to Sheila and said, "How about you, my dear? Care to join in on the wagering? It's the only other thing to do here. We even bet on the weather on slow days."

Sheila squeaked something. It might have been, "Please. Please let us go."

They all laughed at that.

"Let you go?" Wilkes asked. "You're free to go anytime you want, sweetheart. You know, once you've been here long enough you can hear someone's heart beating? I hear yours right now. You're still alive, and we can't hold you here any more than we can find the way home."

He looked down at Keith and said, "He's not one of us, Sheila.

"But you are."

And then she remembered:

***

Morgan's apartment, some shithole above a bowling alley on the edge of town. Keith didn't think Morgan would still be there, not with the meth lab across the street still smoking and DEA agents running everywhere. But there he was, the sorry shit, trying to pack his worldly possessions into a shoebox.

He fell to his knees and blubbered in front of Keith, begging him for some time, enough time to build another lab and recover some of the money they'd lost. Keith had as much extra time to give as he had money and patience. Which is to say, none.

Morgan made one pathetic run at the door, and Keith had no time to grab him.

So Sheila shot him. One bullet to the back of the head. She shot him, and pretended he was Keith.

***

"It doesn't matter if you killed one or a million," Wilkes told her. "If you killed, and you enjoyed it, you're one of us."

Johnny G. flipped the cleaver around, holding it out handle-first.

"It's easy, once you get used to it," he said.

She took it, and looked at her reflection in the blade. It was like she could see her whole life in it: all the hard times when Keith smacked her around, running from one fleabag motel to another, calling her mom at Christmas and hanging up before either of them could start to cry.

The other killers watched her. She realized none of them were breathing, but the thought didn't scare her. It was kind of soothing, in fact. It was nice to belong somewhere for once.

She looked down at Keith, and her smile was a terrible thing.

"Baby--" he whimpered.

"You can go ahead and scream if you want to," Sheila said, raising the cleaver. "It's not like anybody cares."

***

Three weeks later, a dusty Ford Mustang pulled up in front of Johnny G.'s All-Nite Diner. Several young men stepped inside and slid into a booth, looking around with untrusting eyes.

A pretty girl in a tight waitress uniform came to take their order, smiling like she'd just heard the funniest joke. It was hard not to smile back at a girl like that, just the prettiest, most harmless thing you ever did see.

Her nametag read HI, I'M SHEILA! ASK ME ABOUT OUR WORLD-FAMOUS PANCAKES!

The Last Supper
By Steph Ellis

Nobody paid him much attention as they hurried by. Just another down-and-out huddled in the doorway with the obligatory mangy dog. They would draw a glance, nothing more, before their presence was swiftly and conveniently forgotten. If anyone did notice them it was more out of pity for the dog than compassion for its owner. They were a grey pair, dirty, unkempt, unwanted – except by each other. *There but for the Grace of God* .thought many as they passed. They didn't realise however, that God had nothing to do with it.

A man in uniform approached the vagrant; a stark contrast that was all shiny shoes and cleanliness. A cup steamed in one hand whilst the other clutched an open tin of dog food.

"Something a bit stronger would've been appreciated Major," said the man as he accepted the coffee with some distaste and put the tin in front of his dog.

"That stuff'll be the death of you if you're not careful," said the Major. "It's about time you got off the street. We've got a room down at the hostel."

"Persistent bugger aren't you," said the tramp. "Told you. This life suits me. I've got the perfect spot here. It's all in the location."

The Major looked up and down the precinct. It seemed busy enough but the recession had closed many of the shops and there was a growing air of neglect and despair about the place. This had been reflected in the numbers that now queued up at his Salvation Army hostel for either food or a bed. Apart from Jack that is. The man had inhabited the doorway of *The Last Supper* since it had opened three years ago. The owners never seemed to bother him. They were closed during the day so he was left in peace, whilst at night, when it was open, he would appear to move elsewhere. The Major had never come across him when he walked the streets at night, he had no idea where he went; only that he returned once the customers had vanished.

The Major peered in at the tinted windows. As usual he could see nothing. Even the menu had been taken down. Occasionally the thought crossed his mind that it was about time he tried the food there but every time he had neared the place something had happened to distract him and he found himself walking away – even as others went through its doors.

"Don't think it's to your taste," said Jack as the Major gazed up at the restaurant sign.

"Oh, why not?"

"I think you'd find it a bit too hot and spicy ... and I'm not just talking about the food if you know what I mean."

"Ah," said the Major tugging uncomfortably at his collar. "Perhaps I might just give it a miss." But he turned away rather regretfully, his curiosity piqued. He felt that he might return at some point, after all there could be some lost souls to save.

Jack watched the Major walk away, a smile hovering on his lips. His way was now clear to eye up the night's clientele and to plan the menu that would be offered. He was certain it would be to die for. A fragment of conversation reached his ears.

"... get to school. You don't say nothing. Do you hear?"

Jack turned his head in the direction of the man's voice. He saw someone not much cleaner than himself, thickset and shaven-headed. A meaty fist was grasping the arm of a young lad who wore the uniform of the local secondary school. The boy's face was sullen but even from this distance he could sense the youth's fear.

The man moved his face closer to the boy's. "And if you say anything to your mum, you'll get more of this." He raised his other fist to reinforce the message. "Understood?"

The boy nodded and headed off towards the school, head down to hide the black eye he sported.

Jack knew questions would be asked but nothing would be done. The social workers were terrified of Michael Reeves, choosing to accept his assurances that all was well and young David had merely walked into a door.

A flyer brushed Reeves arm and landed at his feet. Michael bent down and picked it up. "Free meal, eh? All you can eat." He looked at the advert for *The Last Supper* and then across at the restaurant itself. He did not see the tramp in the doorway. "Why not?" he thought and tucked the flyer in his pocket.

Jack grinned. The first invitation had been issued, one seat filled. He scanned the road for the next customer. He had a table for six to fill, three of them in fact.

A middle-aged woman, scowl-faced, was going into the supermarket opposite. Her purchases, fags and booze, were paid for with a debit card in the name of Mrs Lilian Wilson. He knew Mrs Wilson, now 80-years old and requiring round-the-clock care, remembered her when she was younger, a kindly district nurse who had time for everyone, even a man like him. This woman was not her; Lilian had been a teetotaller and non-smoker all her life, these purchases were not for her.

In his mind's eye he could see Lilian, bruised, lying in her bed, waiting in terror for the woman who was supposed to care for her. He sent a flyer dancing along the street, floated it into the hand of the false Mrs Wilson who glanced at it absently, not registering that she had not picked it up.

Mrs Jennifer Borden was stressed; she had a long shift ahead of her with old Mrs Wilson. She did not relish the thought, all that dribble, all that … frailty. She had to find her perks where she could and lord knows she deserved them she thought, but still it would be nice to have the day off. Her mobile vibrated. Scanning through the messages – so many missed calls from her husband – or rather avoided – she found the last one was a voicemail from the office. Apologising for the short notice they had given her the day off. Someone else had volunteered to look after Mrs Gray. A big grin appeared on her face, she glanced happily at the advert. Free drinks with every meal. That would do nicely.

Two seats had been filled.

From the opposite direction came two businessmen, sharp-suited sharks, partners in crime.

"We need to send Garvey in," said the thinner of the sharks.

The other laughed. "Yeah, he'll get results all right. Although I think we need to remind him to show some restraint."

"What, no broken teeth and hit them where the marks won't show?"

"Something like that. Should get our cash flow moving again."

"Perhaps we should review our interest rates," said the thin shark. "I could do with a holiday, I think a nice long cruise would go down a treat. The missus has been banging on about it for a while, given me the proverbial earache."

"Same here. What do you reckon? 1%?"

His partner nodded his agreement. They needed to celebrate he thought, his eyes registering the restaurant for the first time.

"Hey, look over there. They've got an offer on tonight, two-for-one. Up for it? We could take the wives, keep 'em sweet."

The men continued on their way. That was one table filled. The first six.

The next table was easier still. Like flies to a corpse they came, clustered together, bleary-eyed, foul in breath and mind. The cream of the nation's girlhood. Their night had only just finished, now they were planning the next.

One of the girls charmingly vomited into the gutter and wiped the specks away with a flyer that had dropped to the pavement beside her. A fitting use thought Jack, you could even call it the perfect analogy to his own plans for them. He allowed another leaflet to find its way to the group.

"Hey, look at this," said the bottle-blonde. "It's for that posh restaurant over there. Really exclusive it is."

"'Cos it's so bleedin' expensive, that's why," said an orange-skinned girl, tugging at her sagging boob tube.

"There's a special discount for groups of 6 tonight *and* a Happy Hour on their cocktails. I'm well up for it. Anyone else?"

The girls eyed the restaurant hungrily. It was rumoured that some of the top footballers dined there. It would make a good hunting ground. Current boyfriends could be dumped, a disposable commodity in their climb to the top. The girls were easily bought, *For Sale* signs glittered in their kohl-caked eyes.

That was the second table filled. The second six. Perhaps he should make sure that the other table did indeed contain the lusted-after footballers, that would really make their night – but no, that would be too easy. He would save the footballers for another time.

The customers he had in mind would not be walking this way that morning; however, there was always the good old postman. He'd ensured that flyers had been delivered with the morning's post. He also knew they would come – there was no choice really, not once they'd been selected.

On the guest list was a politician, wasn't there always one? Pedlar of lies, dealer of deceit. He would make good company with the author, plagiarist of the works of others. Then there was the vicar who was betraying his wife, the spy who was betraying his country, the judge who betrayed justice. That left one seat and it was already taken, by him. He always took part in the festivities. He had his third table filled. The third six. Coincidence? Not really, he was just a sucker for a good allegory. A subtle touch that went over the heads of his clientele but he was pleased with his own sense of the theatrical. He stood up and stretched although making sure that he remained in the shadow of the porch and out of the reach of the morning sun. It really did nothing for his complexion. He cracked his knuckles and gave a low whistle.

"Come on boy," he said to his dog. "We've got a menu to prepare."

The animal bared its teeth in response, forming a curiously malicious grin that sent an unwary child who come over to pet it, scuttling back to its mother.

The woman looked angrily at the vagrant and his dog, ready to do battle with whatever had upset her little angel but when she caught the man's eye she merely smiled and waved. The thought crossed her mind that it'd probably been her son who'd upset the animal. Children really should not torment defenceless creatures. He needed to be punished. The smack echoed down the street, attracting the attention of a passing policeman who in turn noticed the fingermarks forming on the child's face.

Dog and master turned their back on the scene, opened the door to the restaurant and stepped into the gloom. They walked through to the kitchen where spotless stainless steel surfaces gleamed, carving knives glinted. A certificate from Environmental Health hung proudly in its frame. It was a showcase of a kitchen. You'd think no one ever cooked there ... and you'd be right. Service was carried out at the table side to ensure that the customer knew exactly what was coming and so far there had been no complaints. He picked up his chef's whites and moved to the back of the restaurant. The air trembled around him; he could almost taste the anticipation.

"Only a few more hours," he said aloud, watching in mild amusement as his dog sniffed at one of the chairs and then cocked its leg, marking his territory.

"Now, now old fellow. You know you mustn't show any favouritism."

The dog wagged his tail in agreement before meting out the same treatment to all the other chairs. The puddles of urine slowly seeped into the carpet, the colour of which could not be described, soaked as it had been with all manner of bodily fluids since the restaurant had first opened. Today was its third anniversary and the tramp-now-chef thought that warranted a celebration of some kind.

He started to chalk up the day's special on the board. It was certainly an eye-watering dish for any discerning customer. The menu cards were laid out by the till. He scanned the bill of fare, chuckling at his little jokes. *Whores d'oeuvre* for starters, *Taste of Pain* for the mains and *Just Desserts* for afters. A bit lame, a touch cliché but then again wasn't the whole evening one big cliché?

The clock struck 6.00pm. One more hour. Time to fire up the ovens. The diners were on their way.

The girls were already tipsy when they arrived, falling over each other as they crashed through the door. Without a word he led them to their table where he had already placed complimentary cocktails. He could feel six pairs of hungry eyes fixed on him as he walked away.

"He's a bit of alright," said one.

"Mmm," said another, her eyes dreamily following the receding figure.

Jack glanced in the mirror as he made his way towards the door whose jangle had announced further arrivals. His skin was cracked and ravaged, streaked with dirt, grey with age. Greasy hair hung down the sides of his face, framing bloodshot eyes. His whites were still white but they clothed an unwashed body over which an army of lice marched whilst his shoes had split at the toe to reveal yellowing nails. His fingernails weren't much better. None of this however was visible to his customers. They would see what he wanted them to see, free will was left at the door.

He fixed a smile on his face and prepared to meet the new arrivals. Jennifer Borden, Michael Reeves, the loan sharks and their wives.

"May I take your coats ladies?" he asked.

They handed them over without a murmur. Jack briefly disappeared through the door marked *Cloakroom* and chucked the coats into the furnace.

"This place has class," said Shark Wife No.1

"Nothing's too much for you sweetheart," said her husband.

Jennifer Borden eyed Jack appreciatively; salt and pepper hair, firm-jawed, trim, everything Mr Borden was not. Michael Reeves also eyed him approvingly, wondering if he could indulge in some mild flirtation.

Jack left them happily sipping their complimentary champagne. Politician, author, vicar, spy, judge. The last five had arrived. He seated them personally before taking his own seat. The glasses on this table were filled with a blood-red vintage. He raised his glass, admiring the depth of colour as it absorbed the glow of the candles which flickered around them. It was at moments like this, when his sense of anticipation was at its highest, that he felt most happy. He cast a beneficent smile on his gathered guests who all gazed quite contentedly back at him. When the scales eventually fell from their eyes, he knew they would not be as happy. He stood up, ignoring the flies that now buzzed around his head.

"Welcome, my friends," he said. "Tonight you will participate in a gastronomical event unique in both content *and* delivery. A dining sensation that I can guarantee no other living soul has experienced. Of course should our service disappoint in anyway, we will do everything in our power to put things right."

His audience, in their unknowing self-conceit, applauded his speech, ignoring the globs of liquid that fell from his glass as he swung his arms wide in greeting. The scarlet stain crept slowly across the tablecloth. The flies dropped lower.

It was time for the first course. Small slivers of burnt toast appeared on empty plates.

"We pride ourselves on the freshness of our products," he said. "Permit me to prepare these personally."

He walked over to the table of girls who were still positively drooling at the sight of him.

"The *Whores* d'Oeuvres," he announced dramatically. "Ladies Fingers." A razor-sharp cleaver materialized in his hand. Still they smiled, eyes empty and vacant. Much like their brains he thought.

"It is a custom," he continued, "that hands be inspected for cleanliness before their owner is allowed to dine. Personal hygiene is something that this establishment naturally takes very seriously. My dears."

At this command, the girls obediently held out their hands in front of them. He took them gently, caressing their soft skin then raised the hand holding the cleaver. The steel shimmered above his head. Another mirror reflected this heroic pose. *God he was good*, he thought admiringly. Such poise, such finesse. He dropped his arm, watching it arc down, steel slicing through fingers as if they were butter. Six from each woman. Six mouths open in noiseless screams. He put a finger to his lips to hush them. He did not want any sense of pain to disturb the current ambience – just yet. He placed two fingers on each diner's toast. But something wasn't quite right. He gazed at the plate thoughtfully, it was lacking a certain *je ne sais quoi*. Aah, how could he forget? He threw a small piece of limp lettuce and a cherry tomato, only slightly mouldy, on each. There. It was all in the garnish.

"Please, enjoy." His prompt made hands, mutilated or whole, reach for the canapés, crush them into mouths that had not yet registered what they would be ingesting. "Food needs to be experienced by *all* the senses," he expounded as he circulated between the tables. "You must fully engage with your eyes, your ears, your nose, your touch ... your taste. Chew long and hard. Allow the juices to dance across your palate."

Obediently they all bit down, two of the tables still oblivious to what they were eating whilst at the girls' table they gagged and choked as they repeatedly attempted to spit out fingers that had begun to crawl down their throats. Spear-like fingernails, painted in killing colours for the occasion, ripped at gullets, clawed at stomach walls. Jack grinned with satisfaction ... bleeding to death, internally or externally, asphyxiation, shock, he had all his options covered. Life – no, death would be more accurate – was good, and the evening had only just begun. He noticed that there were still two fingers left. He threw them to his dog who swiftly wolfed them down. One of the tables was now silent. Would they be missed? Probably not.

It was time for the main course. He had to admit that for this he had stolen his ideas from South-East Asian cuisine. Dammit but they were creative devils. Such inventiveness was to be admired.

The dirty plates had been replaced by equally filthy plates across which maggots now crawled. He was slightly annoyed. The wriggling larvae were not supposed to appear until the end. He shrugged his shoulders, maintaining perfection was not always possible.

The sushi was placed in front of the diners. Multi-coloured, multi-textured, a real appetite sharpener.

"Please help yourselves. Choose whatever you wish."

The guests did not realise that his comments were not directed at them.

Sushi for loan sharks, little fish eating big fish. Very appropriate. Slowly the lobsters and crabs righted themselves and crawled towards their chosen diners. Gasping fish leapt and gulped across the table, sannakji –

octopus tentacles – writhed and wriggled up chopsticks. Human mouths opened automatically to allow ingress to the moving banquet.

***

Jennifer Borden put down her empty cocktail glass, expecting another instant refill but none was forthcoming. She looked around for a waiter. There was none. The table in the corner was strangely quiet but a shadow hung over it so she was unable to make out what the girls were up to. Perhaps they were getting better service than she. The thought made her angry and she stabbed her knife forcefully into the food in front of her. It reacted violently. Pincers flew at her face, cutting through flesh so that rivulets of blood ran down to mix with the marinade.

Michael Reeves was faring no better. Suckers from the octopus had clamped themselves to his tongue, pushing, rolling it back so that his airway was covered.

The loan shark party in turn had received their meal plus interest, although the wives looked distinctly less than satisfied. But as Jack had said, all the senses needed to be engaged to fully appreciate the meal. He allowed their eyes to see, really see, to touch, to really feel. Now they were awake, albeit only for a brief moment. They would be allowed to taste life and pain to their full before they were sated.

That left one table. Eat, drink and be merry for tomorrow we die. Scratch that. Eat, drink and be merry for *today* we die. They had come so willingly, these pillars of society, it seemed almost a shame.

He resumed his seat, giving his companions a fatherly smile as he did so. They grinned idiotically back. Around them the candles on the other tables had gone out making their own an oasis of light in the encroaching darkness.

They had dined on human flesh and not noticed, they had choked on the living and not noticed. The final dish would only reinforce this metaphor for their own lives. Its pungent smell announced its arrival.

"Ah, the cheeseboard, ladies and gentlemen. Today we have a rare Sicilian delicacy, Casu Marzu."

He flung stale crackers at them. The time for careful presentation had long since passed. It was he who was getting hungry now. The cheese knife hacked out mounds of the roiling yellow substance which he tossed after the crackers.

"Eat, eat, my friends. You must eat your fill. I insist."

Obedient fingers raised the cheese to mouth, to teeth, to tongue. He watched with satisfaction as the light of realisation dawned in their eyes, the horror as they registered the maggots squirming inside it, on top, all over, the desperation as they tried to spit out the intruders but couldn't. More and more larvae exploded from the cheese until the whole table was one writhing surface, spreading towards each guest, covering them, filling them up. They could not scream. He would not allow that. Such bad manners to speak with your mouth full. His stomach rumbled, his dog drooled. It was their turn.

***

Outside, the Major noticed the last lights going out. He had come back to see if Jack needed a bed for the night. The doorway however, was empty. That was a good sign. He hoped the man had been able to get a meal as well, perhaps the restaurant had taken pity and given him some leftovers. Comforted by the thought he turned and walked away, back into a night inhabited by so many suffering souls.

At the far end of the precinct a nightclub disgorged a group of pumped-up, primped-up, boozed-up footballers. One of them noticed a flyer at his feet. He picked it up.

Demons Drink Free
By Shenoa Carroll-Bradd

The burnt-out neon sign on the cafe roof still read "Jay's", but poor Jay Crocker had been dead for two years. Those in the know, if their twisted jaws and forked tongues could make the human sounds, called it "Mavel's".

Mavel Dorset was a good Christian for 47 years, right up until the Rapture, which began on a clear Tuesday morning like any other. Mavel followed her usual routine: rising at five, showering, fixing her hair and painting on a cherry red smile, all so she could get to the cafe by six to start the coffeepots and set the tables.

A few of her regulars came in that morning, and she brought them their usual burgers and slices of pie, each one served with a cup of strong, black coffee. Mavel took a certain pride in her coffee, modest though she was in all other aspects.

Around ten am, a family of four came in and settled in the right corner booth, their eyes downcast, their tones hushed.

Mavel found their somber clothes bit strange, as if they were headed to a particularly casual funeral. When she bustled over with the menus, none of them would meet her eye. Mavel started to wonder if there was something on her face and they were all too kind to point it out. The kids ordered milk, the parents chose water, no ice, and when Mavel offered them her world-famous coffee ("It'll perk you right up!"), the mother shook her head.

"We don't approve of the use of stimulants," she said, as if Mavel had offered them a steaming mug of cocaine.

Shaking her head, she went to fill their drink order, pausing to greet Big Eddie, her burger-with fries, hold the pickles, light mayo regular. "Weird bunch over there," she muttered.

Eddie looked up with a smear of ketchup on his cheek.

Mavel grabbed a napkin and wiped it away like a busy mother. "Real quiet. Real odd."

Eddie glanced over his shoulder at the family, who had joined hands and bowed their heads in prayer around the little Formica table, then went back to stuffing fries in his face without comment.

Mavel poured two glasses of milk for the kids and came around the counter to deliver them, when something caught her attention outside. A flash, in the sky, like a silent silver firework, or a single, soundless lightning strike. She stared at it until the flash burned itself on her retinas, not looking away until it had faded completely from sight.

She turned back to the corner booth. "Sorry for the delay, folks, I thought I just saw-" Her words flew away, and Mavel nearly dropped the glasses of milk.

The booth was deserted, and where each person had sat now lay neat piles of empty clothes. She looked up just in time to see a man's glowing foot disappear through the ceiling.

Mavel did drop the milk then. "The Rapture," she screamed, "It's the Rapture! The Rapture's come to take us up to heaven!" Cheeks flushed and positively giddy, Mavel untied her apron and whipped it over her head, dropping it to the linoleum floor as she dashed out the door to embrace the sunshine. The Lord could not have picked a more beautiful day to end the world upon.

To her right, a car squealed and lost control on the

sun-baked highway, running off the road in a plume of dust as a glimmering man passed through the roof and rose up into the sky.

"Okay, me next," Mavel whispered. "I've been good, Lord. I've been more humble than the rest. It's my time now, time for my reward." She knelt in the pebbly parking lot, clasping her hands before her and resting her forehead on the upraised knuckles, praying, begging, to be drawn up into that holy light.

Mavel stayed there on her knees for nearly half an hour before Big Eddie came to get her, laying a heavy hand on her shoulder.

She turned her face up to him, her red eyes leaking mascara-tinted tears, her bright red lips quivering, waiting for a kind word from her regular, something to put her soul at ease.

"Can you come inside now, so's I can pay?" He said. "Otherwise I'll be late for work."

Mavel's painted lips pulled back over teeth stained from smoking, and she shoved his hand away, struggling to her feet on her own, brushing pebbles and debris from her dented knees.

Not long after that, the handsome drifter came her way, looking like a grunge rocker from the '90s, back when she'd still had hope and a trim figure. He'd stopped in for a chat and a cup of Joe, made her feel safe and useful, like life still had a purpose. He didn't stay long, but when he set out down the highway once more, he left her his favorite pen as a memento.

That had been nearly three years ago. Four more until the Tribulation would end, and one side (or the other) would prove victorious.

Until then, Mavel's was a way station for the hungry, the weary, and the lost.

***

Today dawned brightly, just as it had on that fateful morning, and Mavel was already hard at work, mopping the floors. The once-flat linoleum was cracked and peeling, scored in some places by the rake of claws, and a short scar bisected the counter top from where the swing of a holy sword went wide. No matter how many times she'd told the forces of Good and Evil to leave their quarrels outside, someone always seemed to think the rules didn't apply to them, and it never ended well for the cafe, or for Mavel's mop bucket. Demon blood was hell on the drains.

After mopping, Mavel dusted the windowsills and counters, giving a quick brush to the twin signs in the window, each dying a slow death from sun-fading. The "Help Wanted" sign had been there since Jay died, but Mavel's customers were always travelers passing through. No one wanted to stay and try to set down roots out here, in the dust, and heat, and grit. Her guests were always headed off to some bunker their cousin had read about, or a supposed safe zone just a few states over.

To Mavel, they always sounded like hopeful children writing their letters to Santa. The young, poor travelers were her favorite, the filthy little lambs who couldn't care for themselves now that Mommy and Daddy had been raptured, or, more likely, killed. They never had anything worth bartering, and nine times out of ten, were only too glad to sign up for her credit system. Free food and drink until the end of the tribulation, for just the cost of a signature. Just like writing a check in the old days, before the banks became public mausoleums. Collecting signatures helped Mavel fight the loneliness of spending her last years on earth in an empty cafe. It cheered her to know she'd see them all again, eventually, once the war was over and it came time to pay up.

***

Mavel had lost track of the days long ago, but it felt like a Friday morning, edging toward afternoon. She had just gotten the floor dry when a battered truck pulled up in front of the cafe, right over the asphalt where she had knelt and prayed all those years ago.

A dusty man got out, unshaven, and bearing a foul disposition. He stopped outside the big front windows, (unbroken through what one could only suppose was a miracle) and read the two signs there, back and forth, as if the act of reading one made him forget the other. At last, he stepped inside. Sweat beaded his cheeks and upper lip, and he glared about the place as he wiped it away. "No air conditioning?"

Mavel smiled. "Nope. Enjoy the heat, honey. It's only gonna get worse."

He grunted and seated himself at the counter, looking up and down the scarred bar. "Menus?"

Mavel took the pencil from behind her ear and used it like a baton to point out the chalkboard easel by the door.

"Today's Specials", it declared through a haze of permanent chalk dust.

He frowned at the offerings. Dark circles ringed his eyes, and the lines of his face were drawn tight, as if he hadn't slept well in weeks. "Any meat?"

Mavel twiddled the pencil between two fingers. "There's meat in the chili. Mostly squirrels and the like. Won't be able to do much better until I get a delivery. You got barter?"

He patted a dirty pocket, but didn't answer, eyes still on the menu board. "Sign outside said you were looking for help."

Mavel sized up the stranger with a frown. She knew his look. He wasn't one to stay. "Mhm," she said.

He looked at her then. "How about I work off a meal? Do the dishes, sweep, whatever..." His gaze went past her, to the kitchen doors.

Mavel pursed her lips. "Not looking for temporary help. I need a full-time commitment." She cocked her head. "You look like a prime candidate for credit, though."

That got his attention. The dusty man perked up. "You offer credit?" His expression immediately cooled, and he callously looked her up and down, as if appraising a used car. "On what terms?"

Mavel knew she wasn't much to look at, but neither was this stranger. She began wiping down the counter with a grey rag, trying not to look too offended. "Just takes one little signature to make your meal free."

The stranger grinned. He was young enough, she supposed, and had probably been some kind of handsome, before the tribulations began. He lifted his nose to the air. "Coffee too?"

"Coffee too." Mavel nodded. "Normally it's decaf only for humans, unless they're dining on credit. Gotta save the good stuff for my regulars."

The man chuckled and jabbed a thumb at the front window. "Yeah, I saw your sign. 'Demons Drink Free'? Funny stuff."

Mavel crossed her spotted hands on the counter. Her nails matched her lipstick, not that it mattered. No one saw her as a woman anymore, no matter *what* she painted red.

"Yep," she said. "I'm hilarious. Is that a yes to the credit?"

The stranger nodded. "Yes ma'am. You've got yourself a deal."

Mavel dug behind the counter to fetch her guest book and a sleek gold-tone pen that would have looked right at home on an embezzling CEO's desk. "Here you are," she said, sliding it across the counter to him. "Just pick a line, sign it, and I'll get you some grub."

The stranger frowned down at the crowded paper before him, adjusting his grip on the pen. "This is just a list of names," he said cautiously.

"That's right."

He chewed his stubbly lower lip. "I thought there'd be some kind of form, or promise to pay, or something." He glanced up. "How can you collect payment, if you're just taking down names? You don't even have an address column..."

Mavel slowly fetched a coffee cup and set it by the machine. She made a big show of checking the pot, sniffing it, swirling the dark liquid against the light, and that did the trick.

The man signed.

What her womanly wiles were too dusty to accomplish, her world-famous coffee could still achieve.

"Ow, damn it," the stranger hissed, dropping the pen as if it had bit him. A single drop of blood welled from his fingertip and dropped onto the page, sucked away into the swoop and curve of his signature. "What kind of-"

Mavel clucked her tongue. "Sorry hon, should've warned you. That pen can pinch if you're not careful." She scooped up the guest book and handed him his coffee.

The stranger looked like he might have more to say, then shook his head and took a sip. His face flushed with immediate appreciation. "Any cream?"

Mavel smirked. "Son, does this look like a dairy farm? Ain't been milk around here for years. Besides," she crossed her arms over her sagging chest. "It'd be a sin to dilute my coffee. It's perfect just the way it is."

He took another sip and nodded. "It *is* mighty fine." He set the cup down and gestured to the front window signs again, as if he were trying to hitch a ride from her. "You haven't actually seen a demon, have you?"

Mavel took a long look at him. "I've seen lots of things since the Rapture. Gangs, murders, people acting like animals." She pursed her lips. "I do my best to keep this cafe peaceful. The world may be going to hell outside," she smiled at her little joke, "but I keep order in here."

The stranger glanced at the scar on the counter top to his left.

"When I can," she amended. "Did you want the chili after all, or can I get you something else?"

"Chili please, ma'am."

Mavel nodded. "I'll be just a minute. Don't bother trying to rob the place, I ain't got anything worth stealing. Unless you got a craving for plastic seats and cheap silverware." She slipped through the kitchen doors to fetch the stranger's meal. After fourteen years of service in the cafe, Mavel knew all the squeaks and clicks of the place, and as she ladled up a bowl of chunky red-brown chili, she heard the stranger inspecting the dead cash register. Money had lost all value since the Rapture, but habits don't die of old age. If she had anything to hide, she conceded, it would be in there. Mavel got a spoon, huffed on it, and shone it on her apron. She didn't blame him for checking; no one ever believed her when she said there was nothing worth stealing. Hope springs eternal in the black hearts of thieves.

Mavel made sure her steps were heavy and loud as she approached the dining area, giving him plenty of warning.

The stranger was just returning to his seat when she entered, a guilty look on his face.

She gracefully ignored it, setting the bowl before him. "Here you are, hon."

He tucked in. After the third hasty spoonful, he swallowed hard and looked up at his hostess. "Isn't it kinda wild out here? Seems like rough country for a lady like you."

Mavel winked. "I'm a tough old bird, and I don't scare easy. What about you? Where are you headed?"

The stranger drank some coffee. "There's a preacher I keep hearing on the radio. He's calling everybody to the West coast, to assemble by the sea. Says our sins will be washed clean in the saltwater, and we'll all be Raptured at last." He fished a bit of gristle from between his teeth, wiped it on the counter. "You should come too."

Mavel fetched a napkin and swiped the counter clean again. "That's quite a promise. You believe him?"

The stranger shrugged. "Gotta believe in something, these days."

Mavel nodded and leaned her elbows on the counter with a sigh. "Can't argue with you there."

"What about you? What keeps you going out here?"

Mavel opened her mouth to reply when she was cut off by an unearthly screech, loud enough to rattle the front windows. "Goodness me, what timing. Looks like my delivery's arrived." She came out from behind the counter and stared through the scratched glass, peering around to spot the source of the howl. She heard the stranger swivel on his stool behind her.

For a while, nothing moved outside but swirls of dust on the sun-scorched parking lot. Then, two figures hurtled down from the cloudless sky, locked in a bloody grappling match. One looked like a handsome, winged man wearing brilliant armor, but the other...

Mavel heard the clink of the bowl hitting the counter as her guest sprang from his seat to join her at the window.

The other figure was enormous, with black, hairy skin and deep red leathery wings, like a huge bat. It raked at the angel, for that's what he was, snapping and biting like a rabid coon.

The angel must have lost his weapon somewhere. He smote the demon with his fists, but seemed to inflict no pain until he hit the beast with an armored forearm.

The demon roared and fell back, clutching its face where the bright armor had seared the skin bald.

Momentarily free, the angel struggled to his feet and crouched to launch himself aloft, but only got ten feet in the air before the demon seized his left leg with one talon and slammed him onto the dirty asphalt. The demon pounced on its opponent's back, screaming as the bright armor singed its legs and knees, but not deterred. It grabbed the angel's head with long, wicked claws, and wrenched it around and around like an apple stem until it pulled free in a blinding spray.

Mavel clucked her tongue and retreated behind the counter. She tore the page of signatures from her guest book, tucked it into her pocket, then poured a cup of strong black coffee.

The stranger scrambled back from the window as the demon approached with thundering steps, holding the angel's head in one talon, dragging the body with the other.

Mavel stepped outside to meet it on the concrete ramp.

It threw the body at her feet, splashing her shoes and nylons with bright ichor.

"Always a pleasure," she said, holding out the coffee cup.

The demon took it with surprising grace, holding the little cup between two claws and downing the scalding brew in one gulp. It placed the empty cup in Mavel's hand with the same strange grace.

"And here you are," she said, holding out the guest book page. "My souls for the month. Got some good ones in there. They'll be great company, eventually."

The demon took her offering in its free talon. It looked at the paper for a moment, then brought the angel's head up and took a bite out of it, like a kid with a candy apple.

"Bye now," she said pleasantly.

The demon snorted, then turned and launched itself into the air, flapping away on its great, leathery wings.

Without a word, Mavel walked back inside and erased the chalkboard menu, spreading that graveyard dust into a more even layer of filth. She picked up the stub of chalk and wrote in jagged, squealing letters:

Today's Specials:

Wings

Ribs

Chef's Platter Surprise...

When she caught the stranger's wild, panicked gaze, Mavel shrugged.

"It's like you said, hon. Gotta believe in something these days, dontcha?"

Small Sacrifices
By Matthew Pegg

Layla Kovak makes the best chicken sandwich in London. See her cut the bread so precisely, bread she makes herself. Layla is a surgeon of the sandwich. Two years ago she started as a lowly counter assistant at the Forest Deli, in a side street off Tottenham Court Road, hedged in by bookshops and stage doors. Back then the bread was a loaf from Tesco Metro. Within a month Layla had scouted an artisan baker who did a good deal on fresh ciabatta, bagels, wholemeal baps, sourdough, potato farls, sodabread, and pain rustique. Proceeds went up by 20% in the next two months, which stopped her boss Judy moaning about the expense. Six months later Layla prevailed upon Judy to install a bread oven in the small kitchen behind the shop. Now the Deli sells Layla's fresh bread as well as using it for sandwiches.

Today the loaf has a hint of caraway. Layla makes fresh mayonnaise each day. Lettuce and tomatoes are sourced from smallholdings in Kent and selected for taste over uniformity or shelf life. Layla slices breast meat from a cold roast chicken then augments it with darker thigh for taste and texture. She adds a smear of mustard and thin strips of crispy skin, then crumbles some sage and onion stuffing on top. There is nothing pretentious about the finished sandwich she sends out to the customer. It is just very, very good, hence the 'Best Chicken Sandwich in London' accolade from Time Out.

***

Five months ago Layla used the small inheritance from her father to buy out Judy, who was heading off to run a B&B in Hove. The two women embraced and promised eternal friendship before Judy drove off, never to be seen again, leaving Layla queen of all she surveyed.

Her single minded success in the world of the deli is a surprise to Layla. In every other aspect of life she is beset by fears. She once made a list of them in a notebook. The list filled four pages before she gave up the task, having developed a fear of the list itself. When she moved to London and into a small flat near Alexandra Palace, the city terrified her. She had feared her landlord, Colin, a skinny Irishman, whose gaze slithered over her cleavage and never reached her face. Eight years later she is afraid that Colin's eyes never seem to wander anywhere other than her face. Layla has wrestled some fears into submission, but the sheer number has meant that others have had to be left alone.

Part of Layla's list of fears:

Spiders, ants, wasps, mosquitoes.

Pandemics, eurhythmics, eugenics.

Anaesthesia, neurasthenia, necrosis, psychosis, cirrhosis.

AIDS, SARS. Any other disease with an acronym.

Clowns.

Buttons.

Cane toads.

As far as Layla knew there were no cane toads in England, but having watched a documentary about the Australian monstrosities she developed a fear of them just in case.

It's the end of the day. The last sandwich has been made and the last customer departs, clutching Sicilian Olive Oil, pesto, a jar of Polish *Bigos* and some blue cheese ripened on old saddles at a tiny farm in Dorset. Layla cleans her work surface and sets the dishwasher humming. She pulls apart the chicken carcass, removing remaining meat, skin and gristle. These she chops neatly and divides between plastic bowls. Then she opens the back door and steps into the alley.

The alley is a narrow space for bins and boxes. Layla places the bowls on the ground. Vincent is the first to emerge from the shadows, a handsome ginger tom with most of one ear missing from birth. It gives him a quizzical, lop-sided look. He rubs round her legs and gets a pat on the head before he makes for one of the bowls.

Will is next; a grey feral who has never learned to trust people. He skirts Layla warily and she moves back to give him room to get to the food. He begins to eat, giving her suspicious glances between mouthfuls. The black and white boys are next: big Jack, top cat, leader by consensus, skinny Gizmo with his white moustache like an old colonel, clumsy, fluffy Bill, so uncoordinated and stiff he often trips over his own feet. Others arrive. They begin to eat. Layla reaches down to stroke those that won't be panicked by her touch.

The little colony waxed and waned as cats left, got picked up by the RSPCA and re-homed, died, and were replaced by new kittens. Layla paid for some to be neutered and took any that got sick or hurt to the vet. She released them again if it was feasible, organised homes for some and shed tears for those too far gone to be saved when the only option was to have them put to sleep. She liked the complex social interactions of her tribe.

Layla is not allowed pets in her flat. Once, after a little white cat named Lucy had needed an operation, Layla had bent this rule, taking her home and giving her a box lined with blankets on the fire escape outside the living room window. When Colin turned up unexpectedly Layla was terrified she would lose the flat. She went into the kitchen to find the rent, heart hammering. When she came back Colin was leaning on the window sill and stroking Lucy who was rubbing her face against his hand, purring like a motor. Layla stared and Colin turned to look at her, his face transformed by a big smile. She saw loneliness in his eyes. He wished her good night and didn't mention the illegal lodger he'd been petting. Layla waited a week for an eviction notice but it never came. Eventually Lucy rejoined the colony behind the deli.

Layla goes back into the kitchen. As she tidies and checks the chicken roasting for tomorrow she wonders how she has ended up here. The product of Czech and Egyptian parents, she has inherited her mother's colouring and her father's cheekbones. Layla's mother died of cancer when Layla was seventeen and somehow university got lost in the ensuing chaos. When her father developed early onset Alzheimer's her plans were sacrificed to looking after him. Fear besieged her. Her father died. Layla was working as a part time waitress. She got a grip, took catering courses and decided to move to London to finally begin her life.

There had been a modest succession of boyfriends over the years but Layla seemed to have a Teflon coating and none of the prospective partners had stuck. At 38 she felt she was on the shelf, if not pushed to the back with the jar of fuzzy jam and the forgotten mousetrap. She had good friends, Dora, Anya and Becky, who could be relied on for a raucous night out or a DVD box set marathon fuelled by pizza and white wine. Because of her name and her Egyptian heritage people often assumed she was a Moslem and were surprised to see her attack a pitcher of margaritas. She felt silly explaining her religion.

Life wasn't bad but was it good? What if she ended up

a mad cat lady, like the crazy old woman in *The Simpsons*, hurling cats at strangers?

***

There is shouting and banging from the other side of the serving hatch. Layla moves to see what is going on. She hears Robin the assistant open the door, a crash, more shouting, the 'ting' of the till opening. The kitchen door swings open and a stranger bursts in, a wad of cash in his hand. He shoves it inside his windcheater. He has hollow eyes and a complexion flecked with acne. As the door swings to behind him, Layla sees Robin sprawled on the floor in the shop, amidst spilled conchiglie and broken glass, shaking his head, dazed.

This is a robbery, she thinks and almost laughs at the absurdity of it. The stranger waves something at her. A knife. She backs away, laughter quashed. He steps forward and grabs the front of her blouse, forcing her backwards, blade weaving. She stumbles and nearly falls. The man shoves her and points at the back door. Hurriedly she turns and fumbles it open. He grasps the back of her blouse and forces her into the alley. It is dark now, replete with shadow. She tries to pull away. He grabs her again and pushes her face first into the brick wall. The impact steals her breath. He presses against her back. His breath smells sour. How many of her fears are realised here: pain, injury, disfigurement, powerlessness? She will have to revisit the list and add any that she's missed. If she lives.

For most people helpless acquiescence would be the only choice. Layla has another if she can overcome her paralysing terror. She kicks and her foot catches the bottle standing against the wall. Wine stains the concrete. She paws at the knife and it bites her. Blood drips from cut fingers and mixes with the wine. She speaks the words her mother taught her between giving good advice, "Don't wear orange and purple even when you're a crazy old woman," and dubious advice, "A man who likes cats can't be all bad." The ancient words coil out of her mouth. She offers the libation. The knife is cold at her neck.

It is then that the darkness enfolds them in a blacker grip, and the eyes appear, burning gold and green and orange. She is still and the man pauses, sensing a change. He looks around, moves away. More eyes appear, moon white, fire red. The man takes a step. Her first protector is Will, the scared feral. He leaps from the top of a bin to embed claws in the thief's face. Clumsy Bill runs through his legs and he sprawls to the ground. Vincent and Gizmo hiss and leap onto the man's body. Jack goes for his throat, growling like a puma. And then there are more crowding in from the shadows, little Lucy and all the others Layla has fed and nursed. She sees some she is sure have died or been put to sleep. Shadows and smoke, they flit like silhouettes to embed teeth and claw in the prone, flailing thief. Still more come, out of history, the cats of London, feral packs that haunted bombsites, pampered Edwardian pets, cats killed during the plague for fear they carried the disease. On and on and back and back into the times before the city, when people lived in simple shelters, to before the domestic cat, to the wild ancestors, the beasts, the killers. More pour from the dark, shades of grey and charcoal, piling cat on cat until the man is hidden by a heaving mass of fur and his muffled screams falter and die. And in the murk at the rear of the alley Layla sees *her* watching, a tall silhouette with eyes of jade. Then there is just the purring, a rising cadence reverberating from the walls, that makes Layla's head buzz, and the sound of the pack feeding.

***

Layla stands and watches. In five minutes the feline mound shudders and shrinks. The alley lightens. All that is left is a darker patch on the concrete and some scraps of fabric. Her own cats scatter. Will carries a fragment of something in his mouth. Layla doesn't look too closely. Bill emerges from hiding and plods after the others. Jack pauses for a pat on the head. Layla finds the money scattered on the ground and picks it up. There is no sign of the knife. Vincent limps up to rub around her legs. He has a cut on his side. It is not bad but Layla will take him to the emergency vet. Then maybe take him home and see what else she can discern in Colin's eyes when he finds out. She walks unsteadily towards the door to check on Robin. She will tell him the man dropped the money and ran.

***

Life is not bad. She sometimes cursed her mother for her ridiculous religious responsibility, passed down, generation to generation, from ancient times. But now and then it has its uses. Layla is still scared of many things: last on her list of fears is 'old gods'. But then she does not need to be too brave. She makes the best chicken sandwich in London. And even in London, Bastet looks after her own.

McMurder, McBurger
By Sarah Gibbel

Jackie was excited. He had finally talked Mom into taking him to the new McBurger restaurant with the biggest play place ever. Lily was going to love it. "Finish your burgers, kids," Mom said, "and then you can go play in the ball pit." Mom had finished her burger already. She crumpled up her greasy wax paper and tossed it into a bright yellow bin. Sucking on her shake, she picked up her book with one hand and resumed reading. On the cover, a man with no shirt on held a lady in a funny dress. Jackie had tried to read it the other day, but Mom caught him, and yelled at him to put that trash down.

Jackie bit down on something hard, spitting it out into his napkin the way he'd seen grownups do. "Eww," he shouted, "There's a bone in my burger!" Suddenly his burger didn't taste as good as it had. Bones were gross. Burgers from McBurger tended to taste a little off on the best of days. The shakes were good, though, and he had gotten a toy plastic monster that opened and closed its mouth.

"Mommy, I don't wanna finish my burger," said Lily.

Mom didn't even look up from her book. "You kids finish your Icky B's. You wanted to come here, not me. I paid good money for that food."

Somehow they choked down the rest of their soggy, greasy burgers and french fries. "Come on, Lily," said Jackie. "Let's go play in the ball pit." Jackie crawled into the end of a red plastic tube. The air inside was stale. It smelled plasticy, with another funny metallic scent. He stopped and turned around, crouched in the tube, looking outwards. Lily was hanging back at the entrance. "Don't be a little sissy, Lily." Reluctantly, she followed him. "That's better."

They crawled through endless, spiraling plastic tubes, with here and there a grimy window that looked out on Mom, or the parking lot, or more tubing. In a foul-smelling tank about ten feet across, they discovered a teenager in a McBurger uniform, sitting cross-legged, a pack of cigarettes in one hand and a pack of fries in the other. He grinned at them and held up a large burlap bag. He gestured to it with the french fries, as if to say, *come inside! Come play in here!*

Jackie shook his head, backing away and looking at Lily. Her eyes were round and ringed with white. "Let's go back to Mommy," she whispered. Jackie tilted his head towards the tube, giving her permission to leave. He crawled after Lily, going backwards in case the strange young man with the bag followed them.

As the tubes changed from red to yellow to green to purple, Jackie's heart slowed down. "Lily, you've gotten us lost," he said. "Let me lead now." Lily turned around. Tears were drying on her cheeks. Jackie squeezed past her. He led them up and down, always stopping to peer through the grimy windows. Eventually he got a decent bearing on where they were, and at the last window they stopped at, he got a good view of the play structure. He could see Mom in the corner. It looked like the pipes would lead them back to her.

"There's Mommy," said Lily. "I want to go to Mommy." So did Jackie, but he was a very stubborn little boy, and his sister's fear often brought out a slightly bullying side that was otherwise seldom seen. Plus, he didn't get to go to McBurger very often and he didn't like to waste the experience, even if the play tubes were a little scary.

"In a minute," said Jackie. "I can see how to get to the ball pit too. Now, you *can't* come to a McBurger play place without playing in the ball pit," he said, repeating something one of the cool kids at school had once told him.

They came to a junction made entirely of clear, scuffed plastic. Jackie could clearly see the way to the ball pit now, and as he crawled down that path there was a grinding noise and the plastic beneath their knees vibrated, as if a panel was being slid somewhere. "Wanna go to Mommy," Lily whined.

Jackie told her to shut up.

The children came to an end of the tube. It led directly to the ball pit, like a drain pipe dumping into the sewer. "Cowabunga!" Jackie shouted, leaping into the balls. Balls richoted off the plastic siding. One of them hit Lily in the face, pinging off her. The balls settled down, spread evenly through the pit. "Jackie?" Lily whispered. She put one hand through them, trying to touch the bottom. Lily couldn't feel a floor anywhere, just more and more balls. She lay on her tummy in the tube, her arm in balls up to her shoulder. Still nothing. Lily crawled backwards up the tube, keeping an eye on the ball pit.

***

Jackie hadn't expected the ball pit to be so deep. It felt like he was falling ten or twenty feet before he finally felt something solid beneath his feet. The grinding noise came back, and the position of the balls moved. Jackie felt trapped, as if he were being squeezed to death by stupid plastic balls. He tried to swim upwards through them. It was hard, and every time he slowed down, he felt the ground beneath his feet again. A new motor started up, faster, higher pitched. The balls weren't pressing in on

Jackie's body quite so hard. Something was pumping them out of the tank. Jackie was panting like a dog now, and he couldn't hold his hands steady. When the balls were only going up to his knees, a door opened behind him. It was nice to see some light again. The remaining balls headed out the door, and Jackie turned around.

Skinny, pimpled people in McBurger uniforms crowded around. Several of them used push brooms to herd the balls back into the tank, where they were still being pumped who-knew-where. He was in a large room, kind of like a garage but with more computers. At one end of the room, on a ramp leading up to a garage door, sat a semi truck. Strange noises came from within. Someone swore and muttered something about "only getting one of them." The room was filled with a strange smell. Jackie didn't know what it was.

"Get him in the truck," said a girl with freckles over her acne scars. "It's pretty full. Don't make any more stops before you get to processing."

Jackie didn't know what processing was, but he wanted to go home with Lily and Mom. "I have school tomorrow. If I have any more unexcused absences I can't go on field trips," he said. He didn't like school too much (field trips were sort of fun though), but he'd found it was a good way to get out of things that grownups wanted him to do.

There was some laughter, then the freckled girl began rattling away at her keyboard. "Right. I'll call Ronald and let him know that a shipment is on its way."

The guy who had been hiding in the pipes came down the stairs. He carried a vanilla ice cream cone. "Little boy, I'll give you this ice cream if you go in the truck," said the man.

Jackie shook his head, backing up. He remembered

that Mom had taught him it was better to be polite to people, so he said "No, thank-you."

The boy put his hand on his hip. "We can do this the easy way or the hard way," he said. "Either you trot up there and get ice cream, or I *haul* your butt in the truck and you don't get ice cream."

There was nowhere for Jackie to run to anyway, so he decided to take the ice cream. The truck bore a picture of a gross-looking breakfast burger. "Eat at McBurger today!" it screamed in seizure-inducing shades of red and yellow. "Try a Sausage McBurger, only 99 cents!" Jackie thought if he ever ate a breakfast burger again in his life he would puke.

Jackie obligingly clambered up.

The guy unlatched the door, and opened it just enough for Jackie to be able to slip through. He looked Jackie in the eyes for the first time. "Now, before you get the ice cream, there is one more thing you need to do. Get most of your body through the door - that's right, just leave a hand sticking through. Mm hmm. Well okay." He placed the ice cream cone in Jackie's hand. There was a grating sound as the door was firmly bolted. The motor started, and Jackie stumbled into the door as the truck started moving.

It took a while for his eyes to adjust to his new surroundings. The other children were very quiet. They had dazed looks on their faces. It was like they were sick or something. Some were crying, some were hitting the walls, some were playing with the toys that came in their Happy Meals. But most of them were asleep. There was one grown-up, an obese woman in an electric wheelchair. Most of the light came from little gaps around the door, or from a hole in the other end of the truck. Brief investigation proved this to be a toilet that opened directly onto the road.

There was a FAT PRIDE bumper sticker on the back of the woman's wheelchair. Her stomach was hanging down one leg of her sweatpants. She had several breakfast burgers spread out in front of her and was chewing on one. She offered Jackie some french fries, but he said no thank-you.

His ice cream tasted funny, but he still didn't want to get it mixed up with french fry taste in his mouth. "Why are you the only grown-up here?" Jackie asked.

She shrugged, the fat rolls on her arms swaying gently. "They kicked me off of welfare so I came down to my favorite place, McBurger, to drown my sorrows in french fries. The McBurger people offered me free food for the rest of my life if I rolled my wheelchair up into the truck. I think they're going to kill us, but at least I get to die with a full belly."

Jackie privately thought she was crazy. "Where are we going?"

"The McBurger headquarters, most likely. Hey, I've been watching the other kids and I think they put drugs in that ice cream to make you sleepy and easy to handle. You don't want to be sleepy and easy to handle, do you?"

Jackie shook his head. So that was why it tasted funny.

"I think you should give me that ice cream," said the woman. "Drugs are really bad for you. *Sure* you don't want a french fry?"

Jackie handed her the ice cream, and she took half of it in one bite. "Mmm, ice cream," she murmured. "This is delicious. I finished all my ice cream two hours ago."

After a while, the truck stopped. The woman had finished her burgers and was now on fries and a shake. The doors opened. Several of the children gasped. One even screamed. Those who were sleeping woke up. A clown stood in front of them. Its hair was a dull orange, stiff and yarn-like, sticking out at from under his hat at odd angles. His nose was covered by a paper cup, and his eyes looked stupid but mean, like a crocodile that wanted to eat you up in one bite. "Hi kids," he said, a grin slowly crawling up his mouth. "I'm Ronald McRonald, the hamburger-happy clown." Cheesy music came from somewhere, under his hat perhaps.

He's Ronald McRonald

The hamburger-happy clown.

He's Ronald McRonald

The coolest clown in town!

He won't kill you,

He won't eat you,

He won't boil your fat,

He's a good guy clown,

Now how about that?

"Oh dear," sighed Ronald, shaking his head. "You modern children are too easily scared. You're not as hardy as kids were back in the sixties." There was a poof of magic clown powder, and suddenly Ronald McRonald looked less like a serial killer. Now he had a short red afro, a human nose, and teeth that would make any dentist proud. He was acting differently too. The old Ronald had been quiet and slow. This Ronald was cheerful and bouncy. "Well kiddies! Here I am! Your good old modern safe friendly lovable huggable Ronald McRonald!" He held his arms out. No one else moved, except for the lady in the wheelchair. She stuffed another french fry in her mouth. "Hey Ronald," she said with her mouth full, "Before I die, I just want to know one thing. Whatever happened to those other McBurger characters from when I was a kid?"

"I killed them," Ronald giggled. "They were delicious. Are there any other questions?"

"What are you going to do with us, Ronald?" asked a little girl who still had ketchup smeared across her face.

"Why, I'm going to cook you into burgers! Won't that be fun?" he clapped his hands. "Giant spiders to drain your blood. Then the process begins. Because you're going to be taaaaasty little burgers!" He pulled a bike horn out of nowhere and gave it a few squeezes.

"I got a bone in my burger today," Jackie said.

Ronald chuckled and patted him on the head. Jackie flinched away. He was starting to revert to the old form, the hair fading to a dull orange, lumping together. "Such a dear, sweet little child!" he gushed. "I bet you'll taste extra yummy!"

Ronald skipped away. He returned, limping slowly, his feet making a heavy thumping sound. He was wheeling a ramp. He pushed it against the back of the truck. "Come out," he said, his voice growing thick and raspy. "Come out or I will electrify the back of the truck. Everyone will start screaming and flopping around, and I *hate* when that happens."

Jackie knew what being shocked was like. One time after his dad drank all the beer, he tricked Jackie into licking a nine-volt battery. It had hurt.

The prisoners climbed down, most of them moving very slowly. "Got to finish," mumbled the lady, putting more food in her mouth. "Please, Ronald, let me finish."

The room they were led to was a dingy off-white, scuff marks low on the walls. There were strange symbols and crude drawings, too, written with something crusty and reddish-brown. There was also this message:

The real McBurger mission statement

to cause obesity and heart disease

to promote and increase consumption of children

to prepare for the birth of the ANTICHRIST and,

to make money.

Jackie didn't know what "obesity" or "consumption" were, and he had only the faintest idea of who the Antichrist was (third grade Sunday school tended not to focus on such things), but he did understand that this was probably not the mission statement that was shown to customers.

Ronald grinned at him. His teeth were disturbingly long and yellow, the incisors of a rat. A revolving door began to turn, slowly grinding along on rusty gears. He beckoned the children towards it.

No one moved, fear freezing them to the spot.

"Come on, kiddies, go inside," Ronald whispered.

"But the spiders, Ronald," sobbed the girl with the ketchup face. "I'm scared of spiders."

He knelt, his face now at the children's level. His breath was foul, rancid and sour.   "Oh, but there are no spiders in there, my sweet children. We are going to find your parents. Go through that door. Your parents are there."

"Are my mommy and daddy really in there?" asked a very young boy clutching the same toy Jackie had gotten earlier that day.

Ronald nodded. "Yes. Off you go then. Off to your parents."

The other children entered. Jackie didn't know why they thought the bad clown was going to let them see their parents again. Perhaps it had something to do with the drugs in the ice cream. Only Jackie and the woman in the wheelchair were left outside.

"You know, Ronald," said the wheelchair woman, "I've decided that I don't really want to die. How about I just pay you back for the food? With interest," she added, seeing the look on Ronald's face.

"How about no," said Ronald. The wheelchair began moving forward. The woman shouted, pushing the lever this way and that, but the chair continued moving forward. She dropped the shake, and began to heave herself upwards. Ronald crept up behind her and pulled her back down. "Naughty, naughty," he hissed.

Her chair caught in the door, and was pushed through.

Once she was in the other room Ronald turned to Jackie. "My parents aren't really in there, are they?" Jackie asked.

Ronald pounced forward, toward Jackie quickly, like he was going to hit him. Jackie tried to run, but demonic clowns can be very fast. He scooped Jackie up. His hands were cold and moist. Jackie kicked. Ronald changed his grip, bringing one of his hands higher up, and Jackie bit the clown's wrist. It tasted like makeup and sour milk. Ronald slapped him. Then he began pinching and scratching the back of his neck. While the clown's nails were not long, they were quite sharp.

"Do you like this, little Jackie?" he asked in a singsong voice.

It knows my name, though Jackie. *How does it know my name?*

Ronald stuck him in the door and pushed it around before Jackie had a chance to escape. "Good-bye, kiddies.

Say hi to Mommy and Daddy for me." Jackie tried to get through the other side but something kept pushing him off. It was very dark in the room. Most of the children were wandering around, bumping into each other and calling for their parents. The fat woman had regained control of her wheelchair. She wheeled it around in circles. One of the walls was sheet metal, pulling away from the beams in some areas. In the darkest part of the room (away from the sheet metal holes) was a gate or fence made out of some kind of farm wire. Something black and hairy moved behind it.

Jackie kicked at the biggest hole. He was denting it a little bit, but the hole didn't seem to be getting any larger. The grating sound was back. It sounded just like when they had opened the ball pit. The wire thing was moving. A dark shape crawled forth, and descended on one of the children. Jackie began kicking harder.

"Here," the fat lady said. "Good idea, kid, but move out of the way." She backed her wheelchair up, adjusted the controls, and rocketed towards the hole. The metal crunched. She backed up again. Her legs were bleeding, ripped open. She crashed into the hole a second time. "You kids go on through," she gasped. "Going to have to crawl out. Now!" She lifted herself upwards, inching forward on her seat.

"Come on!" Jackie shouted. "Your parents aren't really in here, they're through that hole. You have to leave, now, before the spider eats you!" The children who were still alive crowded around Jackie. He pushed them through the hole. Some of them pushed back, but Jackie, not being dazed, was able to push harder. There was a loud thump and the dust on the floor rose up. Several of the children, frightened by the noise, staggered back into the shadows. The woman was on the floor. She crawled to the hole, grunting with each push. She left a trail of blood behind her. The children near the hole began escaping by themselves. Soft cries came from the shadows. The lady squeezed through the hole. A piece of metal left a red trail down her back. "You kids come on out," she shouted. Jackie pushed a few more kids through the hole. They wanted to leave now, but were not moving very fast. The dark thing was coming closer. Jackie slipped out behind the others. A pointed black leg, bristling with hair, poked though the hole after him.

"See the road up the hill there?" the lady said. A lot of cars were going by very fast. It looked like a highway. "If we can make it to that, we'll be safe. Everyone needs to stay together, okay?" Some of the children nodded. The group was smaller than it used to be. The girl with the ketchup face wasn't there, which made Jackie sad. He looked back towards the hole. The pointy leg wasn't sticking out anymore. He thought he could still hear the thing swishing around the room, though it might have only been his imagination. The thing had been very quiet.

Jackie grabbed the woman's shirt and tried to pull her up the hill. She moved forward, very slowly. Her legs weren't bleeding as much, but the rocks reopened some of the cuts. "Come on and help me," he said to the other kids. Inch by inch they made it up the hill.

"Thanks kid," she groaned as they reached the cusp of the hill, "Couldn't have done it without you."

"That's okay," Jackie said, "I needed the exercise - all of those burgers, you know?"

The fat lady nodded her agreement.

She doubted she'd be eating burgers anytime soon.

Having A Drink
By T. T. Trestle

"Could you pass me the clicker?" I said to the new bartender. She was a big, sloppy redhead wearing globs of purple mascara and a matching oversized T-shirt.

"The what?" she said. Her short haircut made her red hair stand up in places. Her pals probably called her something like Jo or Sam.

"The clicker," I said. "I can't watch any more of that." I nodded at the bodybuilder being interviewed on the TV above the ratty pool table. He was talking about his work in underdeveloped countries. I wasn't sure if he meant poor countries or skinny countries.

"Hmm," said Sam. "I kind of like it." She folded her arms over her purple T-shirt. She wasn't carrying a crusty dishrag like Bob always did, pretending to clean the grubby glasses that were a specialty of Oges Tavern & Eatery. Sort of ruined the ambience.

I smiled at her, putting some heat in it. "What if I told you I'm allergic to men in thongs?"

She laughed. "Okay, you win, handsome." She reached under the bar for the clicker.

"Thanks," I said, and zapped the bodybuilder. I stopped clicking when I reached a Gilligan's Island rerun. Maryann and Ginger, Technicolor dream women. Why did Gilligan and his buddies want to *leave* the island?

"You like that show?"

I gazed at her, putting some smoke in it. "It's Ginger. I'm a sucker for redheads."

She laughed again but I could see I had slipped one through. Her cheeks were flushing, making her look like the world's largest schoolgirl.

"I have another question for you," I said. I smiled, trying to make more pink appear in her cheeks. She wasn't buying this time. The schoolgirl was hidden back in grade school memories. I'd have to put more heat into it to get a response. I had three thousand green beauties tucked away in the lining of my suit jacket. What did I need to get Sam all hot and bothered for?

She crossed her arms again, waiting.

"It's about the name of this place," I said. "Do you know how to pronounce it?" Bob had said it twice in the five months I'd been coming to Oges Tavern & Eatery. One time it had sounded like Odges and the second time – and I think Bob had been a bit soused – like Ogle.

She gave me a purple shrug. "I dunno...Oggies?"

That's why I loved it here. The element of mystery. Like why it was called an eatery when it didn't even have a kitchen. Heck, the alcohol was so watered down, this hole barely qualified as a tavern.

"Do *you* know how to say it?" She cocked an auburn eyebrow at me.

"Yes, I do." I took a long sip of Glenfiddich, waiting to see what exactly it was I knew. "It was originally two words. During Prohibition, this place was a speakeasy and didn't have a sign. The two words were a secret code for patrons to identify the place without getting nabbed."

She leaned on the bar. "Really?"

"Yup. The two words were 'Oh geez'. So one guy might say, 'Oh geez, I'm thirsty', and the other guy would know exactly what and where he meant."

"That's pretty wild," she said.

I nodded sagely. "Even today, some of us regulars still use the secret code. For example" – I waved at the ratty pool table, the mismatched tables and chairs – "*Oges*, I can't believe I'm in this dump again."

She loved it. "Oh geez," she repeated, laughing. "Is that really true?"

"Would I lie to you?" And then, because I was rich again, because I didn't have a date with Mrs. Welton until next Friday, I broke the most cherished of the Oges Tavern & Eatery rules – I spoke to another patron. He was drinking alone at the other end of the bar.

"What do you think?" I said. "How do you say the name of this place?"

He was large, with a glistening bald head. The first name that jumped into my head seemed more than appropriate. Mung.

"Fuck off," said Mung, without looking at me. He emphasized his point by flexing one bulbous arm.

"Hey," said Sam to me, "don't bother the other customers."

"I know how to say it," said the old black guy sitting at the table next to the entrance. He had a basketball-sized afro, like Linc from the Mod Squad. His papery lumberjack shirt hung down to his knees. I smiled at him, more than a little surprised another patron had spoken.

"It's Ojays," said Linc. He nodded his chin at the dented jukebox on the other side of the entrance. He bopped his afro around, as if he could hear "Love Train" coming from the jukebox.

"Ojays Tavern." I snapped my fingers. "I like the sound of that."

"Damn straight," said Linc.

I turned to the last patron. She was hunched over the PacMan video game table near the hallway leading to the washrooms. A piece of cardboard with OUT OF ORD scrawled on it was taped to the side of the table.

"And what do you think?" I said. I kept my smile friendly. No point wasting any heat on her. She looked too housewifey to be a potential client. Her purse was way too big, almost a sack, to have any real money in it. Her mousy hair was braided into two stiff pigtails. A Doris, if there ever was one.

"Pardon?" she said, looking up. She had a fresh black eye.

"You talk too much, pretty boy," said Mung. He levered his bulk off his stool.

"No trouble," said Sam, reaching under the bar.

"Yo," called Linc, "leave him alone, cueball. We jus' having some fun."

Mung rotated towards Linc. "What the fuck did you just call me?"

The door opened and two people walked in. It was a man and a woman and they were both wearing wolfman masks – black-tipped noses, poofy Michael Landon hair, Elvis sideburns. The woman had a revolver. The man was gigantic, so huge he moved awkwardly, as if each part of his body had its own brain. Bonnie and Clod.

"Oges," I said, thinking of the three thousand green beauties in the lining of my jacket.

Clod stayed in front of the door. He was taller than the door, almost as wide. Bonnie hopped down the short flight of stairs and came over to the bar. She was carrying a frilly white basket with her other hand.

"Hands up, bitch," she barked at Sam. She pointed the revolver at the pool table. "Get over there." She swung the gun towards Doris then me. "You too."

Sam did what she was told. So did Doris.

I stared at the hole at the end of the barrel for a long tick of eternity. My body turned as cold and empty as the distance between stars.

"Now!" roared Bonnie.

I backed towards the pool table, joining Sam and Doris. Sam looked like she was going to cry. Doris was hugging her purse. The only colour in her face was the black eye.

Clod took one giant, stilted step and hauled Linc out of his chair.

"Take it easy, Jack," cried Linc.

Clod shoved him towards the pool table.

"Get over there!" Bonnie barked at Mung, who hadn't budged an inch since the arrival of our two trick-or-treaters. She set the frilly white basket on the bar and leveled the revolver at Mung.

"Or what?" snorted Mung. "You gonna shoot me with that?" He turned his back on Bonnie and pointed at Clod. "I don't care about the size of you. Get in my way and I'll make you eat that stupid mask." He strode towards the door, bald head glistening.

Bonnie didn't shoot him. I squinted at the revolver in her hand. It was a toy. I slipped my fingers under the left cuff of my suit jacket. My three thousand green beauties weren't going anywhere tonight. Thank you very much, Mung.

Clod blocked Mung's path. Mung never hesitated.

He swung one bulbous arm, ramming a fist up into Clod's face. If Mung had hit me like that it'd all be over. My face would be an eyesore. I'd never get another client.

Veins were rising all over Mung's arms and scalp. You had to hand it to him. He looked sort of...transcendent. He launched another fist but Clod's arms shot out and yanked Mung into the air. Clod whirled and threw Mung towards the PacMan table. Mung sailed across the room, bounced over the table, knocking it on its side. The PacMan table made an electronic burp and the blank screen filled with glowing yellow dots and chomping ghosts.

"Holy croak," said Linc.

Sam started crying.

My fingers turned to icicles and fell out of the sleeve of my jacket. It didn't matter that Bonnie's gun was a toy.

Clod went over to Mung, picked him up by his wide leather belt and carried him down the hallway to the ladies' room. He kicked open the door and tossed Mung inside.

Bonnie and Clod kissed, tongues slurping. Bonnie strolled off towards to the washroom. Clod came and stood in front of the pool table. He crossed his arms and loomed.

"Hey Jack," said Linc, "here, you can have it, man. It's all yours." He was holding out a greasy brown wallet. Crumpled paper, bus transfers and a TOPPS baseball card were sticking out of it.

Clod regarded the wallet.

"Take it," said Linc. "There's three Mastercards in it and two Visa. They still good."

"I could open the safe for you," offered Sam. She had stopped crying. Her mascara had run, leaving big, sloppy purple runnels down her face.

A scream came from inside the ladies' room. It was a chorus of all the worst things in life – profound agony, hopeless pleading, abject fear.

The scream stopped.

Sam started crying again.

Clod watched our faces, his gigantic body shaking with laughter. "You can keep your money." He pointed at Linc. "We want you." Then Sam. "And you." Then Doris. "And you."

Then me.

"And you."

Sam bent forward and puked. Clod looked down at the mess, nostrils flaring in disgust. Linc took off, darting forward and ducking under Clod. Clod lunged for him but he was too late. Linc's basketball afro was already bouncing through the mismatched tables and chairs, his lumberjack shirt flying back like a cape.

"See ya!" cried Linc as he hurtled towards the entrance. Clod turned to follow, tripped, caught his balance on the bar. For a moment, Clod's mammoth back was to me, as wide and inviting as a door. My fingers tensed, ready…

But what if you miss?

Clod went after Linc. He plowed through tables and chairs. But Linc was quick. He was already springing up the entrance steps, lumberjack shirt flapping.

Don't look back, don't look back.

Linc reached for the doorknob. He didn't look back. That's why he didn't see Bonnie. She slammed him into the door. She tore at him, shredding his shirt. He fought wildly, punching her, kicking. Then Clod joined the tangle. Linc tried to keep fighting but Clod was too much for him. Linc never screamed, never made a sound while they killed him. I don't know why. Whether he didn't know what was happening or was hurt too badly to scream or just wouldn't give them the satisfaction. His afro had been snatched bald in places.

I didn't remember the emergency exit at the end of washroom hallway until they were finished.

So what? You going to run for it? Like Linc? Long odds and you've never been one to risk your pretty face, have you?

Bonnie and Clod walked back to the pool table.

"Who's next?" said Clod.

Sam retched again. Nothing came out this time but a dribble of complete terror. Doris clutched her sack purse.

"How about you, bitch?" said Bonnie, flicking a finger through Sam's red hair.

I stepped forward, away from the pool table, into a vast, desolate place. Bonnie and Clod both glanced at me in surprise.

Take it back, take it back. You don't protect *women. That's not what you do for women.*

"What do we have here?" said Clod. "A hero?" He turned to Bonnie, grinning. "Isn't that just so sweet?"

I felt something take form inside me, something clean and dense with potential. An ember of rage.

"Hey Rover," I said to Clod.

They stopped laughing.

"Bite me," I said.

Doris inhaled sharply. Sam looked up at me, purple eyes wide.

Clod snorted. "You think you're something special, huh? You're nothin' but a walkin', talkin' Big Mac." He picked me up and shook me until it felt like my skeleton was liquefying. He carried me over to the washroom hallway. He kicked open the door of the ladies' room and threw me inside. I covered my head and gritted my teeth, bracing for impact. But I landed on something soft, was grateful until I realized what it was – Mung. Sort of.

I scrambled off him. I saw why Mung had screamed the way he had. She had eaten him, or parts of him.

I closed my eyes, to keep the sickening, pulsing soup inside me from boiling over into the room and dissolving the world. I turned away from the sort-of-Mung sprawled on the drenched floor. My hip bumped into something hard and my eyes opened. I was at the sink.

They ate him, she's going to eat you, eat you while you're still alive, Linc never screamed, never stopped fighting them while they murdered him.

I splashed water on my face, hid in its simple cold wetness.

The door opened and Bonnie sauntered in. "Hi there," she said. She came towards me, hips swaying. She raised her long arms, stained hands reaching for me.

"Wait," I said, smiling with all the heat and smoke in me, as if I had the sun hidden behind my eyes.

She paused. "Are you going to beg for your life, pretty little dinner?"

I almost lost my smile. The boiling, pulsing soup tickled the back of my throat, scratched at the edge of my mind, wanting in. But I kept smiling, giving her everything I had.

She swayed towards me.

"I know how to touch you," I said. I caressed my fingertips over the back of her hand.

She stopped. She stared at the goosebumps on her hand.

"Let me show you." I slid the tip of one finger across her palm. She shuddered. I traced intricate, spider-leg patterns over her wrist and down her forearm. I brought up my other hand and did the same to her other arm, leaving a trail of shivery goosebumps.

"I could touch you other places…"

She moved closer. "Oh, such a clever little dinner."

I made a circle with thumb and forefinger, floated the circle towards one of her breasts. She arched her back. I paused. She buried her stained nails into the palms of her hands, waiting, waiting for my touch.

I gently flicked my forefinger across her nipple. She groaned. I flicked again, harder, the shock of the pain exaggerating the pleasure.

"Take off your shirt," I whispered.

She grabbed at her black turtleneck and tore it open.

I gazed at her dark, avid eyes, promising her ecstasy. I drew an S down one breast, ending at the straining nipple. She wasn't wearing a bra. She locked urgent fingers around the back of my neck and pulled me to her. My head lowered to her breast and –

Oges.

Her breast was covered with wavy, brown swirls of hair. Fur. Light and downy, but still fur. From this close, I could see individual follicles coming out of the pale, blue-veined skin. Her nipples were a deep satiny black.

She dug her nails into the back of my neck. "What's

wrong, bitch? Why have you stopped?" Her nails burrowed deeper. Blood trickled down my neck and nestled in the collar of my shirt.

And you know something else, don't you? You'd already figured out that something wasn't right about Bonnie and Clod. You knew when you saw what they did to Mung. So what are you waiting for?

I placed both hands on Bonnie's muscular back. I pulled her to me. I put my mouth over one of her nipples. I almost wrenched my head away from her breast when I felt something hot squirt into my mouth. I swallowed, knowing the only thing keeping her other appetites at bay was a flimsy gauze of bliss.

At first, I thought it was my own blood, that I had bitten the inside of my mouth when Clod was shaking me. But the taste was wrong. Sweet as a soft peach, smoother than hundred year old Scotch, radiant in my belly, spreading glowing tendrils throughout my body. I almost let the boiling, pulsing soup inhabit my mind but my mouth, trained and obedient all these years, kept trying to make her forget anything else existed in the world but ecstasy.

And it worked. Because she was still groaning with pleasure while I slipped my fingers under the left cuff of my suit jacket, drew Mac out of his sheath and thrust the knife into her back.

I'm good at two things. One I use to make money. The other thing I use, every once in a while, to make sure no one takes my money away from me. To make sure no one takes *anything* away from me.

"I just killed you," I whispered like a lover.

She stared at me, panting, breasts heaving. She hadn't realized she wasn't in ecstasy.

I held up Mac, his serrated blade glistened with her life. She bent an arm around behind her and touched the hole in her back. Her eyes were confused, clouded with imminent agony.

"Pretty little corpse," I said and cut her neck from Elvis sideburn to sideburn. She staggered away from me, tripped over Mung and fell into his contorted embrace.

I went over to the sink, stuck two fingers down my throat and emptied my stomach onto the cracked porcelain. I rinsed my mouth out with cold water. I walked across the drenched floor and opened the door. Clod's massive, shaggy head turned towards the washroom hallway as soon as he heard the door open.

"Hey Jack," I said.

He actually did a double take, eyes bulging out of his hairy face.

"Surprised to see me?" I ambled down the hallway. "Oh, by the way – " I held up Mac. "I made lamb chops out of her."

"Marsha?" said Clod. He shook his head then clawed at his cheeks, leaving tears of blood. "Marsha..."

I stopped at the end of the hallway. Marsha?

Clod bent his head back and howled.

I waited.

He charged, bounding across the room. Each leap toppled mismatched tables and chairs. His last jump flattened a table decorated with pink flamingoes. I threw Mac. Clod saw the knife flickering towards his head and raised his arms but Mac dipped suddenly and thunked into his chest. He spun past me and crashed into the wall.

I'm good at two things. Sometimes I'm very good.

I went over to Clod.   He was still alive.   But the only place he'd be going any time soon was to meet his maker.

And who would that be?   Who made him?   And who made the other one, lying on the floor with sort-of-Mung, deep black satiny nipples, milk like the birth of the universe?

I looked away from Clod, over at Sam and Doris. They were frozen, as still and unreal as a portrait – Two Astonished Women.

I walked over to them.   I smiled.   Damned if I didn't wink, too.   "Boy, I should could use a dri–"

Neither woman was looking at me any more.   Another portrait – Two Petrified Women.   I didn't bother turning around.

Can't kill one that easy, dummy.

I took off for the bar, hearing tables and chairs toppling behind me, snuffling breath.   I dove over the bar.   I plunged to the mucky floor in a shower of cigarette butts and peanut shells.   I scrabbled on all fours over to the spot where Sam had been when Bonnie and Clod came in.   I flung glasses off shelves, searching for whatever weapon Sam had been reaching for under the bar.

Clod landed on the bar over my head, splintering wood.   He lowered one arm towards me.   Mac was still sticking out of his chest, as if it were just some kind of trendy new bling.   I found what Sam had been reaching for – a cellphone.

Clod latched his hand around my neck and dragged me towards his maw.   I tried to scream but something else came out.

"She was mine before she died!"

He hesitated.

"Can't you smell her on me?" I said.

His black nostrils flared then quivered with the knowledge he was inhaling.

"No...Marsha would never – "

His head exploded, coming apart like a jigsaw puzzle tipped off its table. Slowly, limb by limb, his freight train body toppled down behind the bar. I slid away from the mass of hair and muscle and gore. I climbed to my feet using a Guinness spigot as a handhold.

Doris was standing in front of the bar, sack purse in one hand, a very large, very shiny silver handgun in the other.

"I think," I said, "I love you, Doris."

She nodded grimly and lowered the gun. "Storm," she said. "With an h."

"Storm?" I said, glancing up at the ceiling, expecting to see dark clouds. "With an h?"

"My name's Storm," said Doris. "With a silent h on the end."

"Oh," I said.

She leaned over the bar and looked at Clod. One of his boots was stuck in the bar sink. Clod had worn a size 18. I tugged Mac out of his chest.

Monsters roam the world, eat you alive, knife in the chest won't kill them, deep black satiny nipples, milk like the beginning of life.

"Sorry it took me so long to get him," said Doris, no, Storm with a silent h on the end. "I never had a chance to do anything until you distracted him. Thropes are way too dangerous to take on alone." She shook her head, making her pigtails swing. "I came here as an afterthought. I've always had a bad feeling about the other bartender. Tonight confirms he's a collaborator."

"Bob knew these two?"

She nodded, mouth tight. "I think it's a certainty that he was part of this."

"What are you talking about?" said Sam. She had floated over to the bar and was looking back and forth between us.

"What did you call them?" I said.

"Thropes, as in lycanthropes." Stormh pointed at Clod. "Him and his mate were skinpoppers."

"Huh?" said Sam.

"Werewolves," I said. "Just like in the movies. American Werewolf In London, I Was A Teenaged Werewolf, Abbot and Costello Meet The Wolfma—

"Yes yes, that's right," said Stormh. "Just like that. Give or take a few details." She tapped the shiny silver gun on the sole of Clod's boot, like a professor pointing out some fascinating concept on a blackboard. "We think they're using some kind of mutagenized transgenic retrovirus."

"Ah," I nodded. "That explains everything."

Stormh gave me a hard look hovering somewhere between impatience and ire. She turned to Sam. "Could you make us some coffee? I think we could all use something hot to drink."

Oh no, none for me, thanks. Had enough hot drinks to last a lifetime.

"Okay, sure." Sam floated down to the end of the bar.

Stormh went over and picked up the frilly white

basket on the bar – the one Bonnie had brought into this fine establishment. She set the basket in front of me. I peered inside. There was a baby inside, pudgy face, fresh baby smell, big saucer eyes. Two tiny fangs teeth poking through pink gums, as sharp as pins.

"Give me your knife," said Stormh. She held out a hand.

I looked up. "What?"

"Give me your knife. I have to finish the job."

"It's just a – "

She slammed a fist on the bar. "It's an abomination!"

A sound came from the basket. "Blug," said he, she, it, I don't know. I poked my head inside the basket. The baby was smiling.

"Blug!"

"Don't worry," I whispered. "Don't worry, little... guy."

What are you doing? You hate *babies. Woman cooing over them because that's what they're supposed to do. No past, no mistakes, only a coddled present, a rosy-cheeked future.*

"Get away from it," said Stormh, raising the silver handgun.

"Are you serious?" I said.

She didn't say anything. The answer was in her eyes.

"You get that shiner battling werewolves?" I said. "Like you did tonight? Watching while other people fight and die?"

She stared at me, eyes steady, gun steady.

I backed away from the basket.

"Mog!" said the baby.

Sam came back carrying a tray with three grubby mugs of coffee and Kit Kats that had been broken into individual fingers. She looked down at Clod. "I thought these – these…things could only be killed by silver bullets or something like that?"

I regarded the blood-spattered corpse for a second. The slug had torn a chunk off the side of his head. "Evidently massive brain damage also does the trick."

She nodded. "Lucky for us all those movies got it wrong." She set the tray on the bar. "I made some coffee for you."

"Thanks," said Stormh and shot the baby.

Monsters roam the world, beasts with Elvis sideburns and Michael Landon hair and –

Stormh pointed the gun at my chest.

And pigtails.

"I wouldn't do that if I were you," she said.

"What?" I stared at the maw at the end of the shiny silver barrel. "Do what?"

"Put the knife down," she said. "I don't want to hurt you."

I looked at Mac, surprised. He was by my ear, throwing position. "Okay, take it easy." I slowly lowered Mac and slid him back in his sheath. "I won't do anything stupid."

I turned to Sam. She was crying again. I squeezed her shoulder and since I couldn't think of anything else, I said, "Your mascara's running." I walked out from behind the bar.

"Hey," called Stormh, "where are you going?" She

followed me as I headed towards the washroom hallway. "We need to talk. Bane could use someone like you."

I passed the shattered PacMan table.

"Are you just going to leave?" she said. "You've seen true evil and now you're running away?"

I went down the hallway to the emergency exit. I looked back. Stormh was glaring at me, shiny silver handgun resting on her shoulder like a rifle. Sam was still holding the tray. The frilly white basket had a gaping black hole.

"What's your name?" I said to Sam.

"Joanna, my name is Joanna."

Joanna…Jo. I smiled at her, no heat or smoke. A real one. She tried to smile back. I opened the emergency exit and stepped out into the narrow alley.

"We'll be seeing you again!" yelled Stormh. "That's a promise!"

***

The alley stank. The dumpster near the exit was a lodestone of foulness, drawing and magnifying every horrid odour in the alley. A host of stenches clawed at my nose – rancid oranges, maggoty fish, the sour old stink of a man's running shoe, wet moldy cardboard, the sickly sweetness of sun-fried cola –

A man's running shoe?

I stopped. I stared at the dumpster. How did I know there was a man's running shoe in there?

Something moved on the other side of an old car halfway down the alley. A padded, stealthy movement. Mac leaped into my hand. I crouched low, waited. A cat dashed out from under the car.

You drank some.

There were no lights in the alley. The surrounding buildings were high enough to block out the streetlights but I could see the colour of the fleeing cat, a pudgy, nutmeg-coloured tom. I could smell the piquant vapours of the tom's fear, the tart hone of its sex.

You drank some of her –

I ran down the alley. I passed the cat before he reached the street. The tom froze, looking up at me as I bounded over him, fur bristling, ears back. The scent of its terror reminded me of Glenfiddich.

My car was parked beside the mouth of the alley. The fumy cloggy metal smell of the Porsche made my stomach churn. I unlocked the door and got in. The inside of the car smelled like blood. I snatched Mac back out but the car was empty. The blood smell was coming from me, from my suit. I breathed in the sweet, narcotic aroma.

It reminded me of Glenfiddich that had been aged since the birth of the universe. I gulped down the aroma, couldn't stop sucking it in, until the car began to turn to mist and the only real thing in the world was Bonnie and Clod, their hot, warm, smothering nectar.

I ran Mac across the palm of one hand, grasping onto the pain, the private, comforting smell of my own existence. When the car started to feel solid again, I put Mac down on the passenger seat, tugged off my tie and wrapped it around my bleeding hand. I jammed the Porsche in gear and pulled away from the alley.

I glanced up at the moon. It was a crescent, as fine and bright as the blade of a scimitar. Shouldn't it be full? Wasn't that one of the rules?

There was half a city between me and Oges Tavern

& Eatery before it dawned on me why the bar's decrepit sign advertised the availability of both drink and food even though there was no kitchen in that screaming hellhole.

I took the flask of Glenfiddich out of the glove compartment. I took a long, long swig – or started to. I opened the car window and spat out the foul liquid. It tasted like distilled poison.

I looked up at the bright crescent moon and decided Storm with a silent h at the end had been right when she promised I'd be seeing her again. I would definitely be seeing Stormh and her Bane, whoever or whatever that was, again. And Bob, Bob the collaborator.

And…Sam, Joanna. Maybe I would call her some time and ask her how she's doing? Maybe ask her if she wanted to go for a coffee. But I wouldn't be seeing Mrs. Welton or any of my other clients again. I was through with trick or treating.

Acquired Taste
By William Holden

"Oh my god." I groaned as I slipped it into my mouth. I closed my eyes savoring every drop of the warm, salty cream. I didn't swallow. I wanted to hold out a little longer. The earthy flavors lingered on my taste buds. I licked my lips to catch the cream that dribbled from the corner of my mouth. A wave of heat swept over my body. Beads of sweat broke out across my brow. My balls contracted. My cock stretched. I gave into the urge. I swallowed.

"Christ, Dean, keep your voice down, people are staring at us." Cameron whispered from across the table. "It's fucking spaghetti and meatballs."

"I know, but the cream sauce is unbelievable." I opened my eyes. Cameron did not look amused. "You have to try this." I twirled my fork in the mass of carbohydrate goodness. I stabbed one of the oversized meatballs and severed a piece of it to add to the sauce and pasta.

"No thanks." He pushed the fork out of my hand. It fell on the table splattering bits of meat and cream over the red and green-flecked Formica table. "Jesus, fucking, Christ, Dean."

"What's your problem?" I took another mouthful letting the flavors take me to a more pleasurable place so that I could ignore Cameron's shitty attitude. My cock pushed against the shrinking space in my underwear. I felt a drizzle of pre-come trickle down my thigh. The urge to fuck rushed through me. I moved my right hand up my leg. My cock was a solid shaft of flesh. "Did you say something, Cameron?"

"Never mind, I've lost my appetite. I'm going out for a smoke." Cameron threw his napkin over the plate and left the diner. I took another bite, leaned back against the seat, and let the pleasure rush through me.

The pit of my arms became wet and sticky. I could smell my own perfumed coated sweat seeping through my t-shirt. I took a sip of water and noticed a man watching me from a set of double swing doors. He looked to be in his early forty's. A dark five o'clock shadow covered his otherwise hairless, rectangular head. Bright orange flames etched into his skin snaked their way out of the collar of his chef's coat. The flames licked the ridge of his jaw-line. Our eyes met. A half smile crossed his thick lips. He ducked back behind the doors. The whoosh of the doors echoed in my head. The other patrons didn't seem to notice.

I heard the front door open. I looked behind me. Through the window, I saw Cameron outside on the sidewalk. He lit up a cigarette. His red hair appeared darker under the streetlights. I tried to think of him naked. His pale skin covered in those soft, silky red hairs always sent me over the edge. Even as horny as I was, the idea of having sex with him did nothing to quench my desire.

A fit of laughter erupted. I turned my attention away from my boyfriend and focused on two couples sitting in a booth across from me. They raised their beer bottles. They laughed. I twirled my fork, took a bite, and continued to stroke myself while watching the odd behavior of the two couples.

The men kept glancing up from their steaks to look at one another. Their glances grew to long stares. A few moments later, I noticed one of the men slipping the dress shoe off of his foot. He took a bite of his T-bone steak. He licked the bloody juice from his lips as he stretched his leg out and began to caress the ankle of the other man.

He slipped his toes under the hem of his friend's pants. They looked at each other with a secret desire. The younger of the two moved closer to the edge of the seat spreading his legs further apart. He reached down and grasped the curious foot. He brought the man's toes to rest upon his crotch. They smiled at one another as if their wives were not sitting next to them.

The sweat continued to slide down my neck and into the collar of my shirt. My breathing came in heavy bursts. I took a sip of my water without taking my eyes off the two couples.

"Honestly, Helen." One of the women continued. "He's useless in bed after eight." The two women giggled. She looked at her husband and winked.

"You can be such a bitch, Darlene." He said as he caressed the man's foot that was nestled in his crotch. "Excuse us a moment." He pushed his friend's foot away and grabbed his wife's hand. He pulled her from the booth. "I'll show you who's useless." He hissed as he pulled her through the diner and into the back hallway where the restrooms were."

I smiled at the thought of what would be happening in one of the restroom stalls. The man who sat alone with his wife caught my smile. His face was as flushed with need as was mine. He winked at me and slipped his hand between his legs. He seemed oblivious to his wife's presence. With an agitated look, she pulled his hand from his crotch and settled it underneath her skirt. Her head fell back. She closed her eyes and spread her legs further apart. He didn't notice his wife pleasuring herself with his hand. His attention was focused on me, and the motion of my hand beneath the table.

It wasn't more than ten minutes before the second couple came out from the back hallway. She paused to adjust her skirt. He zipped up his pants. His neck covered in red splotches told of his recent pleasure.

"Dean," a distant voice called. I ignored the voice as I watched the couple return to the table as if nothing had happened. All four of them picked up their conversations where they left off. The two women laughed. The men just stared at each other.

"Goddammit Dean, let's go." Cameron dropped into his seat. "I've been out there for over twenty minutes."

"So?" I spoke to him as I continued to watch the events unfold across from me. I forced myself to look away. "Sorry..."

"Don't bother apologizing. I've paid the bill, let's go."

"But I haven't finished my meal." I looked up as our waitress walked by. "Excuse me, could I get this to go?"

"Of course, honey." She picked up the plate as she passed our table. I watched her old sagging ass sway back and forth. Her greyish wrinkled skin sagged at her ankles. My vision blurred. She turned to look at me. She stood naked fondling herself in front of everyone. As she masturbated, she grinned exposing a row of yellow crooked teeth. I looked away and shook my head. When I looked up again, she was fully clothed and scraping my meal into a box.

"I need to go to the bathroom." I scooted across the booth with my head swimming with thoughts of the old woman fucking the two men across from me.

"Can't you fucking wait?" He grabbed my arm.

"No. Can't you see I'm not feeling well?" He looked at me with a confused look. "What is your problem tonight? I'm just going to go into the bathroom. I'll be right back." I stood up at an angle so that Cameron couldn't see my raging hard-on, or the wet spot in my crotch. I turned my back on him as my body cleared the edge of the table.

I stopped halfway to the bathroom and leaned against a chair as a wave of pleasure rippled through my body. *"Holy shit. I'm going to come."* I gripped the edge of the chair with both hands. My body shook as the orgasm raced through me. I held a hand over my mouth to quiet my mounting pleasure. I ran to the bathroom as the waves of pleasure increased. I stumbled into the first stall as another surge swept through my cock. I leaned my head against the cool metal surface. "Oh, shit!" I leaned against the door bracing myself with the metal walls. My knees buckled. "Oh, Jesus." I grabbed the top edge of the walls. "Fuck!" My body shook as another orgasm rushed through me.

"Fuck." I opened the door of the stall and stumbled against the washbasin. I grabbed a paper towel to clean up the mess, and then left the bathroom. I stood in the small hallway with my eyes closed, hoping to slow my breathing before going back to Cameron.

"Let's go." I said as I approached the table. I grabbed the Styrofoam box that contained my half-eaten dinner.

"I've been ready for," he hesitated." His hand settled on my shoulder. "Is that what I think it is?" He turned me around. "Jesus, did you fuck someone in the bathroom?"

"Don't be ridiculous."

"Your neck." He reached up and stretched the collar of my t-shirt. "And your chest, you have sex blush. You fucked someone in there didn't you?"

"No, I didn't." I looked around the restaurant. The two women sat with solemn expressions on their faces, talking. I turned my attention back to Cameron. "We are not having this conversation here." I turned and left the restaurant.

"Don't walk away from me." Cameron yelled as he stepped out onto the sidewalk. "I know how you get after sex. You can't tell me those red splotches came from something else."

"Look, I can't explain it. I'm having these feelings, these spontaneous orgasms. Is that what you wanted to hear? Are you satisfied, now?" I glared at him. "And put that cigarette away. I can't stand to kiss you after you smoke. It's disgusting."

"You couldn't have waited till we got back to my place?" He lit the cigarette despite my comment.

"No." I wanted to say more, to get him to understand it was out of my control, but with my anger toward him growing, I knew I would regret every word of it. I held my tongue.

"No." That's all you're going to say?"

"Maybe it's because you were not the one I wanted to fuck tonight." The words escaped before I could stop them. I could see the hurt in his eyes. "Look, I'm sorry, I didn't mean it. I can't explain what happened in there."

"You don't have to worry about kissing this mouth tonight." He took a drag of his cigarette and blew the smoke in my direction.

"Cameron."

"Don't." He pulled away from me. "Thanks for a great evening, Dean. I'll walk home from here. I need to clear my head."

"Aren't you over-reacting? So I came in my pants. Big fucking deal." I shouted down the street. "Jesus, I masturbate all the time."

"It isn't. Never mind. I'll call you in the morning." I watched his body disappear into the shadows.

I walked to my car, opened the door, and waited for the door light to dim. I felt comforted by the darkness. As I sat among the silence, the smell of the rich vodka cream sauce filled the car with its tantalizing aroma. I slipped the Styrofoam container out of the bag and opened it. Nestled in the center of the leftovers was a smaller container with a note attached to it. I pulled the note from the box and read it. "You left without ordering dessert." As I read the note, I felt someone watching me. I turned on the headlights, and I looked out across the parking lot. There was no one around, yet the feeling persisted. I opened the smaller container. Inside was a five-layered dessert cut into a perfect circle. A tiny plastic fork rested against the side of the box.

A nerve twitched in the pit of my stomach as the craving for pleasure rose through my body. My hand trembled like an addict needing his next fix. I tore into the alternating layers of cake and mousse. The chocolate, butterscotch, rum, and hazelnut flavors opened a flood of emotions. A chill ran over my body. Gooseflesh broke out over my skin causing the hair on my arms to rise. I took another bite. I threw my head back against the seat and let the rush of a building orgasm overtake me.

"Son-of-a-bitch." I braced my head with my hand. I felt lightheaded. My body ached as if I had been fucked senseless. I set the container in the passenger seat. I stared at the food. Its aroma beckoned me to take another bite. I closed my eyes trying to clear my head. I held the key in the ignition praying I could get home. I looked across the parking lot. The man that I had seen earlier stood watching me from the door in the alley. I felt his eyes upon me. His presence filled the air as if he were sitting next to me. I looked down in my lap as I felt my cock stir.

I looked up. The man was gone, but the door remained open. I took the keys from the ignition, paused, and then opened the door and stepped out into the night. I shivered from the icy sweat that ran down my back. My footsteps crunched against the rough surface of the ground as I approached the alley.

I hesitated at the door, and then stepped inside. I slid my hand along the door to soften the noise when the lock engaged. The kitchen was immense, impeccably clean, and empty. I looked at my watch. It was only nine fifteen, too early for the kitchen to close. I walked toward the two-way doors. They rocked back and forth in opposite directions as if someone had recently walked through them. I held them open and looked into the dining room. Customers filled nearly every table, yet their laughter; their spoken words were silent to me as if someone had pushed the mute button on the television. The silence became deafening.

I left the door and walked through the kitchen. I felt I was playing a game of hide-and-seek with no knowledge of whom I was seeking. As I walked through the kitchen and into the large pantry, I felt the familiar feeling of being watched. I began to think that perhaps I was not the seeker, but the one who should be hiding. An enormous refrigeration unit stood in the back of the pantry. Its door was ajar. As I approached, I felt the icy grip of the air. I rubbed my arms to warm them. I heard footsteps coming from within the refrigeration unit. I stepped inside. My breath crystalized in thick white puffs. Metal shelves covered in a light frost lined the left side of the room. To my right, various cuts of meat, hung from hooks suspended from the ceiling. I turned to leave when a voice came out of the darkness.

"Did you like your dinner?" The man's voice was sensual, deep, and hypnotic.

"Jesus." I turned around. Even in the dim light, I could see the flames coming out of his collar. My cock stirred in my pants as the strange cravings rushed through my body. "I…it was…"

"I make the meatballs myself. In fact, I make all the meat myself. I have a secret way of smoking it." He pulled a knife from his breast pocket and walked toward me. I took a step back, to distance myself from him, and the knife he gripped in his hand.

"I should go." I eyed the knife in his hand. The dull light of the room reflected off the sharp, metal blade. "I'm sure you have customers to attend to."

"No." His voice was immediate and angered. "Why do you want to leave?" His tone softened. He placed his hand on my shoulder. His gentle, firm touch ignited my cravings. "I'm Benjamin, the owner and chef. Here, have another piece of my meat." He slipped the knife through a slab of meat that hung from one of the hooks. He pulled it away with his thumb. I opened my mouth taking in the salty meat. "Tell me Dean, What is it you desire?"

"How do you know my name?" I swallowed letting the heat swell within me. The uncontrollable urge to come returned. My balls tightened. My cock pulsed.

"I know that you want me, Dean, almost as much as I want you. You may even say that you need me, Dean."

"Why me?" I grabbed hold of the edge of a shelf to support my weakening legs as an orgasm raced through my body. "Oh, Shit. Not again." I doubled over holding onto my knees.

"I love you, Dean. Why else would I give you so much pleasure?" He leaned into me and licked my neck. I came in my pants.

"But I don't…"

"Shh…' He held a finger to my lips. "Don't say it,

Dean. The words would wound me, and I've suffered intolerable pain over the years. I cannot take that from you, not ever. I need you to want me Dean. You do want me, don't you?"

He took the knife and raised it to his neck. He smiled as he brought the blade down, cutting the threads that held each of the buttons on his coat. He exposed himself to me. His chest was a solid mass of muscles and covered in short, clipped hair. He let the chef's coat fall to the floor. The orange flames etched into his neck continued in a single fiery line down the center of his chest, and then branched out into burning reds and yellows across his stomach. He pulled me to him. I pushed against him trying to resist the urge, yet knowing it was no use. The sharp blades of his chest hair poked at my skin. "Tell me that you want me Dean."

"I want you." I moaned as my lips brushed across his sunless skin.

"Liar!" He shouted and shoved me from his body. I fell against the icy shelves. He looked at me with a slight tilt of his head. "Oh, Dean, I am sorry. I just don't like when people lie to me." He came to me. His thick finger traced the line of my jaw. "Why, did you lie to me?"

"I don't know what you want from me?" I pulled away from his touch even though his touch, his love was what I desired.

"Want?" He looked at me with a hurt expression. "What I want is you, Dean – all of you." He raised the knife to my throat. "I'm sorry." He pulled the knife away with a quick flick. "I sometimes get carried away." His smile melted any fear I had for him. In that moment, I wanted him to take me. I wanted to give myself to him with complete and total abandonment. "God, please kiss me." I took a step closer to him.

"God?" He laughed. "I am not God." He pushed me away from his body. "God does not exist here, Dean. Take your pants off."

I pulled the shoes from my feet. He curled his finger and smiled. I tossed one of them in his direction. He caught it. He held it to his face. I could hear his deep inhaled breaths. He moaned and took another long, deep breath of the odors of my sneakers.

"That's good. I can smell your desire for me. I have chosen well." He tossed the shoe in his hand as he waited for me to undress.

I unbuckled the belt, and then released the buttons of my jeans, keeping an eye on the knife that he licked and moved in and out of his mouth. I pulled the pants off my legs and tossed them to the floor. The arctic air covered me like a wet blanket. Despite the cold, my cock was rock-hard. I shivered as the temperature continued to drop.

"All of it."

"Please make these cravings stop." I looked down my naked body as I pulled my underwear off. Crystals of ice from my sweat-dampened body clung to the hairs of my chest. I approached him.

"You don't want the cravings to stop do you?" He pushed me away from him. I slipped on the cold, icy floor and landed on my ass. The pain was instant. "Do you want to go back to the passionless existence you had with Cameron?"

"It was great with Cameron, but how did you...?"

"I know everything. Tell me, Dean is Cameron who you want?"

"No." I gasped, shocked at my own admission.

"Than tell me Dean, who do you want?"

"I want you." My voice cracked as the frosty air caught in my throat. I sat on the chilled tiles as my cock ached for release.

"Beg for it, Dean. I need to know that you want me."

"Please, I want you. Don't deny me anymore."

"That's more like it. Tell me that you love me, Dean."

"I..." The words caught in my throat. I shook my head. I watched as he took the knife to the slab of meat. He licked the thin slice, and then bent down in front of me. The urge was too much to resist. I wanted the tiny sliver of flesh, but knew what I had to do to get it. "I love you Benjamin." Tears welled in my eyes from the release of emotions as I bit into the meat. I fell against the tile floor in a rush of desire and passion.

"Yes, that's it. Don't fight it, Dean. Give into the pleasure. It's not going to do you any good to fight it. The cravings won't stop until I make them stop." He picked me up and threw me against the metal shelves. I felt the cold metal attaching itself to my exposed skin. "Let's get down to business." He entered me. The pain ripped through my body. I coughed and choked against his invasion of me. I wanted him to stop, yet I knew this is what I needed. I clung to the frozen metal shelf in a state of pleasure as he fucked me.

The sound of metal against metal filled the room. I raised my head from the shelf. Benjamin hadn't touched me, yet I could feel myself being fucked. He stood across the room with his butcher knife and a honing stone. His dark pearl-like eyes sparkled as he focused on the blade running along the edge of the stone.

"Please, don't hurt me." I feel to the floor in a rush of exhaustion and desire.

"Hurt you?" He stopped and looked at me. "I would never hurt you. I love you, Dean. Don't you know that by now?" In two short steps, he was upon me. He knelt down and stroked my hair. "The only one who can hurt you now is you. Are you feeling okay? You look needy." He fondled me. "Do you need more?" He waited for a response. I nodded my head. "Perhaps later, right now we have some business to attend to." He pulled me off the floor and propped me up against the shelves. "Your pleasure or pain depends on you." He walked in the direction of the back wall of the unit. A heavy tarp that I had not noticed before hung from the wall. It appeared to be covering something. "You are now my apprentice. You will learn my trade tonight, or die." He pulled the heavy plastic from the wall.

"No, God, please no." I cried in disbelief and horror as I looked at Cameron crucified to the wall. His feet rested on a wooden plank. His arms stretched out perpendicular to his body with a single nail in the center of each palm.

"Don't worry my love, he's not dead. The angry mood I placed him during dinner had a little something extra to relax him. It will also ease his pain. Trust me, he's very much alive. It has to be that way. That's part of my secret. The meat has to be fresh from the bones." His laughter filled the room. "Most people think that warm skin makes for a closer shave, but I have to disagree with that conclusion. The hair comes off much cleaner when the skin is chilled." He took the blade of his knife and ran in through the fire-red hair that covered Cameron's chest. The thin fibers of his hair gathered on the floor. I sat paralyzed with fear and grief as Benjamin scraped the hair from Cameron's body, stroke by careful stroke.

"I'll do whatever you ask." I crawled over to him and grabbed his leg. "Please, don't do this. Let him go. It's me you want, not him."

"Oh, my dear little Dean, I cannot do that. Redheads have the most delicious flavor. Besides, it is the only way that I can have you. " He looked down at me and patted my head.

"You have me, please do not hurt him." I begged.

"I'm sorry. You misunderstand the situation here. I'm not going to do this. You are." He began to laugh as he licked the remnants of hair from the blade of his knife.

"You're fucking crazy. I'm not butchering my boyfriend." I let go of his leg. I crawled away from him. "No, no, no." I shook my head in slow back and forth motions. I felt the shelves against my back. I continued to chant my response until it was just a whisper.

"You said that you love me, Dean." He took a small paring knife from his pocket and pressed the tip of it under Cameron's navel. The tip slipped under the skin with ease. He drew a half circle with the knife just below the skin. "See? It's as simple as this." He cut a small one-inch piece of meat from Cameron's body. Cameron mumbled. His body quivered. "Would you like a taste of him?" He placed the piece of Cameron's skin on the tip of the blade and slipped it into his mouth. He ran the blade across his own tongue, painting his mouth with Cameron's blood. "There's nothing better than a fresh piece of meat. I realize it's an acquired taste, but one you'll get accustomed to."

He came to me then.

"It's your turn, Dean."

He handed me the knife. "Do it quick before he wakes up, or the last thing he'll see is his boyfriend cutting away his flesh."

"No." I took the knife and threw it across the floor.

"I know what you want."

He grabbed my cock. I couldn't help but groan from the pleasure his touch ignited in me. He removed his hand and let my cock drop to the cold floor. "You need to understand where I'm coming from don't you?"

"Please stop this."

"Don't worry my love. I'll make it better." He walked over to the hanging slabs of meat. He looked a couple of them over, and then shaved a sample from one of them. He brought it to me. I opened my mouth, no longer caring who or what he fed to me. I chewed the tougher piece of meat, waiting for the pleasure to rush through my body, and with it relief. Instead, sadness consumed me. I began to cry with heavy sobs. "Yes, that's it. Feel the pain of my sadness. It has been my sole companion for centuries. The knowledge that it shall never leave burns a hole inside of you. Cry all you want, the tears may end, but the sadness will live forever." He walked across the room and cut a piece of meat from another slab.

"No." I said through the tears. "Please, make the pain stop. How can you live with so much sadness?" I sat there sobbing, feeling the grief and sorrow that Benjamin gave me. I cried not for myself, or even Cameron. I wept for everyone in the world that had ever suffered. If Benjamin wouldn't stop the grief, then I would have to. I crawled across the room and grabbed the knife. I turned my wrist over. I pressed the edge of the knife against my skin wanting nothing more than to end the pain and suffering I...he... we felt.

"No, you fucking coward!" He ran toward me. He pulled the knife from my hand. "You don't get to take the easy way out. This is your destiny. I will not let you disappoint me."

"Please, make it stop." I begged through a wave of despair.

"You want the sadness to end?" His tone was soft, sensual. He touched my shoulder as if he cared. "My love, you must eat this. If you don't, I'm afraid I might have to wake up your boyfriend and rip him to shreds. You will hear his agonizing screams for the rest of your life. You wouldn't want that now would you?" He grabbed my hair and dragged me across the floor. I screamed and kicked my feet against the cold tile floor trying to throw him off balance. He was too strong for my weakened state. He pulled me to the back wall and released me under Cameron's body. He knelt beside me. He embraced me. He rocked me like a mother comforting her sick child.

"Will you please eat this for me? I do not want to lose my temper with you. I so hate violence." He ran his thick tongue up my check. His hot saliva clung to my skin. I opened my mouth and let him slip the meat onto my tongue. It was bitter and spicy. The sadness faded. We continued to rock. I looked up at him. He smiled at me. "There, that's better than crying isn't it?" He kissed my head. "It's more productive anyway." He laughed.

"Fuck." I groaned as my body became flushed with a searing heat. My heart pounded in my chest as I felt an incredible anger rise inside of me. "What…You…Son-of-a-bitch. How can you…?" Despite the frigid air and the ice that clung to the hair of my body a fever unlike anything I had ever experienced rose within me.

"You'll want this." He handed me the knife. "Don't fight it my love. It will only make things worse."

"You son-of-a-bitch!" I raised the knife and pointed it in his direction. The rage, his rage ripped through me. I gripped the handle of the knife enjoying the weight of it in my hand. I met his stare. I repositioned my fingers around the handle and then slammed the knife into his chest. I felt the blade tear through his skin. I shoved it deeper into him. Blood seeped from the wound and ran down his chest. He laughed as he took his fingers and smeared the blood over his body. He licked the blood off his fingers, and then pressed his lips to mine. The warm metallic taste of his blood filled my mouth. The rage consumed me. He broke our bloody kiss. He chuckled and laughed as he took my hand and pulled the knife out of his chest. His body lurched against me. He threw his head back and moaned as if he had just suffered an orgasm.

"You can't hurt me, though I know that is where the anger lies." He raised the knife to his mouth and licked the edge of the blade. "You know what you must do."

"I want to hurt something. I need to release the anger." I looked up at Cameron crucified to the wall. He moaned in his sleep-induced state. "Why are you doing this to me?"

"Isn't it obvious? I am the teacher, and you are my pupil. Though I hate to do so, it is time for me to go. You must take over for me. Carry on my traditions here in the diner."

"I don't want this." I looked over the blade and stared at Cameron. The rage grew inside of me, taunting me, calling me.

"It will come. It always does. No student has ever failed the final exam." He stood and lifted me with him. "Embrace the anger, Dean. Feel the control. Feel the power that it gives you."

"No." Even as I spoke my response, I could feel my heart hardening. The pulse felt hollow as I adjusted my grip on the handle of the knife. The anger screamed through my body. Yet behind the burning fires of hell, I felt the control and power that Benjamin talked of. I tasted it behind the anger, behind the sadness, behind the seduction. Yes, this is what I had longed for. What I had waited my entire life for, and it was finally at hand.

"Do it. Give over your life to me. Free yourself from this world, and from those you are about to leave behind.

"I don't know how."

"Yes, you do. Follow the instincts that I have given you. With me by your side you cannot fail." Benjamin stood next to me. I looked at Cameron, the man I once loved, the man who would smoke, and then want to kiss me with his soiled breath; the man who use to tell me how to do things his way because his way was the only way; the man who wanted everything and gave nothing in return.

"I can feel the anger rising." Benjamin's voice held excitement. "Yes, there you go. Embrace my gifts."

I felt a smile curl the side of my mouth as I let the emotions take control. I plunged the knife into Cameron's chest. I felt the tip of the blade strike the metal wall behind him. My mind flashed images of dying memories. I tasted Cameron's body on my tongue. I felt his cock pulsing inside of me as he fucked me. I dragged the knife downward letting the knife come to rest on the pelvic bone. There was no time for him to scream. His death was quick, easy, and satisfying. His warm blood saturated my hands and body. I became aroused at the thought of his body covering mine – a full body orgasm that spewed his life out onto the floor. I gutted him being careful not to damage the precious meat. I carved a small sliver of his stomach and placed the bloody piece of meat in my mouth. He was sweet and tender.

"You are doing well, my love." Benjamin's voice echoed in my head. "Give into my pleasures, my emotions, and my tastes that you have acquired."

I walked out of the refrigeration unit while Cameron's body drained. I looked at the clock while I sharpened my knife. My cock pulsed with excitement and desire as I contemplated the dinner menu, with Cameron as the blue plate special.

The Fine Print
By Rebecca Snow

You couldn't tell it from looking at me now, wearing an eyepatch and a frayed knit cap, resting in a corner booth, watching the rain fall, but I used to have a life. The shadows sitting with me used to tether people....real live people. The flakes before me used to be full meals. Now, I lick my thumb to catch any leftover bread crumbs. The empty spaces in this booth used to hold my family. My wife and daughters and anyone who happened by...they were all family to me. I didn't have far to go for work, but even a fry cook can have a life.

I loved the breakfast shift. Tired customers downing coffee to stay awake. Sleepy kids on their way to school, stopping in for Danishes. My favorites were the families heading out on vacation. Everyone was glowing and hungry, except for maybe the restless teenager being forced to leave her first crush behind for a few weeks. Ah, young love...but I digress. This isn't about them, at least not directly.

One morning, about 9 o'clock, I was tossing some cheese and eggs into the pan. Omelet 101, never let the eggs burn. The bell above the door jingled. You know the one. You always hear it on TV shows about diners. I glanced up, and the doorframe was empty. I shrugged it off, figuring it was just kids pushing the door wide on their way past. The lights flickered, and I let the moment go. It's an old building. Look at it. The mice probably dare each other to walk past the wiring in the joint. The busboy dropped a tray of plates, but that was normal too. I took notice when flames shot from the fryer, and the sizzling oil whispered my name.

"Simon," it hissed. "Simon, we're here."

I didn't dare leave the omelet. I had to turn it in thirty seconds. You see, I time my eggs. They're better that way if you have a reliable burner.

"Simon, we know you can hear us." The –s dragged like a cooling steam engine.

"You'll have to wait." I flipped the cheesy mess once. "Can't you see I'm busy here?"

"We have waited long enough." A flash of sparks popped from the fixture above me. "It is time to fulfill your end of the bargain."

"Bargain? What bargain? I didn't make a deal with you." I sprinkled some peppers onto the eggs and folded the concoction like a taco, letting the bottom brown a bit longer than the top.

Silence echoed from behind me. The grease fire went out, and the fizzing bubbles quieted. The door chime rang once again. I removed the breakfast from the heat and placed it on a plate with a side of home fries. Slapping the bell on the counter, I wiped the back of my hand across my forehead. Sweat trickled down my neck. "Order up."

***

"I'm tired of this racket. Last vacation I took, people knew what I did for a living because I smelled like bacon," Louie said. "The stuff oozes out of my pores." The man sniffed. "I'd sell my soul for a few comfortable years."

"Aw, you don't mean that," Mona said, sweeping the broken plate shards and egg remains into a dustpan. "And I like the smell of bacon."

She flashed a wicked grin. The man ignored it.

"Course I do." Louie kicked a slice of fried meat onto

the pile and stared at the broom straws as they swept. "I do, indeed."

"Why don't you grab a smoke? You're all thumbs this morning." Mona groaned as she straightened her knees. "This arthritis is gonna kill me, and I don't think you're in your right mind."

Louie nodded. "Simon, take over for a minute," he called to his second.

Not waiting for an answer, he slid out the back screen door. It creaked and slammed as if angry. Lighting up, he inhaled and held the breath for a beat before blowing several successful smoke rings. His mind wandered to his wife. Just that morning, she'd mentioned losing the baby as an afterthought. He'd been looking forward to being a father even if it had just come about from a drunken night with Delia. They'd been married for twelve years without as much as a scare. Then, the stick and the three extras, just to be sure, had all shown little pluses in the windows.

Louie squashed the cigarette butt under the toe of his scuffed boot. He hadn't wanted them, but Delia had insisted since he spent most of his days on his feet. She had grown tired of his complaints of corns and callouses.

The constant fly buzz in the dumpster quieted. A rat scurried into a crack in the far wall. A swirl of smoke filled the alley's entrance, and a man strode from it, displacing foggy wisps.

"Are you Louis Castiglia?" the stranger asked from behind pitch black glasses.

Louie tilted his head. "Who's asking?"

"I am, sir." He proffered a leather clad hand. "I believe Mr. Castiglia requested my services. Are you he?"

"That's me, but I don't remember ordering anything." Louie stuffed his fingers behind his doubled apron string.

"I've come to offer you a deal." The man lowered his offered palm and clasped his gloves behind his back. "You may call me Douglas."

"Well, Mr. Douglas," Louie stammered. "I don't know what you're sellin', but I'm above board here. I don't sell my customers outdated meat."

"Just Douglas." A grin spread across Douglas' face. His cheeks puffed enough to raise the sunglasses half an inch. "That's not the nature of the deal I'm offering."

Louie pulled his lips into a thin line and narrowed his eyes.

"What *is* the nature, then?"

"I grant wishes." Douglas stood motionless.

"Like a genie or one of those little green guys?" Louie stared at his own reflection in the man's lenses. His head looked huge in the contour.

"The process is quite different, but the outcomes are often similar."

"So I don't need to rub a lamp or follow a rainbow?" Louie raised an eyebrow. His reflection did the same.

Douglas shook his head. A quiet smile rested on his face.

"Can I wish for anything?" Louie's forehead wrinkled.

"Anything," Douglas said. "Within reason."

Louie lifted his chin. "Who decides what's reasonable?"

"I do." The man gave a slight nod as if acknowledging his power.

"How many wishes do I get?" Louie crossed his arms and rested them on his protruding gut.

"The limit is dependent on what you are willing to offer in return." Douglas remained still.

"The diner's all I got." Louie thrust a thumb over his shoulder before recrossing his arms. "Apartment's a rental, so I don't know what I got that you might want."

"The diner is one option, but we shall discuss payment terms upon the submission of your list of requests."

The screen door squawked. Louie turned to investigate the noise. Mona's head emerged from the door.

"We need ya back inside, hon," she said, glancing around the empty alley. "Who you talkin' to?"

Louie's eyes searched the empty alley. A cloud of buzzing flies rose from the dumpster.

He must be losing it, he figured.

***

The next day, the bell rang again. This time, I was flipping pancakes. When the voices hissed, I took a chance and peeked over my shoulder. Shadows danced in the oily flames. Faces, some I had known, or thought I had, leered at me with agonized howling mouths. No shrieks bubbled, but the hissing voice continued.

"We've come for payment," they said.

"I'm all paid up 'til the end of the month." At that point, I still had my wits about me.

"You will honor the contract." A flame lifted the top off of a nearby pot and slammed it to the floor.

"Everything all right in there?" Mona called from the counter.

"Everything's fine," I yelled back. "I just dropped a lid."

I turned my attention back to the griddle.

"Don't you remember us?" the occupants of the fryer cried.

I shook my head and tossed a flapjack onto the waiting plate. "Nope. Can't say that I do." The backs of my knees were cold with perspiration. I was hoping they couldn't sense it. "Were you there when I renewed my driver's license?"

The fire extinguished in a spark of blue. A moment later, the front door jingled.

I slid pancakes and a side of baked apples across the counter. "Order up."

***

"Hello?" Louie whispered into the empty alley.

A scruffy cat slunk from the shadows, curling around Louie's ankles. Distracted, the man reached to scratch the fuzzy head. The stray shot a glance to the street and hissed before diving behind a pile of filled garbage bags. A low growl rumbled from the now invisible animal.

"Louis."

Louie flinched. The man had returned. Curls of smoky mist clung to his elbows. A gold molar gleamed from his smile.

"Call me Louie," Louie said.

Douglas's face drooped. "I prefer Louis."

"No problem." Louie's smile brightened as if attempting to reignite the other man's happiness. "I'll answer to either."

"I am not surprised." Douglas's upper lip curled. "Your requests, have you collected them?"

Louie nodded his head as if it hung from a loose hinge. He pulled a folded, grease-stained sheet of torn notebook paper from a back pocket and passed it to the outstretched, black gloved hand.

The tips of Douglas' fingers peeled open the scribbled note as if the text were covered in acid. Pursed lips hid his shiny tooth. Dropping the offending item onto an upturned crate, he smoothed the creases and read, nodding his head here, shaking it there. He plucked an enamel clad fountain pen from a hidden coat pocket and placed a red mark next to each line. Sliding the paper back to Louie, he recapped his pen and waited.

Louie's eyes darted down the page. A crease grew between his brows. A concerned half smile tickled the corners of his mouth.

"Do I have to accept these or can I ask a few questions?"

"Speak."

Douglas flicked a hand as if waving away a waiter.

With a sausage finger smudging the page, Louie dragged a bitten nail down the list. He stopped after passing a third of the items. "What're the stars next to the private island, mansion, and cherry red Camaro?" he asked.

"The stars represent a necessary clause."

Louie waited for Douglas to elaborate. When no explanation came, he asked for one.

"These things will require an action from you if you are willing."

"I don't have to kill somebody, do I?"

A tiny mumbled meow whispered from the mound of trash bags.

"No need. Such things happen without intervention from your kind."

"What is it I need to do?" Louie tilted his head sideways as if waiting for a right hook.

"You are aware of the lottery, are you not?"

"Yeah, they sell tickets all over the place."

"You will need to purchase a pick six ticket from the nearest vendor at precisely eleven minutes past three o'clock in the afternoon a week from today. The numbers you choose are irrelevant."

"That's it?" Louie squinted one eye and stared at his reflection again. His huge head looked skeptical.

"Yes, you must sacrifice a dollar for those things on your list that require monetary gain."

Louie nodded and went back to the paper's red marks. Lower down, he stopped and returned his gaze to Douglas.

"Why can't you make my wife pregnant again?"

The man barked a laugh. "You should rephrase such a question, as it was not I who made her with child."

Louie's face contorted into a confused scowl.

"From your list, you requested that I bring your unborn child back." Douglas shook his head. "Your child's soul has moved on to its next departure point."

Louie remained silent and sullen.

Douglas's features softened. "That does not mean you are not allowed to ask for your wife to carry another child to term."

Brightening like a switched on bulb, Louie scrambled for the pencil he kept in his apron. He rewrote his request and held it up for approval. Douglas removed his pen and placed a star next to the line.

"What's kind of clause do you need for a baby?" Louie's shoulders slumped.

"You must sacrifice your seed to impregnate your beloved once more."

Laughter exploded from Louie's lungs. He snorted a chuckle as his amusement lessened.

"No sacrifice there." A smirk slithered under his nose. "None...at...all."

"Very well, do you require more clarification on this documentation?"

Louie scanned the hash marks and shook his head. "Nope, the rest are clear enough, but how do I pay?"

A flash of lightning streaked the sky. The sheet of paper combusted in a quick spark. The flames reduced the ink to ashes. From the voluminous folds of his dark trench coat, Douglas procured a rolled piece of parchment tied with a black velvet ribbon. He presented it to Louie who pulled the end of the ribbon and unrolled it over the remains of the scorched requests.

"The terms are spelled out clearly in the contract."

Louie skimmed the document, taking note of several blank spaces. One was for his signature, one was for the date, and a third and fourth were mysteries.

"What're these spots for?" he asked.

"You own this property, am I correct?" Douglas's eyes flicked to the diner's rear door.

"Free and clear." Louie's chest puffed like a courting robin. "All the fried food I can eat."

"And that, my friend, is why, currently, you have seven years, three months, and fourteen days left with this body."

Louie's eyes widened. "Excuse me?"

"Please forgive my impertinence," Douglas sighed. "The end of this life may come at any moment."

An uncertain silence filled the alley. Louie shuffled his feet on the cracked blacktop.

"You requested an explanation of the necessary information?" Douglas's gloved finger pointed to the final spaces.

Louie stared at the lines, waiting for an answer.

"Those blocks are for those who will benefit from your contractual agreement." Douglas presented Louie with his fountain pen.

"That's easy." Louie poised the nib above the paper before scraping his wife's name on the first line.

Douglas cringed at the instrument's abuse. A new pen tip would be his next order of business after the soul was acquired.

"Will she receive the diner as well?"

Louie's nose wrinkled and drew his lips into a line. Letting out a burst of air, he shook his head.

"No, Simon can have it." He scrawled his employee's name across the paper in red ink and signed his own name and the date on the bottom line.

Before the marks were dry, Douglas whisked the paper into a roll and retied the ribbon. Secreting it back into his coat, he nodded with a slight bow and turned on his well shod heel. Louie noticed the cuffs on the man's pants were scorched.

"One more question." Louie's voice cracked.

Douglas looked back and lowered his shades, unveiling a set of burning red irises.

"Are you the devil?" Louie croaked.

"No, of course not." Douglas smirked, replacing the sunglasses on his nose. "I'm his lawyer."

The screen door creaked.

"Who *are* you talking to?" Mona asked.

A week later, Louie bought a lottery ticket like he'd been told.

In Friday's drawing, all of Louie's numbers appeared like magic.

***

On the third day, I was ready. The tinkling sounded, but no one visible entered. The lights sparked. The plates fell. When the oil fire burst to life, I tossed a twenty pound sack of baking soda into the flames. The blaze disappeared. Seconds later, the front bell fell off the door.

The fryer was a mess and would need a cleaning and some fresh oil before I could use it again. The good news was that it already had the baking soda in it for a good scrub.

"Mona, tell Colleen and the others that the fryer's on the fritz." I ran a towel across my reddened face. "Nothing deep fried today."

"That's ninety percent of the menu?" She popped her gum and pulled a pencil from behind her ear. Jotting a note on her order pad, she shrugged and turned back to the diner.

I reached to the plug and yanked it from the wall. A large bubble rose from the bottom of the chamber. Two eyes glared up at me. When the leering air pocket burst, it splashed my face with hot oil. My left eye felt as though it seeped down my cheek. Tripping backwards, I shrieked and tried to wipe the burning grease from my skin.

"We told you it was time to pay," the voice hissed inside my head.

"I didn't order anything." I pressed my palms to my eyes, trying to block out the pain.

"We have a signature." Sparks flew from the wall socket. "And you are Simon."

"Yeah, but I didn't sign any papers," I shouted from the floor by the griddle. "I didn't make any deals!"

The face I'd seen as it rose from the oil had been the one that haunted my nightmares. I'd seen the man out back by the dumpsters with my old partner Louie. His back stooped with age. His fingers gnarled with time. That was a week before Louie won the lottery and gave me the diner. When he handed me the deed, he said he'd made a deal with some guy to get a few good years. At the time, I'd thought he meant tires.

A few years later, he was found in his island home with his wife. Both of them had been skinned, chopped into tiny pieces, and deep fried. The running joke was that whoever did it left a side of fries on the counter with a bottle of ketchup. The police never found the culprit or Louie's toddler, but I was certain it had something to do with that deal he'd made.

"But you were named as Louis Castiglia's beneficiary," the hissing sizzled again. "You must pay the price."

A howling pierced my eardrums as I cowered, pressing my back as far as it could go into the corner of the lower cabinets. I scanned the area with my one good eye and saw the frying pan. I grasped the handle and slammed the skillet against my head.

"Get out of there! I didn't sign any papers! I don't want any benefits!"

I spun in circles and broke as many bones as I knew how.

The awful voice kept whispering.

It's quieted since.

***

From what I've pieced together in the years that have escaped me, Colleen found me.

My wife had to sell the diner to pay my medical and psychiatric bills.

They say I'm psychotic. The girls stay with their mother upstate with a restraining order against me. I can usually scrape together enough for a cup of coffee.

"Spare some change, sir?, just a dollar?"

Big Night
By Jason Norton

She kept looking through the scratched plastic crystal at the hands moving ever so slowly beneath, and pulled her threadbare scarf tighter around her neck. Two forty-five. Fifteen minutes. Fifteen minutes and Mr. Browning would be here. He never kept any of them waiting; he prided himself on punctuality. With any luck, she may have a new watch by the end of the night. The one residing on her grimy wrist had seen lots of damage, lots of bitterly cold nights and bitterly cold sidewalks. So had she.

She hoped that tonight may be her lucky night; that Mr. Browning might take her away from all this. They all had the same wish. Some of them had been able to escape, thanks to Mr. Browning's generosity. Mary went last year; Jerome departed in September. Mr. Browning picked up lots of the others, but most had returned, usually with new clothes, an expensive souvenir and stories of their fairytale evening.

No one knew how Mr. Browning decided whom to offer salvation to. Did it require some recompense, and if so, to what degree? What could a homeless vagabond give to a man of Mr. Browning's means that he hadn't seen or experienced? What would they have that he would even want?

Natalie was determined to do whatever it took to win his favour. Mr. Browning was her only hope. There was no other way for her to escape the life that she had found—or the life that had found her.

She'd tried, of course. She wasn't like some of the others, who just stuck one hand out while holding a bottle in the other. But restaurants and shops don't hire based upon good intentions, and it's difficult to make a pleasant first impression when you share your bed with street creatures. When all other employment options failed, she'd resorted to sleeping with a different, yet no less disturbing breed of vermin.

Ten minutes. Just ten minutes and he'd arrive, and her Big Night would begin. She wondered which car he'd bring. It had been the Jag when he'd pulled up last week and called her over. Maybe he'd choose the Rolls tonight. If Andre was driving, so much the better. He was beautiful, as if he'd been sculpted with a chisel. He always smelled like what she'd imagined Colorado must smell like—clean and fresh and wild. If Mr. Browning took her away tonight, maybe she'd go there, to test her hypothesis.

She watched the others milling around her. They squabbled over pavement, arguing for the corners they claimed. They panhandled. They drank. They loitered.

She couldn't live like this. Not anymore.

There had to be something else.

***

It was the Bentley; the green one. He hadn't brought that one around in months. Natalie had only seen it once. But it was hard to miss as it rounded the corner. It purred to a stop alongside the curb in front of her. Mr. Browning's window dropped silently. He leaned out toward Natalie, his ever-present smile intact.

"Good evening Natalie," he said enthusiastically. "Are you ready to go?"

"Hello, Mr. Browning. Yes, I'm ready," she responded.

"Well then, climb in," he said.

Andre left the engine running as he exited the driver's seat. "Ma'am," he said deeply, with a tip of his hat. She breathed him in as he escorted her around the car. His fragrance was even better than she remembered—woody and sweet. He escorted her around the car, his arm under hers, the dust from her jacket soiling his. She was mortified but Andre didn't seem to notice. He opened her door and she scooted inside, trying her best not to drag dirt across the back seat.

Mr. Browning noticed her timidity. "Oh please, Natalie; don't fret," he said, trying to ease her apprehension. "How are you? How have the nights been; it's been chilly lately," he said, resting his gloved hands across the waist of his black wool coat.

"I'm doing okay," she said. "You learn how to cope. Right now I sleep in an alleyway between buildings, to block the wind. We usually get a barrel fire going too, so that helps."

"We?" he asked, running a finger under his slightly greying beard.

"Oh, yeah. There's about four of us, besides me. Three guys, another girl. We try to stay together when we can; strength in numbers and all," she explained.

"And food? Are you getting enough to eat?"

"We do okay. Folks are still fairly generous. I don't deliberately beg, but I won't turn down charity, either. We don't have to scavenge that often, thankfully," she said, deliberately avoiding the lengths she had to go to receive food from some of those "charitable" sources.

"Well I'm glad to know that," Mr. Browning said, smiling again. "Have you ever visited the Beacon Street Mission?"

"A couple of times for meals," she said. "It's just too crowded to sleep there. They're pretty much maxed out every night by the time I can walk that far," she said.

"I donate food to that shelter each month. I'm sure I could get you a more permanent spot there," he told her.

"I appreciate that, Mr. Browning. I really do. I'll be sure to check it out," she said, hoping that after tonight, her regular dining accommodations wouldn't be so uncertain.

Browning paused, flashing another smile. "So, tell me; are you excited about tonight?"

Natalie returned his gesture, doing her best not to tip an overzealous hand. She had learned how to hide emotion. It had become nearly a nightly practice. Most of the men she gave herself to—traded herself to—rarely detected her revulsion.

"I am excited," she said. She hoped he couldn't see the extent of her enthusiasm; how she'd smiled, even laughed all week, bragging to the others in anticipation of the impending evening. She didn't want to seem too eager. Coming on too strong could ruin her chances. But she didn't want to seem indifferent, either. She had no frame of reference. The others hadn't been much help. She'd listened to their advice about how to act on the Big Night; little good it did. Each had their own opinion, but what did they know? All of them had come back.

Natalie looked out the window. The sun was low, but still powerful enough to silhouette the buildings that sped past. They were foreign to her. They were only blocks away from her corner, but they may as well have been on the other side of the globe.

"So, what's on the itinerary?" she asked, politely turning back to her host.

"I have a fitting scheduled for you at Braddock's at four. You can pick out something for the evening and maybe something for later," he said.

She'd never been to a dress fitting, but she'd always dreamed that one day she would. Maybe there'd be champagne, strawberries. She couldn't even remember the last time she'd worn a dress. High school maybe. Her mind raced to sequins, v-cuts, side slits.

The appeal faded quickly. *Something for later?* What did he mean? Something new to go home in? Not a day went by that she didn't wish for new, warm, clean clothes. But that kind of gift would condemn her to resignation. New clothes would mean going back to the corner. New clothes equalled old life.

Maybe she was reading too much into it. Maybe he meant—Jesus, maybe he meant something lacy with silk—

"Then dinner," he said, disrupting her contemplation. "It's one of my favourite places—Phago. I hope you'll like it. They have a very eclectic menu. The chef prides himself on preparing authentic regional cuisine from around the world. Just last week I enjoyed a marvellous dish from Chile. I'm sure you'll be able to find something you'll enjoy," he said.

Browning continued to pine about the restaurant's constantly evolving menu, but Natalie lost him somewhere around the word "crepes." She was busy dreaming of a steak, one large enough to hang off the sides of the plate it was served on. Maybe a baked potato, a salad. Screw a salad, she'd just double up on dessert. Cheesecake, baklava, chocolate—God only knew what she would do for quality chocolate.

On second thought, maybe He didn't.

"At any rate, I hope by the end of the evening we'll

know each other better," Browning said, reaching across the seat to cover Natalie's hand with his own.

Ah. So maybe she still had a chance at more than a rented dress and a cosy meal. Mr. Browning was attractive enough; more so than most over the past three years. She returned to her earlier internal conundrum. What did she have to possibly offer Browning? Perhaps he was answering that question for her.

"I really like this car," she said, attempting to steer the conversation elsewhere. "It's a beautiful colour."

"Midnight Emerald. It came down to this and Pale Velvet—a bold purple. It just seemed a little too flashy," he said.

Natalie wasn't sure how much flashier a $300,000 car could get. Chances are, it would attract the same level of attention whatever colour it was.

Andre hung a left. Minutes later, he took the Mt. Vincent exit. Soon, they were out of the city.

"Where are we going?" Natalie asked, confused by the detour.

"Forgive me; I forgot to explain," Browning said. "I typically allow guests to freshen up before a fitting. We're going to stop at my home…if that is acceptable?"

Natalie grinned, captivated by the idea of a behind-the-scenes tour of Browning's mansion (or at least one of them). "Of course that's acceptable, Mr. Browning," she said.

"Please," he told her, patting her still-covered hand; "call me Edgar."

"Thank you—Edgar," Natalie said, returning his pat with her free hand.

From her window, she watched trees—actual living, non-fenced-in, non-lone-standing, non-municipal-department-of-public-works-maintained trees—blur into the thousands as the Bentley raced smoothly around gentle curves. The stalwart stance of the oaks and poplars was soon challenged; iron gates and paved drives interrupting the green.

"Here we are," Browning said, gesturing toward an entrance to the right. It reminded her of the photos of Civil War-era southern plantations she'd seen in tenth grade history. Wrought iron fencing, black and ornately spiralled, climbed into the air. Stone lions guarded their flanks; scripted Bs hung like metal breastplates from their crossbars.

It took Andre nearly two minutes to summit the length of the inclined drive. The home at the end of it was magnificent. Natalie pressed her face against the glass, trying to count the spires and arches. By the time Andre opened her door, she'd gotten up to fourteen.

Browning came around to meet her, taking her hand as he led her toward the main entrance.

"Welcome to Northwood," he told her.

***

If she knew how to swim, she would have attempted laps in the tub. Undoubtedly, she could have fit her closest streetmates in there with her and still had room for a small-scale orchestra.

In the first thirty minutes, she'd tried every one of the shampoos and soaps the maid had left out for her—and there were a lot of both. She reclined for the next quarter hour, soaking away days of the city.

The robe was thick and fluffy; the clothes slightly

oversized, but sufficient for the trip to Braddock's. The attendant was as polite as she was meticulous. Natalie believed she would have stayed all night to select the perfect dress for her. She was right. The attendant had fitted nearly all of Browning's guests; she knew how generous he could be, and not only to those he treated to a Big Night. For a little extra effort, Browning would reward her with a tip that dwarfed her weekly check.

"I think it's down to this one and the blue one," Natalie said, checking the hem as she twirled in front of the multi-panelled mirror.

"No, this is the one," Martha, the attendant, confirmed.

"This is definitely your dress," she said.

It was a tight number, and complimented her surprisingly enviable frame. Its coppery shimmer was a strikingly flattering contrast to her dark eyes and hair. The slit came up to the middle of her left thigh. The neckline came down to the centre of her chest. Thin straps hugged her shoulders.

"You think? It doesn't make me look too skinny?" Natalie asked, self-conscious about the unintentional results of her unavoidable diet plan.

"Not at all, Natalie. You have the perfect body for this dress. We'll get you some jewellery and put your hair up. And I've got the perfect pair of heels to go along with it. Trust me, Natalie," she said, as they both admired the transformation reflected in the mirror. "You're gonna knock 'em dead tonight."

***

Phago was crowded but surprisingly quiet. Natalie wagered that the tailoring bills represented were at least equal to a down payment on Browning's mansion.

The walls of the place were rich amber. Sconces allowed enough lighting to enjoy intimate interaction, but kept intrusion upon the other diners to a minimum. Widely-spaced tables helped to augment the feeling of communal privacy.

The entrance had been unexpected. When Mr. Browning—Edgar—led Natalie down the concrete steps to the equally non-impressive concrete door, she'd wondered if he had decided to skip dinner in lieu of a rave.

After six distinctly punctuated raps from Browning, an eye-level panel slid across the door. The eyes on the far side staring back at them signalled noticeable recognition, but still demanded a password for entry.

"Anardana," Edgar said.

Immediately, the door opened. The bald, massive doorman greeted the couple as they entered. "Good to see you again, Mr. Browning. I hope you will enjoy your dinner," he said.

"I trust I will, Terrance," Browning replied, passing the man a fifty dollar bill as they parted.

Natalie felt the warmth of Browning's hand on the small of her back. "This way," he said, gesturing down a dim hallway that bent left, then right. Natalie lifted her hem high enough to climb the stairs to the closed double doors. Another attendant opened them with a polite nod to the couple after taking their coats; he was rewarded with another fifty from Browning.

The Maître d' greeted them as they entered—a strong handshake and personal "Good evening," for Browning; a lightly pressed kiss onto Natalie's cheek. He led them to a table in the centre of the room. Browning, dapper in his gray double-breasted Zegna original, must have shaken two dozen hands before they were seated.

"You're very popular," Natalie told him, after she'd thanked the Maître d' for sliding her chair out for her.

"I owe some of them money," he joked, before adding, "Some of them owe me."

As Natalie placed her napkin in her lap, a waiter filled her empty wine glass with some variety of red so pleasantly aromatic she smiled as it trickled from the bottle. Nope; you wouldn't find this on her block, she was sure.

"And what are we drinking tonight?" Browning asked the server between pours.

"This is a 1982 Chateau Haut Brion Pessac-Lognan. Chef Ramiel was very deliberate with his pairing tonight. I think you'll find this vintage compliments the entrée perfectly," the waiter said.

Browning lifted his glass to his nose, inhaling the aroma as he swirled the deep crimson liquid around the rim. He sipped, rolling it around on his tongue before swallowing. "Exquisite," he said to the server; his radiance testament to his satisfaction.

Natalie tasted hers. She wasn't exactly sure what good wine was supposed to taste like, but she was all too familiar with the taste of bad wine. This was a long ways away from bad.

"Do you like it, ma'am?" the server asked Natalie.

"Yes. Yes, it's very nice," she said sheepishly, unsure of the proper response.

The server left the bottle in the clay cylinder at the edge of the table, vowing to return quickly with bread.

"So tell me a little bit about yourself Natalie," Browning said, before taking another drink.

Natalie paused, weighing just what and just how much she would share.

"I was born in Colorado. I've lived in Idaho, North Dakota, New Mexico, and Maryland. I'm a military brat—Air Force. Dad died not long after we moved to Andrews. Mom was tired of moving and she liked Maryland so we stayed. I wasn't such a fan. I'd seen a lot of the country, but all of it was on military bases. I was ready to experience more than what mess halls and PXs had to offer."

"So you lit out for the big city," Browning surmised.

"With big dreams and little talent," she said.

"Broadway?"

"Theatre. I couldn't carry a tune in a bucket," she admitted.

"Did you have training?"

"Just a couple of drama classes my junior and senior year. God bless Coach Simchick, but his tutelage didn't exactly make me a threat to the American Conservatory grads. I worked just about every crappy part-time job I could find to pay for acting coaches and agents. They were all just interested in my money…or whatever form of compensation I could trade. I wound up falling in with the wrong crowd—not criminals, just stoners. Within a year, I'd been fired from all my jobs and was out on the street. That was three years ago," she said.

Browning calmly sipped his wine, seemingly unfazed by Natalie's confession. "Are you clean now?" he asked, matter-of-factly, just before their server fulfilled his promise of bread.

It smelled divine. To Natalie, the fragrance was positively intoxicating. She marshalled restraint, stifling the compulsion to snatch the crispy loaf from its wooden cutting board and devour it before Browning could even taste it.

He recognized her struggle. He'd seen it on many a Big Night. Lifting the serrated knife, he cut and buttered a hearty wedge. He placed it on one of the two small plates the waiter had left, and gently shoved it toward Natalie. "Please," he said.

"Thank you," she said, nearly inhaling it. It was warm and crusty and chewy and yeasty and perfect. Her stomach grumbled in appreciation and anticipation of another piece. She suddenly realized Edgar had been intently watching the spectacle, and figured it must have resembled feeding time at a zoo.

"Sorry," she said with a self-deprecating smirk.

"Not at all," he responded, preparing another piece for her.

"Thanks," she said, accepting seconds. "So, to answer your question," she said, pausing to chew another bite, "I've been clean for a little over a year now. It wasn't easy at first, but I honestly don't ever see myself going back. I know all the twelve-step programs espouse the once-an-addict-always-an-addict philosophy, but I don't buy it. I won't allow myself to. That would make it too easy to relapse, and I never ever want to go back to that…lifestyle," Natalie said.

Browning leaned forward, tearing the remainder of his bread with his fingers. "But what about your current lifestyle? Is that any better?" he asked, in what Natalie perceived as a condescending tone.

She bristled, but Edgar missed it as he dipped his morsel in the dwindling butter and popped it into his mouth. She pressed her tongue against the back of her teeth, paused, and responded.

"I do what I feel is necessary to survive," she said, with a sip of wine. "I don't use it as a means to finance a habit.

I don't do it because I have daddy issues. And I damn sure don't do it because I enjoy it. I do it because I have to," she said.

"Would you walk away from it if you could?"

"Absolutely. There is nothing in the world I've ever wanted more than to get off the street. I'm not like the others. I still have my mind. I still have dreams. I want a job and a home and a husband and 1.5 kids and a dog and picket fence and the whole nine yards. And I'm scraping and scratching to get to that point. It will happen; I can make it happen. But it just can't come soon enough," she said.

The waiter returned with a tray hoisted so high Natalie couldn't see what was on it until he lowered it to the table. Salads; huge and multi-coloured filled with unfamiliar vegetables and fruits and seeds, were laid before them. The server scooped up the remnants of the bread. "More, please," Browning called after him, as he turned toward the kitchen. "Right away, sir," the waiter replied.

"This looks wonderful," Natalie said, reaching for her salad fork. Her first bite—a medley of purpley-red tomato, bright crispy green leaf and a deep yellow pepper— maybe?—was tangy and spicy. Her tongue tingled from the eclectically tart combination.

"Oh my God, is that good," she tried to say to herself. Browning's laughter confirmed that she had voiced her opinion aloud. "Yes, it is delicious," he agreed.

"Seriously, what kind of dressing is this?" she asked, gulping another forkful.

"My guess is some type of champagne Dijon, if I know Paolo."

Natalie looked confused. "I thought the waiter said Ramiel was the chef," she said.

"Paolo Ramiel," Browning explained. "He and I are old friends. I helped finance the restaurant. We have a common interest in fine cuisine."

"So that explains why they treat you so well," Natalie said.

"It helps," Browning replied.

They continued with their salads, mutually silent for the first time since the meal began. Natalie boldly breached the respite.

"What happened to Mary and Jerome? Where are they now?" she asked.

Browning dabbed the corners of his mouth and returned his napkin to his lap. "I have a number of very wealthy friends who are always looking for special people like Mary and Jerome. I brought both of them here for their Big Night—that is what you all call it, correct?"

"Best we could come up with," Natalie grinned. "We're not the most creative lot."

Browning chuckled. "But charm goes a long way," he said. "That was what did it for Mary and Jerome. I introduced them to a few of my friends here who fell in love with them. They saw just how special they were, and they were impressed enough to—" Browning paused, searching for the right words— "liberate them."

"So did you keep up with them? Do you know where they ended up?" Natalie repeated.

"I'm not quite sure," Browning said, picking through the last few bites of his salad. "Despite our common interests and opulence, my friends and I all enjoy a healthy degree of discretion. Believe it or not, we don't kiss and tell," Browning said.

Natalie swallowed the last salty seeds from her salad, leaving the plate at the edge of the table. Immediately the waiter retrieved it, along with the one Browning handed to him.

"So do you think I'm…special, Mr. Browning?"

"Edgar," he reminded her. "And yes, Natalie, I think you are very special. And very beautiful."

She smiled at him, a slight blush on her cheek illuminated by the intimate glow.

"Which reminds me," he continued. "It would be a good time for me to introduce you to Paolo. He'll have a moment to take a breath before the soup is served."

"That would be wonderful," she said.

Browning motioned the waiter over, disclosing his plan. "Of course, Mr. Browning. I'm sure you know the way," the waiter replied.

"Indeed," Browning smiled, as he stood to get Natalie's chair. Taking her by the hand, he led her toward the kitchen.

"I've been meaning to ask you about this place anyway, but we got busy talking about me," Natalie said.

"How so?"

"Well, there's no sign outside, it's located in an underground basement, there's a password to get in, and no menus. What's up?" she asked light-heartedly.

"I must apologize," Browning said. "Phago isn't actually a 'restaurant' per se; it's a very exclusive dining club. A personal invitation from Paolo—and the aforementioned password—is required for entry. There's no menu because Paolo serves what he wants, when he wants. A very select group eats here; they have very discriminating taste. But they trust Paolo implicitly. Without fail, he knows what to prepare, every time."

"Well, I can't wait for the entrée," Natalie said, as Browning pushed open the swinging IN door to the kitchen.

"I'm sure it will be a thing of beauty," he said.

The kitchen was a flurry of chaotic precision. A horde of white-coated chefs pared vegetables, their silvery blades moving in a blur of staccato tap-tap-taps. Without missing a beat, one of them took the plastic flexible board to a gigantic chrome oven. He folded the board, taco like, over the large pot boiling on the front burner, allowing the fragmented veggies to slide in with a red splash. A lone sous chef stood by, stirring the pot, ordering others to bring spices, barking at one more to hurry with the cream. In a separate corner, pastry chefs used brushes and pipettes to glaze and frost something that couldn't help but be delectable, based solely on its appearance.

In the midst of it all, a lone dark man, wearing a chef's hat that was taller than any of his colleagues', floated amidst the maelstrom, overseeing it all with firm yet peaceful instruction.

"Ah, here's the maestro himself," Browning said, gesturing toward the stoic chef.

Paolo glimpsed his friend just as he finished sampling a green sauce from a simmering pot. He encouraged the chef tending it to add more stock and a dash of basil, draped his towel on his shoulder and greeted Browning and his guest.

"Edgar! Who let you in?" he boomed, with a grin.

"I can't tell you that. I'd hate for Terry to lose his job," Browning said, returning the joke.

"Good to see you, my friend," Paolo said, punctuating his greeting with a sturdy embrace.

"And who is this...vision?" Paolo asked, releasing Browning, as he kissed Natalie's hand. She smiled with another blush.

"This is Natalie. She is very excited about your work," Browning said.

Paolo placed his hands on his hips. He smiled at Natalie; pride and appreciation showing on his charismatic face. "I am flattered," he told her. "The soup will be ready soon; I hope you will enjoy it."

"What is it?" she asked.

"Well, normally I don't even give out hints until it hits the table, but since you're back here already and it is the next course, I'll let you in on a secret," he said, allowing his pregnant pause to build suspense. "It has water in it," he finally revealed, without cracking a smile.

"Well that sounds delightful," Natalie said, as deadpan as possible, holding out as long as she could before bursting into a laugh.

"*What?* You'd want me to tell you what you got for Christmas before you opened your presents? I'm not going to ruin the surprise. You'll see what it is soon enough," Paolo told her.

Browning interrupted. "Speaking of surprises, this is Natalie's Big Night," he said to Paolo.

Paolo paused again, but when he spoke this time, his voice had lost its lilt. His friendly grin had also disappeared.

"Oh, your Big Night," Paolo said, turning toward Natalie. "Edgar's right. You're in for all kinds of surprises."

Paolo turned, apparently announcing Natalie's Big Night to the kitchen staff, based upon the little Spanish she remembered from her sophomore year.

Their furious activity ground to a screeching halt. Ovens were turned down, ingredients were abandoned. Boisterous chefs fell immediately silent.

But none of them dropped their knives.

Paolo turned, halting beside a large rectangular stainless steel prep table.

It was empty.

A few of the other chefs joined him, still silent with each step.

Nervous confusion ignited the full length of Natalie's spine. When she felt Browning's hand on her lower back—firmer than it had been when they first entered Phago—her unease erupted into full-scale panic. As she tried to twist from his grasp, he cinched his arms around her waist, bear-hugging her tight enough to seize her breath. She tried to choke out a scream as the remaining chefs overtook her. Natalie did her best to fend them off, but within seconds they wrestled her to the cold prep table.

Pairs grabbed her arms and legs, splaying her wide. Others wound yards of meat wrapping twine around her torso and neck, immobilizing her. The final trio forced her jaw open, wedging a red waxy apple in her mouth. She tasted sugary blood as one of her bottom incisors pierced the fruit before ripping from her gum.

Blinking against the tears flooding her eyes, she saw a watery Browning leaning above her.

"You're special, Natalie; just like Mary and Jerome. You're unique; not like all that street trash that's out there. Just look at you. You're beautiful. Lean, young and tender… you're not the type of dish that you can just get anywhere. I told you the clientele here had very specific tastes. They're going to love you," he said.

Natalie unleashed her loudest scream—despite her obstructed mouth—at Browning's full disclosure of the eventual outcome of her Big Night.

Kneeling, Browning whispered in her ear. "Now, now, Natalie. Isn't this what you wanted? Just think: you'll never have to return to that old lifestyle again."

Standing, he planted a kiss on her forehead. "Now Paolo," he said, turning to his friend. "Work your magic."

Natalie kept screaming and closed her eyes so she wouldn't be able to see what was about to transpire.

The first incision began cold, but warmed quickly.

Just before she passed out, the aroma from the pastry table wafted past her.

Chocolate.

Damn.

Leftovers
By Daniel Hale

"Mitch. Mitch! Pay attention when I'm talking to you, you dipshit!"

Mitchell Graves looked up from the fryer, his round face somber and attentive. "Huh?"

"Take the grease and dump it, dumbass. I don't wanna be stuck here any later than I have to because of you, understand?"

Dave the manager, on grill duty, thrust a tray slopping over with watery grease to Mitchell, splashing his apron.

"Okay" Mitchell took the tray and lumbered out of the kitchen. Dave scowled at his back. "Fucking 'tard," he muttered, not quite under his breath.

Mitchell took no notice. He never seemed to hear anything anybody said to him when he was focused on the job. He would just stand there, frying fries or washing dishes, working slowly and carefully like he was disarming a bomb. It was a diner, for fuck's sake, it wasn't like it took a genius to do the job. Dave supposed that being the manager's nephew got Mitch special treatment for being so slow; he had been working there for more years than Dave knew and he would probably still be there long after Dave had left. He never made small talk, he never complained, and if you did manage to get his attention he would just stare at you with that stupid look on his face. He gave Dave the creeps, that was for sure.

Dave sneered at Mitch's back. He wondered if the moron knew how much Dave hated him.

***

In the backroom Mitch dumped the contents of the tray into a plastic bucket. The level rose to the top, so Mitch heaved the bucket up and exited out the backdoor, to the barrels where the grease was collected for pickup.

Mitch glanced at the security cameras set on the wall above the barrels. He knew his aunt did not check the footage as well as she used to, and chances were that she wouldn't notice if he took the whole bucket. But no; best to play it safe. He removed the lid from one of the barrels and dumped almost the entire contents inside it. Then he replaced the lid and went back inside.

The bucket was now a quarter full as Mitch took it down to the cellar. There, hidden beneath a shelf packed with buns and bread, Mitch had discovered a pipe protruding from the wall. A large cork had been wedged in it some time ago. Mitch removed the cork and with a great air of solemnity, dumped the remaining grease down the pipe.

Mitch knew precisely what Dave thought of him, but he hardly cared. Mitch had more important matters to concern him. He had been chosen for a greater calling, and to stoop to Dave's level would be to betray that sacred duty. He was the instrument of a power Dave would not understand; that his impurities would not let him understand.

No matter. It was no concern of Mitch's.

"Seeping be praised," Mitch whispered down the pipe. A gurgling echoed from far below.

***

When you see them, you don't need to be told. You can recognize it in the vacant look, the wide eyes, and the mouth that is open just slightly. If you talk to them, you recognize the halting, hesitant tone and the too loud voice. It is an easy thing to spot when someone is a little bit different in the head. It is an easier thing to spot those trying not to show that they know.

When you see them, you look away, telling yourself that you don't want to stare. In truth you don't want to witness this travesty, this perversion of the human condition. Only when someone else turns and sees and points them out, only *then* can you regain sight to defend them. You reprise the role of Good Samaritan, casting scorn on the insensitivity of some people. They must get enough of that, you think. Poor things.

Mitch did get enough of it. He'd had enough of being treated like a thing, day in and day out. He could deal with the ones who insulted him, made fun of the way he looked and the way he sounded, and laughed at the way he wrung his hands in frustration and shook in bewilderment when people got impatient with him. At least it meant they were treating him like a person, albeit one they could bully. It was the others, who would look away the minute they saw him, who spoke to him in condescending, sugary sweet tones as if he were child …those were the ones he couldn't stomach.

It's very hard to live anything like a normal life when people decide that you are not complete.

So Mitch had resigned himself to his status as a non-person. The best he could hope for was to be the tragic prop for people to practice their compassion on. If you could ignore the artificiality of it all, it wasn't so bad. There were benefits; Mitch kept his job at his aunt's diner, so he could at least feel like he wasn't a burden, even with the certain amount of leeway he was granted. He could never be everything that it took to be normal, never be a whole person, but at least he could be useful.

If people got angry at Mitch for how slow he worked, it didn't stop them from turning over the tedious jobs to him; sweeping up, filling the condiments, wiping down the shelves, emptying the garbage cans. Mitch would stay behind and finish the jobs that were not his responsibility and nobody would question it. So long as it got done—and if Mitch was doing it then it would be done, eventually—then nobody thought to care.

And so it would go, with people being either spiteful or pitying at Mitch, giving him work to keep him busy, and he would pursue every task put to him, alone in his mind and in his life, just as he was one night in the restaurant, after closing when everyone else had gone home, and his god revealed itself to him.

During the day the kitchen floor was covered with red rubber mats, in theory to keep the workers from slipping. In practice the things were such raggedy tripping-hazards that it would be safer to do without them. At closing time Mitch took them in the back and hosed them off. Beneath them the floor was yellowish tile, scuffed and filthy. Mitch dragged a sopping wet mop over the floor, and the water sluiced into the drain set in the tiles.

This night the water pooled over the grate but did not drain away. Mitch looked down at it anxiously. Obviously the pipe was blocked. He moaned, already thinking about the trouble he would surely get in, and wondered what he should do.

Beneath his feet Mitch heard a low gurgling noise, and a few bubbles floated to the top. Swirly strands of a viscous black substance seeped through the grate. Then the level of the water started to rise, flowing over the walls of the drain and onto the floor. The black gunk was pulled along with it, dragging more stringy strands of it up from the pipe, before meeting a dip in the floor and staying in place. It was thick; it didn't pull apart as more of the gunk was dragged up, but coagulated into an amorphous lump. A length of it—an actual *weave* of spiked greasy strands—trailed back down the pipe.

Mitch stared down at it. His mouth was hanging open and he wrung his hands. He wondered what he should do about this. He wondered which would get him in the most trouble; dealing with the mess immediately without the go-ahead from someone else, or failing to do so. In Mitch's experience it was either one or the other. It made quick thinking somewhat difficult.

The lump continued to squat there like a crusty, oozing scab, studded with bits of yellow and brown. More bubbles broke on its surface.

Mitch started and peered closer at the lump. Its body seemed to be coiled into ropey tentacles. Unless he imagined it the lump had moved—

Thunk. The thing jerked, splashing muck onto Mitch's shoes. He backed away as the thing prickled and convulsed at his feet. He made to bolt but his fascination—disgusted and appalled fascination but fascination nonetheless—held him still.

The 'creature' was covered in short black spines that were wavering sickly on its flesh. Its bristly limbs waved lazily in the air, like a recumbent octopus. He realized they were the burnt scraps left over from meals cooked on the grill.

Mitch sat and watched the thing. Fear was easing away, replaced by something akin to awe. Slowly he raised a hand and reached out.

Snap! A slimy tentacle gripped Mitch's finger. Mitch gaped as a rough, ropey limb slithered over and around his hand, leaving oily trails over his skin. Its slithering movements seemed curious, enthusiastic; almost affectionate.

On some level Mitch was aware that it was very late, and he should be getting home if he wanted to make an early start of it in the morning. But here and now, there was only the creature, and a small yet rapidly growing sense of duty.

This is mine, he thought. *And I will protect it.*

***

For the rest of the night Mitch stayed at the diner, letting the creature or whatever it was run its feelers over his hands, his arms, his face. He watch as it dragged itself across the kitchen floor, exploring every corner and crevice. By the time he wondered about getting home it was an hour before opening, and he began to panic.

The creature, thankfully, seemed to know this as well, and pulled itself down the drain. With haste Mitch mopped up the kitchen and replaced the cleaned mats, with only minutes to spare before his aunt arrived. Fortunately he had a set of keys, and it was not unheard of for him to get there before her.

She smiled widely at seeing him, and Mitch was surprised that it annoyed him more than usual. It seemed an automatic reaction and empty of meaning. His curt nod in response must have reflected this; Aunt Catherine hesitated, and peered at his shirt. He realized it was still covered in the grease and sweat from yesterday. "Laundry day?" she asked, and laughed uncertainly.

He muttered some excuse, and she nodded before he finished. *Nobody listens. What's it matter what I say?* He headed to the backroom for an apron.

Dave was already there, tying one on. As usual he ignored Mitch—or at least pretended to. *Why do you try so hard to show me that you hate me?* He shook his head and rubbed his temples at the unfamiliarly harsh thought.

"Move it." Dave shoved past Mitch, and glared back at him. "Fuck, you stink, man! When was the last time you had a shower?"

"Don't shout," Mitch said under his breath.

Dave turned back, his face clouded. "What did you say? Huh?" He marched up to Mitch and pushed him.

"I said don't shout!" Mitch stood his ground, standing over Dave, uncertain but assertive.

Dave blinked, confused. Mitch was *taller* than him. He usually seemed so small, crouched and shaking like a hunchbacked freak. He regained himself enough to say "Don't start shit with me," and left.

Mitch's heart was beating quickly. His fists were clenched. His head, usually clouded over with the urge to be quietly helpful, was blazing with something else. He didn't recognize it at first because he had never really felt it before. But he knew it was confidence.

Mitch heard a liquid sound, like something disturbing the flow of water in the pipes beneath the floor.

***

Very little changed over the next few months, at least visibly. Mitch continued to pursue his jobs with diligence, only now he was driven by the pride of his secret. Every day he could feel it beneath him, swimming through whatever pipes it needed to be nearest to him. Knowing it was there, watching and waiting, filled Mitch with a sense of assurance he had never known before. It was the confidence of one who knew he was the concern of a greater force. It was faith, pure and unsullied.

And at night, when everyone else had left, Mitch would wait for it to rise up. When it did he would sit on his stool and just watch it slither and explore the corners of the kitchen. He would marvel at its shape, and the ease with which it crawled about the kitchen, the spiky chunks of burnt remnants flowing over its skin like so many feelers. It would pull itself as far as it could, an umbilical trail of bile and scraps leading back to the drain. Apparently it could go no further than the kitchen. Occasionally it would sit in front of Mitch, pulsating and writhing, and Mitch would reverentially brush his hands over its skin.

Every moment of every day Mitch would think about it—he took to calling it the Seeping. He thought of the little drips of grease scattered about the kitchen that he had never been able to clean; under the shelves, in the corners of the ceiling. He wondered how long it had been beneath the diner, crawling through the pipes. He wondered what could have brought it to life. Most of all he wondered how long it had been watching him before it chose him.

His co-workers noticed that there was something different about Mitch, but weren't able to put their fingers on it. It seemed as though he had a lot on his mind, and was anxious to get back to it, whatever it was. She was rather relieved about that; Mitch had always seemed so devoted to his job that he neglected having an actual life.

To Dave, it was as if Mitch was starting to get uppity. Not in an out-in-the-open sense, but subtly. Whenever he had told him to do something before, the retard would usually grovel like a faggot. He still did what Dave asked, but like it was *his* decision to do so. And he smiled all the time now, like he knew something about Dave that he was just itching to hold over his head.

If only he could tell them; beyond the growing contempt he felt for his aunt and the amused pity he was beginning to feel for Dave, Mitch had few emotional ties to the world around him. His only concern now was the Seeping. Every night he would sneak some more scraps and fat for it, allowing it to grow. After hours he would see the fruits of his labor as the Seeping pulled itself along by a few more precious inches. Soon it was able to drag itself out of the kitchen and into the dining room.

More and more Mitch would plunge his hands into the thing, letting it investigate every crevice in his palms and every hair along his arms. An idea was starting to take shape in his mind. Mitch knew that the Seeping was intelligent in its way but still limited. There was something of the farm animal in it, sitting placidly in its spot before moving on a little ways, and then settling down again. He thought of the years of grease and scraps that had accumulated in the Seeping that gave it its form; the remnants of burgers and hotdogs and chicken, flakes of metal and hair, all sloshing together in a watery mix. The animals that had been made into the food had presumably not been particularly clever.

Mitch was beginning to feel very firmly what he must do to help the Seeping. The god had chosen him, had made its decision that he was the only one it could rely on to help it. He was *chosen*, and he needed to prove himself worthy of that choice. He would give the Seeping what it needed to be greater. To be smarter.

Mitch had to do it. He knew he could. He had *faith*.

***

It was night. The customers were gone. The waitresses were gone. Mitch's Aunt Catherine was gone. Dave was on his way out.

Mitch kept his head down, studiously scrubbing the counter, as Dave brushed past him to the back door. Technically, as manager, he was supposed to stay behind after closing to make sure everything was wrapped up. That he left anyway was something that Mitch used to tell Catherine and that she would always promise to look into. If she did it had done no good. It was still pretty much a given that Dave would leave early.

Tonight, Mitch was counting on it. He reached under the counter as he heard the door slam back open.

"*Shit!*" Dave rushed past the kitchen and to the office. Mitch hurried after him quietly, the knife in his right hand and the grease bucket in his left, suddenly anxious. "What's wrong, Dave?"

"You stay the hell away from me right now if you know what's good for you, Mitch. My fucking tires are slashed and I can't find my auto club card." He was sitting on the desk with a phonebook open on his lap, swiping at the pages. Quickly, before he could think about it, before Dave could react, Mitch made his move. By the time he was aware of it he had already stabbed him a dozen times in the chest.

Dave was gasping in pain and disbelief, and Mitch regained his senses enough to grab him by the hair and hold his neck over the bucket. Gingerly, he slit Dave's throat. A small amount of blood oozed into the bucket, mixing with the bit of water and grease that was left at the bottom. Mitch hoped that it would be enough.

Dave fell to the floor, wheezing his last scraps of breath. "*Hwhat…hyou…*"

Mitch backed away. He was starting to shake. The certainty, the rightness of his cause, was beginning to waver. "It's…it's for the god, Dave. My god. You're going to be a part of it now. It'll be better now…" He stuttered and hesitated, angry with himself. To show doubt now, at this vital moment, when the Seeping most needed him! "You're nothing, Dave. Not compared to the Seeping."

Dave stared without seeing, his breathing getting fainter and fainter. Mitch marveled for just a moment at the power he held now over his tormentor. In that moment, however brief it was, he reveled in it.

***

Mitch dumped Dave's blood down the pipe, using a spatula to scrape out the last of the slimy ichor. He wondered if the blood was too watered down, but reasoned that enough of the Seeping must be made of water at this point that it would make no visible difference. 'Reasoned' may not be the most accurate word to describe the miasmic slurry of emotions that were currently running through his mind; aghast horror at what he had done was being completely consumed by the heady sense of power he had felt as he did it, which was likewise subsumed by the fiery possession of his devotion to the Seeping.

The Seeping was one thing made from several others, but they were all animals. But if it knew what humans were like, how they thought, how they could be dealt with, it would be unstoppable. The world would witness his miracle, his god, and be amazed. And he would be revered as a prophet. The First Prophet in the Seeping Congregation.

Mitch knelt before the pipe, eyes to the floor, ready to welcome his god.

He waited. He heard the gurgling far below that usually signaled the Seeping's rise, and then nothing.

He continued to wait. His knees were starting to hurt but he was fearful of showing disrespect. He would prove his faith, however long it took.

After an hour a new noise was rising up the pipe. Mitch was momentarily relieved until he began to hear it properly; a trickle, faint but getting louder. As it reached the top he realized it was the sound of water quickly filling a space—

A spray of brownish fluid blasted Mitch full in the face. He fell back, sputtering at the filthy taste of it. Metallic and greasy, like blood.

The water gushed into the air for a few seconds, a brief, messy geyser, the last of it spurting out as something—a bloated black-and-red scab-like thing—popped up out of the end. It pulsed its way up, a solid, thick log of dark crimson meat, bulging as more of it was exposed to the air. The tip of it jerked around, as if looking for something, and dropped to the floor.

Mitch scooted away, still on the ground.

The end of the blob attached itself to the floor. Mitch could see bulges in its flesh as it pulled itself up from below and collected on the spot before him, like something lumpy being sucked up a straw. At the end it morphed into a meaty mass, like crimson dough, growing larger and larger as more of it was pulled up.

Mitch backed further away. This was not what he expected. The utter wrongness of this thing, this creature his god had become, was diminishing the fire that had possessed his mind. He whimpered uncertain, fearful things to himself, as he watched.

The confusion was back, replacing the serene certainty that had driven Mitch for so long now. He curled into a ball, crying as he listened to the slushing mess of the creature as it formed. Hot tears streaked down his cheeks as he muttered, and the pillars of his faith twisted into knots of grief and loneliness and guilt.

Mitch scarcely noticed when a hand was laid gently on his face. When a finger brushed a tear from his eye he began to stop shaking. It felt coarse and bristly, but smooth and slick, as though coated in gel. Mitch opened his eyes and for a moment felt comforted again.

The face was red as muscle, and covered with dark bristles that waved in swirling patterns of mesmeric complexity. Its eyes were two empty holes, ragged around the edges. Viscous yellow tears leaked down its cheeks. Its mouth was a jagged tear, gaping in the suppurating meat. The edges shivered as the thing wheezed, and the creature— the Seeping—the *god*—spoke.

"*Mitch…*"Its voice was low and deep, and sounded like a man drowning in blood. Mitch smiled in awe and gazed at his god through ecstatic tears. He held the tips of his fingers to the face of the Seeping, letting the yellow ooze stream down his hands.

The Seeping pushed him down, and sat on his chest. Mitch gasped as rubbery meat fingers clamped around his neck. He struggled as the creature brought its face to his ear.

"*You…teach me…worship. Teach…me strength. Teach me move. Teach me praise*" The Seeping smelt of rotted meat. Mitch's vision became spotty. "*Teach me I am…a god. Teach me sacrifice. Now I…I know. I know. Sacrifice teach me. I know dominance. I know fear.*"

It forced its fingers between Mitch's lips. The flavor of dry sausage skins caused Mitch to gag as his mouth was held open. He coughed and hacked, but the Seeping took no notice as it looked down his throat.

"*I take you. Shit. You sacrifice. I give. I give fear. I take worship.*"

Mitch could not scream as a rancid meaty hand was shoved into his mouth.

***

The coroner's report was as succinct as could be expected, in the circumstances. Dave Trenton, the manager of Cathy's Homey Diner, had sustained several stab wounds to his chest and stomach, and his throat had been slit. His body had been found on the floor of the office. The details were gruesome, but recognizable. Familiar.

The initial investigation seemed to suggest that Mitchell Graves, the owner's nephew, had committed the crime. Certainly the man seemed to have had a long history of mental difficulties, and the fact of his own corpse would seem to suggest his committing suicide directly after the crime. But one look at his corpse was enough to set the officers on the scene against that theory.

The coroner couldn't help but agree. For a start there were bruises on the man's neck, obviously indicating strangulation. His body was unnaturally pale for the recently dead. His mouth was wide open, the sides split, and several teeth were loose in their sockets. An autopsy revealed that his esophagus had been stretched and split, but otherwise nothing that should not have been there. He was, however, missing a few things that *should* have been there, mainly fluids: blood, bile, even stomach acid seemed to have been sucked from his body. There were no visible puncture wounds, seeming to suggest that they had been sucked straight from his throat.

There were footprints, of a sort, next to the body. They started in a pool of greasy water that had gushed from a nearby pipe. The suspect had apparently wandered about the diner for a bit before returning to the pool. Security footage outside the restaurant showed that no one had exited through the doors or windows.

But for all that, Mitch's fingerprints found on a knife confirmed him as the killer and thus closed the case for most of the authorities, there were those who would keep thinking back to that evening, to the puddle, to the bits of meat found in Graves' mouth.

And in the weeks to come, after the wave of kidnapping, the victims of 'vampiric' murders discovered; after the groups in ragged dirty clothing who called themselves the Seeping Congregation rioted in the streets; after the nights of terror when families barricaded their doors against the men of blood and bile; after even the day that would be called the Rising, when the bloated mass of fat and human fluid burst through the sewer grates and flooded the city, and the mad and the downtrodden screamed in horrid rejoicing; even then, the coroner would never forget the hint of blissful acceptance on the face of Mitch Graves.

A Real Slice of Americana
By Lisamarie Lamb

I think I want a divorce.

The words sprung to life in Joanne's head, and stayed there, growing, thriving, until they were running around on stubby little legs that tap-tapped at her brain, having a tiny temper tantrum when they knew they'd been heard, just to complete the utter annihilation of comfort and ease. They dared her to notice them. And, really, she couldn't do anything else *but* notice them, stuck in a car with the air conditioning competing with the country music blaring from the radio to make her equally nauseated and cold.

I'm fairly sure I want a divorce.

Joanne glanced across at Martin. She saw his hands resting lazily on the steering wheel, his sparkling wedding ring gleaming happily on his finger, pleased to be there, a brand new band, ready for anything. She looked down at her own; a bulky thing, not as pretty as the one she had admired and hinted at, circled in the catalogue, and then outright asked for. No diamonds for her. No swirls and graceful twirls. Just this ring that she would be stuck with for a while yet, and it was already scuffed and a little tarnished. It wasn't even engraved. She hid her hands in her lap and sighed. Martin didn't hear over the din of frigid air and Waylon Jennings. Or Willie Nelson. Or Johnny Cash. One of those guys, anyway.

Yes. Pretty sure I want a divorce.

Joanne and Martin had been married for ten days.

Joanne and Martin were on their honeymoon.

Joanne and Martin. Joanne and Martin. That was it

now. Coupled together until death and so on and so forth. It sounded painful. Joanne and Martin. It sounded final. Very final indeed.

Martin and Joanne sounded even worse.

Joanne stared out of the window and made herself deliberately dizzy, trying to catch and hold a fence or bush or – what was that? A cactus? Tumbleweed? – in her eye-line for as long as possible. It wasn't a fun game by any means, but what else was there to do? Sleep? She'd done enough of that. Too much. More than she ever thought she would, and it wasn't as good as she had imagined it would be. Twelve hours in bed? Wonderful! Only, no, it wasn't really. It was hot and sticky, it gave her a headache, and it was deadly dull. Eat? Well, yes, that would be good. Very good, since her stomach had been gurgling for the best part of the morning, shouting, screaming at her to do something, to give it anything, just to stop it from caving in on itself and fizzing away in its own juices.

And that was part of the problem, wasn't it? Part of the reason she was so pissed off.

"I'm starving," she'd said as Martin filled up with fuel. "Can you grab me a snack or something when you pay? A chocolate bar or something? Bag of crisps?"

Martin had shaken his head and grinned at her. "Nah, it's not that long to lunch time, babe. You can hold out a little bit longer, can't you? I promise, it'll be worth the wait."

Really? Joanne had forced out a smile, not wanting to cause a scene in front of the other motorists. "Sure. Okay. Only, I'm famished, and breakfast wasn't really much-"

"Oh?" Martin had asked, eyebrows raised. He carefully placed the fuel nozzle back where he'd got it and leaned into the car, through the open driver's window. "I thought it was pretty good. Pancakes. Maple syrup. Bacon. Really American. You don't get that at home, do you?"

Joanne had to agree. "True, but I'm still hungry. Just a bit of chocolate?"

Martin winked at her, banged the roof of the car and laughed. "We'll see."

Which meant he'd do exactly what he wanted to do and sod what she wanted. This was a little fact about Martin that Joanne had learned over the past ten days. She wondered how she'd missed it before. Too much in love to care. Too blind to see. Too stupid to deserve much more.

"Fine," Joanne had muttered through thin lips. Her eyes had narrowed, her forehead had furrowed, and she'd been in a bad – more than bad; utterly repulsive – mood ever since. Two hours now.

It was getting ridiculous.

And Martin had not bought her any snacks at the petrol station.

Joanne was so hungry she was beginning to wonder how the headrest would taste. She was beginning to wonder what the hell was wrong with all the perfectly fine fast food chains they were passing every bloody mile.

"We could stop there," she ventured. "It's got a few places to choose from. Pizza. You fancy a pizza?" *If you don't want a pizza, I'm definitely leaving you.*

Martin sucked at his teeth. "Nah, I don't think so. I know what I'm looking for. When I find it, we'll stop. I promise, babe." He reached across to Joanne's naked knee and squeezed. Joanne shuddered. His fat fingers did nothing for her except make her think of sausages. Delicious, moist, juicy, greasy sausages… Damn him. Damn his fingers and his plan, whatever it was. If it even existed.

"Not long now, I'm sure of it," Martin added, giving Joanne's leg a final pinch and then sliding his hand away, back to the steering wheel.

Not long now. True. One more week. One more week of hell. One more week and they'd be home. Back to work, back to life, and maybe, perhaps, possibly, things would work out okay.

Would she still be hungry then? Was this it, some kind of purgatory in which she was forced to pass by mouthwateringly perfect eateries in the search for something more, something better, something mythical? Like Sisyphus and his boulder, there was Joanne and her need for a juicy burger smothered in ketchup. Oh yes.

Just the idea of it made her stomach cramp up and her throat squeeze itself shut in tired submission. No food for you. Not yet.

And then…

"Here! This is it, this is the place!"

Joanne jumped at the sound of Martin's voice, unsure of what she had just heard. All she knew was that he was turning off of the motorway – highway – and parking. Actually stopping. In between a couple of giant trucks, their once-huge-now-tiny rental car sighed as its engine died, and they sat there, the two of them, newly weds in a parking lot in the heat.

"What do you think? Looks incredible, doesn't it?" Martin leaned forward, pressing his chest against the steering wheel, sweat already beading across his receding hairline now that the air conditioning was no longer wheezing out of the dashboard.

Joanne blinked through the windscreen. In front of her was a diner. A dusty, dirty looking diner that appeared to be empty of anyone other than truckers and the staff. "This?" she asked, unable to keep the disappointment out of her voice. Not really wanting to. Not caring enough. "This place? You mean you *intended* to come here all along?"

"Ha, that would have been a good trick!" laughed Martin, obtuse as ever. "No, I had no idea this was here, but it's just the place I was looking for. Who wants a chain when they can have a one-off piece of Americana like this? With real people in it, proper food. And the coffee! Can't you just smell it now?"

Joanne thought she could smell something, and it wasn't the coffee. *Bullshit. You are so full of it, Martin. I'm leaving you. Today. That's it. After we've eaten.*

"Shall we?" asked Martin, his eyes shining, his face one big, excited smile. "I'm buying."

"You'd better be," said Joanne. Martin glanced up at her, his happy mood failing for just an instant as they locked eyes. But then Joanne cracked a smile, just a tiny one, the smallest, and he relaxed again.

"Right."

"Right."

"Right." Martin exited the car and ran around the back of it to open Joanne's door for her. "Madam," he said, winking strangely as she slid from the fetid interior. Her legs were stuck to the faux leather seat and she was sure she had a wet patch on the back of her t-shirt. And possibly her shorts. She stood by the side of the car and plucked them from between her buttocks. "Are you sure?" she asked, nodding towards the diner. "It's a bit... Isn't it rather..." *Shabby? Shit? Shocking? Should we even dare enter when the likelihood is that the locals will rip us to bits as soon as pour us a coffee?*

But no one was listening to her words or her thoughts. She found herself alone, trapped between the big rigs, watching Martin's flabby back as he jogged towards the diner.

Damn you! "Damn you." Joanne hissed the words and then moved, not wanting to expel any energy but not wanting to take her chances out here with the trucks and the weirdos. Although they were probably already inside.

She didn't want to go in. It was a sudden and important thought that settled between her eyes and gave her an instant headache. She did not want to go in. It was not good. They probably did not serve pizza.

The slow molasses movement became a jog and then a run and then a sprint, but she was still too late. She couldn't stop her husband.

It seemed that Martin pushed open the door of the diner in slow motion, his hand outstretched, his head turning just so, staring at her, grinning like a kid with cake. He inhaled and, if it was possible, his mouth stretched wider. And then he was gone, through the door, into the diner, onwards without her.

Joanne wasn't that far behind when he entered the place, near enough for him to wait, but she knew, just *knew* after all these days or weeks or possibly millennia that they had been trudging around in that God-awful vehicle-car-*thing*, that Martin would be so happy to have found a dirty old truck-stop in the middle of Nowhere, USA, that he would forget about her and that the smeary glass door with its oh-so-jolly *Hi! We're Open!* Sign was going to hit her right in the face.

It did.

Joanne's anger slammed her palm into the door so hard that it stung and jarred all the way up her arm, and it made her hate her new husband even more. *I'm getting that divorce.* She glared at his back as he happily ran, like an over-excited child, to the counter and hoisted himself onto one of the red leather covered stools, the corrugated rim of chrome shining brightly under his arse.

At least she could understand what it was that was making Martin so happy, even if she couldn't understand *why* it did. Her breath caught in her throat before she could speak, and the more she coughed the worse it got. The smell. The musty, crusty smell. It smelled of grease and coffee and air conditioning and *America*. It was perfectly vile. But for Martin, it was perfect. It was just what he'd been looking for. It was another slice of pure cliché he could tick off his holiday list.

Joanne was sure Martin was happier than he had ever been, and that included standing at the altar with her. She wondered, briefly, and then the thought stuck and she wondered longer, whether he had only married her so that he could go on holiday. Live his dream. Drive around searching for the untainted, the real, the everyday.

She wouldn't put it past him.

Glancing around, Joanne spotted a few shifty looking individuals, all bib overalls and sun hats, all chewing gum or tobacco or manure for all she knew. Martin was the expert. Martin was the one who was so desperate to taste everything Americana that he had taken the money she had given him for their honeymoon, the money that was supposed to go on a trip to the Seychelles, or to Hawaii (still America, right?), anywhere that had a beach and cocktails and lots and lots of sun, and spent it on this trip. *This* trip. This was not a honeymoon. This was some kind of punishment. And Joanne spent much of the time when she was in the car – which was a lot of time – wondering what she had done to piss Martin off enough to do this to her.

She had wanted a beach. She didn't get it. She had wanted relaxation. Nope, not forthcoming. She was also keen on sun. Now *that* she was getting. She was getting that in bucket-loads. But it was not the sun she had wanted. It was not the warming, calming, tanning sort of sun that she had dreamed of as she leafed through the holiday brochures and grew more and more excited about a time after the wedding, the preparations for which had taken over her life for the past year. No, *this* sun was a blazing, burning, unrelenting sun that made her temper short and her body melt. It made her think bad thoughts and want to do bad things.

And she didn't deserve it.

The air conditioning in the diner was beautiful, gently kissing her boiled skin and then enveloping her in its dry coolness. She wiped the sweat from her brow, not caring that everyone was staring, not caring about the stains under her armpits or her straggly, rattail hair. She didn't care about anything other than getting some food (pizza? Get your pizza here!) and something to drink and forgiving Martin. It was the heat, she knew. It cooked her and her temper until they were both ready to explode. Arguments were bound to happen. Not that Martin had actually noticed.

Okay. Maybe not a divorce. Let's see what the food's like. Let's see... let's see...

Joanne pushed every nasty, naughty thought from her head and joined her husband at the counter. Husband. That was the key word. She had to remember that. She had to try. She plucked her sweaty shorts from between her buttocks and jumped ungracefully onto the seat. "There are booths, you know. Tables. With benches. Nice and private." She shifted, her thighs sticking to the seat and making a scratching, sucking sound as she moved. "We could have sat in one of them." The words were out before she could stop them and when she saw Martin's poor, happy, irritating face she wished she'd been more forceful – *I want to sit in a booth. We need to talk.*

But no. For Martin, the counter was the place. That's where they sat in the movies eating sweet potato pie and sipping iced tea.

She sighed, and picked up a menu. It was ketchup stained, sticky and laminated. More words; "We could sit in a greasy spoon at home, you know." Punching with them, hitting out at him with syllables rather than fists. And he just took the blows, not even seeming to take any heed. Did they touch him? Didn't he know she was getting ready to forgive him if he'd only acknowledge his mistakes? Didn't he know that her forgiveness was a time limited offer, and that if he did one more thing, just one more thing…

Martin turned to her. "We can go somewhere else if you like?" But his eyes were pleading and his voice was hesitant. And so she shook her head.

"No, here's fine." She let him win. Again. Too tired and hot and regretful to do anything else.

Joanne scanned the menu. No pizza, of course. But a burger seemed safe. She didn't recognise half of the items; grits and biscuits (the picture looked like a scone, and the idea of one of them smothered in strawberry jam and clotted cream was suddenly in her head, in her *mouth,* and she might have been drooling) and such like, and she didn't trust the idea of chicken when the slapdash state of the cleaning might be replicated in the slapdash way of cooking. *Yeah, that's about done, I reckon. Bit o' pink in the middle's good for ya.* At least undercooked beef wouldn't kill her.

"Howdy, sweethearts, what can I getcha?"

Joanne looked up from the menu and saw a peroxide perm under a red and white paper hat, and under that a gaunt face with the reddest lipstick and thickest mascara she had ever seen. The face was chewing gum, clacking and clicking it with her tongue. Joanne was, at that moment, sure that she had walked onto a movie set and wondered exactly what lines she was supposed to say and had instantly forgotten. Everything was so set up, so clichéd, that she could hardly believe it was real.

But it was real.

She knew that by the way that Martin gleefully asked for a coffee even though he never drank coffee. She thought about asking him why he'd done it, but the answer came to her before she could form the words. *Free refills.* He wanted to know whether the place really offered *free refills.* And he'd caffeinate himself to death to find out.

So instead of asking Martin why he had ordered coffee (she ordered a glass of iced tea – she never drank tea, iced or otherwise, but it was the first thing she saw on the menu and with the over-coiffed gum-clacking waitress hovering with a notepad and a pencil, she panicked and tea gushed out), she asked him why they were there. "And, also, where are we going? Do we even have a plan or are we just going to drive around until something happens to us? Just drive around until we die?"

Martin just shook his head. "No need for a plan, darlin'," he said in that coddling way she had loved before they had come on holiday (not honeymoon, she could not call it that) together for the first time. Now the tone seemed to smother her in its sweetly saccharine stupidity, seemed to suffocate her like a comfortable but nonetheless deadly pillow.

"Don't call me 'darling'," she said. What a rebuttal! What a response! She knew it was weak but she felt weak and all she wanted to do was find a nice – no, beautiful – hotel with no mould, no dust and no rust, and sink into the bubbliest bath she had ever had the pleasure to sink into. Hot. Red hot. And to cool her down a glass of crisp white wine. Tonight her prospects were either a crumbling motel run by potential psychopaths or a crumbling motel run by potential rapists. It had been the same every night.

Martin rubbed her back in his nauseating loving way. "Whatever you say, Jo, whatever you say." He grinned at her and she really and truly wanted to smack his face round to the back of his head. Smack him so hard that her fingers stung and then lost feeling. Smack him so hard that her own cheek hurt in sympathy. Although that was the only sympathy she would ever give him.

Forgiveness was no longer an option.

She was over that little moment of madness.

"Any food?" asked the waitress who had been listening to the entire conversation, such as it was, without blinking. Joanne wondered whether the waitress' eyes would open again if she closed them, the mascara was so thick. She wondered whether that was the reason the woman never blinked. "Grits and gravy," ordered Martin. He and the waitress (her name was probably Candi or Bambi or something) both looked at Joanne expectantly. "Oh, I'm not hu-" she began, but her stomach gave her away, growling viciously. "A burger," she said instead. "And chips. I mean fries. Fries."

"Coming up!" Clack, click, *smack*. And that sound was a dream to Joanne.

"Can you make that coffee decaffeinated?" called Joanne. It was a way of getting back at Martin. A subtle way. Joanne didn't think he had heard her, although the waitress waved in acknowledgement.

The food was a long time coming. Joanne's stomach was getting more and more agitated, and Martin had drunk four cups of coffee. *Thank Christ it's decaf,* Joanne thought, shuddering at the idea of a wired Martin, unable to sleep and plotting their next move, wherever and whatever that might be. But then again, she corrected herself, he never plotted, never planned, and that was half of the problem. The other half was that he was himself.

The *other,* other half was that she had known none of this before she'd married him. Romance was all very fine, and it had its place, but reality was better in the long run. *Now, Martin, I know you're having the time of your life, but I've got something to say...* She'd do it when the food was done with, not wanting to chance not being able to eat. And she had to word it so that she didn't sound like one of his damned country songs.

"I've got to go to the loo," Martin told her. He squeezed her shoulder on his way past. Joanne refused to put her hand out to squeeze back.

The waitress appeared behind the counter again. "Gone for a wander?" she asked, looking at Martin's empty seat.

Joanne smiled as politely as she could and shook her head. "Toilet. Restroom. Sorry."

"Well, now, don't be sorry, honey," oozed the waitress. She tilted her head to one side and then shot forward suddenly, quickly, leaning across the counter and staring into Joanne's eyes. Too close, but Joanne was too shocked to back up. Not that she had anywhere to go.

Candi/Bambi gushed a sweet cloud of breath over Joanne. "Nice guy? Your husband? He looks cute." And then she stepped back, jumping down, putting her feet back on the floor.

"Er," said Joanne. "Um." She blinked a few times. "Cute? Is he?"

"Isn't he?" asked Candi/Bambi. "I'd say he looks good enough to eat. But then, it's not my place."

No, it's damn well not! But instead of saying that or similar, Joanne half grinned, half grimaced. "I'm sure he'd be flattered." The words felt flat in her mouth.

The waitress noticed. "Everything all right with you guys? Of course, it's not my place…"

It may not have been her place, and it was certainly none of her business, but Joanne had to speak. Just had to.

"I think we might be getting a divorce. Or something. He's… Well, he's not what I thought."

The waitress nodded, understanding. "Divorces are messy. I should know, I've had three of 'em. Then I found this place. Job saved me."

"Sounds great," said Joanne, wishing she'd kept her mouth shut.

Candi/Bambi winked. "I'll chase up that burger for you."

After ten minutes Joanne began to get restless. Where the hell was Martin? Had that waitress said something? Hinted? What was going on?

After twenty minutes her burger arrived. But still no Martin. *Don't say he's gone.* Not when *she* was the one who was going to be doing any leaving that was going to be done. No. He was not that sort of man. Or at least, she didn't think he was. She realised she didn't actually know.

Joanne stared at the enormous, clearly homemade and handmade burger that was sizzling on the plate in front of her, and thought about waiting for Martin. She *definitely* thought about it. But she was so hungry and it smelled so surprisingly good that she took a big bite, just one bite, and she'd have the rest when he returned. But ten more minutes passed and the burger was getting cold. She could see its goodness draining away.

It wasn't fair.

She couldn't wait.

It really was the best burger she'd ever had. And she completely forgave Martin for everything, there and then, because of it.

She ate, bite after bite after mouthful after mouthful, not caring that the juice was running down her chin, not caring that she was dripping ketchup and fat down her top. Not caring that she could barely breathe with the effort of eating. She just wanted more.

"Good?" asked Candi/Bambi when she reappeared, wiping red tinged hands on her red tinged apron and smiling widely, nodding, already knowing the answer.

Joanne licked her lips enthusiastically. "Really good," she said even though her mother had told her never to talk with her mouth full. And then something occurred to her, just a little thing, hardly worth mentioning really, in the scheme of things, in the presence of the crumbs of the world's greatest burger; "Have you seen my husband?" she asked. "He's been gone for ages, he only nipped to the toilet."

Candi/Bambi smiled. It was a kind, pious sort of smile, the sort of smile that means someone's done something that they were secretly proud of but that might be frowned upon and so they couldn't possible comment. "Now, now, sweetheart, there's no need to be coy," she said, the words causing Joanne's brow to wrinkle and her chewing to stop. Reluctantly.

Joanne swallowed. *An empty mouth is all the better to question you with, my dear.* "What do you mean?" The words sounded thick with meat and bread and sauce. And was that relish? Pickle? Difficult to tell. Joanne took another bite. She hadn't meant to, but it really was the best... Was it beef? Pork? A mixture? Or was it something new, something exciting?

And then she got it. Understood the wait, the red, the meaning behind the secretive smirks and the understanding waitress and all of it.

Divorce was messy indeed.

Through a mouthful of her husband, Joanne ordered a second burger.

To go.

A Good Bit of Crackling
By Stewart Hotston

The clutch finally gave up the ghost a hundred miles east of Seattle's outskirts on US 2. John had been suspicious about the hire car price but he didn't have the luxury of choice. The journey to Spokane had to be made by car. It was bad enough that the only way to Seattle from London had been by jet; there was no way he'd willingly jump on some two bit internal flight where you could feel each and every vibration as the plane shook itself apart. The trip would take five times as long this way but he'd be on the ground and in control.

The acne ridden boy who'd rented him the car, the only manual shift in the entire place, couldn't have been nineteen yet already displayed the world weary cynicism of someone who had to deal with stupid all day, every day. John tried to be pleasant but the lad wasn't even remotely interested; he'd almost had to force his credit card into the man's hands. *Still,* thought John, *got to be positive. Even if,* he squinted at the youth's name badge, *Stew, isn't interested, I'll be gone in two minutes, on my way to meet Peach.*

Peach - the girl he'd met on the internet. The girl from Washington State, six thousand miles from home. *A woman,* he corrected himself, *who shares my soul, who understood me.* Not for the first time he wondered how it was that his soul mate lived half a world away. He didn't dwell on it except to remind himself that it didn't matter because he'd found her now. They'd have a chance. A green eyed, curly haired, red head with freckles so dense they merged in places. He was still uncertain about what he was doing, but if TV had taught him anything it was that chances like this didn't come back for people who watched them sail by. So he'd taken all his holiday at once then booked the plane. A dozen vodkas later he had unsteadily disembarked from the flight, waited in arrivals until he'd sobered up, then rented a tiny little three door box on wheels.

He leaned against the car, squinting as he remembered the scraping sound when he'd tried to change gears; a noise which had forced him to pull over in a cold sweat. He could still hear the car's painful shriek as he'd asked it shift to fifth. He was no mechanic, being more comfortable with the Care Standards Act 2000 than the care of sparkplugs, but he was pretty sure it was fatal.

He stood on the car, held his phone above his head and swung it about hopelessly; there was no signal out here. The road was straight as an arrow in both directions with giant firs and pines crowding close to its edges on each side as if they were only waiting for him to look away before invading the tarmac and erasing man's intrusion completely.

At least it isn't raining, he thought. The guidebooks had taken great joy in informing him that Washington was at the heart of a temperate rain forest where it rained, on average, for three hundred days every year. Two sights were on his list while he was out here; a giant red wood towering taller than a skyscraper and a foot long yellow slug robust enough to throw mountain bikers who ran over it.

He remembered passing a diner three miles back. He remembered because it wasn't the classic American curved aluminium pre-fab lovingly plonked on the side of the road surrounded by eighteen wheelers. Instead it was like the witch's house from Hansel and Gretel - but lit in neon spots and strips rather than candy and gingerbread. The car park had been empty, a rusting pick up without wheels with a popped hood sat in one corner.

In typical Yankee style is was called Oink's diner. The

sign glowed a frail pink in daylight and stretched along the whole length of the building. John popped open the boot of the car and unzipped the smaller of his two suitcases. He pulled out a neatly folded coat. He put the coat on, zipped it up, then carefully repacked the case. Locking the car he stared at the little three-door hatch back, trying to fathom what exactly he was going to do with it. In a moment of indecision he sat in the front passenger side seat and read the paperwork he'd signed. Breakdown cover was part of the deal, *so all I have to do is find a signal for my phone,* he thought with relief.

He walked for forty minutes. Just as the diner came into view an SUV pulled up alongside him. A gruff older man wearing mirror sun glasses in the thick blue evening light leant out of his window, "Fella, where're you headed?"

"Me?" asked John in surprise.

"Ain't no one else walking along US 2 is there," said the man looking over the top of the lenses at John as if he was mentally deficient. "You need any help?"

John looked at the unkempt beard and the rust patches holding the SUV together then at the diner a few dozen yards away. "I just need a phone."

The man looked with John at the diner and chewed on his whiskers. "They got nothing for you in there, son, jump in and I'll take you to Sheena's. Her eggs and strip bacon are just perfect."

"How far's that?" asked John, surprising himself by considering it. *There's something just a bit too whacky about Oink's,* he thought.

"Some twenty miles as the crow flies. Reckon an hour's driving. You coming?"

"Thanks for the offer, but all I need's a phone and

somewhere to wait for the tow truck," said John. He couldn't face adding another two hours to his journey.

The glasses came off and the driver looked at him long and hard, as a vegetarian might a turkey the night before thanksgiving. "This ain't a place for someone like you. Remember that."

John's heart leapt into his throat as scenes from horror movies about red necks and city slickers came unbidden to his mind. "Uh, thanks. I'll be fine." John backed away from the car. The man put his glasses back on, pulled the truck into gear and drove away in a cloud of midge-infested dust.

John stopped at the door to the diner, took in the tarnished chrome handle held onto the wooden frame by rusted in nails that was bathed in the glow of neon. The door opened silently onto an equally quiet room. He checked the closed/open sign on the door, *if the door's unlocked they've got to be open.*

"Slug, is that you?" called a woman's voice from the kitchen.

John looked around but he was the only person in the diner. "Hello?" he said hesitantly.

A woman in her late forties came through from another room to stand behind the counter. She whacked a grimy dishcloth over her shoulder and blew out a heavy breath, "You're a bit early. We dun't normally open till gone 6."

John was crestfallen. Seeing his dismay she said, "Oh it's ok, just sit yerself down an' let me know what you want. Slug's due now anyway and he'll cook you up fine." She walked back into the kitchen.

John looked around - the sheer choice left him standing there like an imbecile. He blushed, sat down at the nearest seat and pulled a laminated menu from between the ketchup and mustard.

"There you go," said the woman. "Tea. In a pot." She smiled at him expectantly.

He lifted the lid of the steel pot. Through the steam he could see two bags swirling gently. He didn't hold out much hope for the taste. Regardless, he was unspeakably grateful to this stranger. "Thanks, that's perfect."

She thrust a hand in his face, "Candice. Friends call me Candy."

He looked at the hand with its trimmed nails and then her face. "John. Thank you for this. You're a life saver."

"You're welcome," she beamed.

"And what do we have here then?" asked a booming voice behind them. Candy twirled to face the front door. John twisted in his seat. A gut wrenchingly huge man, carrying half a dozen bursting carrier bags, walked across the diner and behind the counter. He had piggy little eyes with short brown hair on a head whose folds of pale fatty skin hid a well structured jaw and cheekbones. John couldn't stop staring at his bulk, trying to imagine himself stood next to the man; he guessed he'd be staring moobs straight in the eye.

"Cat got your tongue has it?" asked the man with a toothy smile. *Like the Cheshire Cat*, he thought.

"Sorry." stammered John, "my car; it broke down a few miles back." *When did I forget to make the call?*

"You'll be needing a phone then?" asked the giant. John thought he detected a hint of an accent from the north of England. It was swallowed by a strong American twang but there were definitely guttural vowels hiding in there whose home was north of Watford.

"If you have one," said John.

Candy swung back to him, "By the restrooms honey. Do you need change?"

He patted his pockets theatrically but knew without checking that he had four hundred dollars in twenties in his wallet. He nodded before following her to the counter where she retrieved a handful of quarters from the tip jar.

"What can I cook for you while you wait?" asked the man.

"Um," said John, casting around for the menu.

"On the table. I'm Slug by the way. Least my friends call me that. Anything you want let you me know." The side of beef that was Slug's hand was thrust out in greeting. John shook it gingerly but was overwhelmingly relieved when he was neither crushed nor drowned in the man's sweat.

Returning to his table he picked up the menu and leant against the back of the chair. *Eggs with ham; bacon and waffles; bacon and sausage; sausage and pancakes; pork chops*...everything was pig. Even the steak came with crackling and ribs. The sides of corn on the cob, fries, hash browns and the like were cooked in pig fat. It didn't stop there either - the deserts had something swinish to them. *Jell-O, chocolate ice cream, now you're just being silly,* he thought. His eyes wandered back up the menu to the starters and mains; John was amazed to see pickled eggs, trotters, roasted belly, fried liver and potted tongue. He half expected to find the bones being sold out the back to corset makers.

"You guys like your pork." he said to Candy as he ordered.

"I'm a pickled eggs man," said Slug through the serving hatch. "Although a good pork chop does me fine."

"A good half dozen chops he means," said Candy sotto voce.

The diner's door opened. Through it came a small sweaty man with long, thin greasy hair that barely covered his liver spotted scalp. His nose was pressed up against his face in a manner so reminiscent of a pig's snout that John knew instantly he was looking at Oink himself. In contrast to Slug, Oink was short and lanky, like a collection of different peoples' bones in a sack of loose skin. Oink walked past John ducking into the kitchen without a glance.

John ordered eggs with ham, waffles and maple syrup, *when in Rome.* Candy shuffled back to the kitchen as well, leaving him alone among the red edged, white Formica tables and chairs. An ancient jukebox sat in the corner covered in greasy grime. *I hope the kitchen is cleaner - still beggars can't be choosers I suppose.*

Slug emerged from the kitchen a little later wiping his hands on a dishcloth. "So you're from Great Britain huh? Lived there once. Food was small."

Looking at the size of him John could well believe Slug's experience back home. "Where'd you live?" he asked.

"Leeds, father worked on a US base up north but wanted us to experience Britain. He figured it would broaden our horizons." He paused to stick a finger deep into his ear. When he was finished probing he examined the results of his excavation before sucking his finger clean. "Lived in Wales for a year. Great cafe there, a bit racist," he said as if remarking on the weather, "but they served a great black."

"I'm sorry?" said John awkwardly.

Slug frowned, but John had the sense that the man knew exactly what he was doing. "Black sheep? Beautiful breed, huge depth of flavour. Real flames render the fat down but leave it juicy and sweet." His eyes had glazed over.

"I'll have to try it," said John, trying to make the best of a conversation in which he felt he wasn't really a necessary part.

"Slug!" bawled a nasal New York accent through the hatch, "That delivery good for you?"

"I've seen it, I'm just checking so stop your belly aching," he shouted back. He turned back to John, "Chuffing owner thinks he can dump the supplies out here and I'll jump to it."

"Same the world over. Shit rolls down hill," said John.

Slug laughed, "you got that right. Hey, you travelling with family?" The giant squeezed himself into one side of a four-seater table.

"Family died when I was young. Brought up by an aunt." He sighed, "but in typical fashion she died too."

"Sorry man, didn't mean to make it deep."

"It's ok, I've been alone for most of my life at this point." He grunted with resignation and smiled at Slug, "Thing about us Brits is we're known for our stiff upper lips."

"You leave your girl with the car?" asked Slug.

"Girl? No. No girl." He paused, "nor man neither. Not my thing you know. Definitely girls for me." He stopped himself from continuing. He felt too nervous about Peach to tell anyone, let alone a stranger, that he had come half way across the world determined to fall in love with someone he'd never met.

"So what brings you so far from home?" said the chef. "Work?"

John shrugged, "nah, just travelling. Was hoping to get to Spokane today but," he realised he hadn't yet made the call to the car hire company, "Shit. Excuse me, I've got to call for help for my car."

"How far are you?" said Slug, small eyes twinkling as John started towards the phone.

"Two, maybe three miles east." said John.

"You know," said Slug, thoughtfully, "one of the locals could give you a lift to Spokane if you want. It'll be easier to fix your car there than getting someone out here."

John stopped fumbling with the coins Candy had given him and looked at Slug, "really? You'd do that?"

Slug laughed. "Why wouldn't we? You never know when you might need someone's help. Pass it on my sister says. Feed those that are hungry."

"It's a long drive. I'm not sure I could ask anyone to do that."

"You're not asking," said Slug. "I'm offering. At least a couple of the folks we see most days do this drive two, maybe three times a week. Any one of them would be happy to take you."

"What about the car?" asked John, thinking of how the obstinate car hire company. *Anything to avoid being dependent on them.*

"This is the United States. Everyone's got a tow bar."

That made up John's mind. He walked over to the counter and put the quarters in the tip jar. *I'll leave a proper tip too,* he thought, feeling more grateful than he could express.

"Guess I'd better get the dinner cooked," said Slug, who stood up like a floppy earthquake and strode back into the kitchen.

Over the next fifteen minutes people started to file in and take their seats. They mostly arrived alone, saying hello to Candy before choosing their spots based on where they had sat every single visit for all the years they had been coming. *It's like a memory played out in slow motion. A place where history, the present and the future are the same as each other,* mused John. His stomach rumbled its greedy response to the smell of frying that was wafting through the diner.

The sounds of people chatting to one another filled the diner with warmth. John spent the time watching these strangers live their lives, whether alone or with people they knew. He sat there trying to guess what they did or where they were going when they had finished. Candy took orders from most of them but nothing was served.

A glass of thick orange juice was placed in front of him, "On the house." said Candy. It was sweet like candy-floss making him wince at the taste.

"Is it okay?" she asked, her face tight with worry.

"No. It's fine," said John, feeling under the judgement of a dozen unknown faces. "More *orangey* than I'm used to."

A few minutes later his ham and eggs came out. The eggs were cleanly fried, the yolks runny and intact. The smell of heat, salt and corn oil made his mouth flood in anticipation. He felt tired looking down at his plate but was famished.

The ham wasn't like gammon or any roast pork he'd ever eaten; the flavour was peppercorn, woodlands, earth and caramel. *I'll bring Peach here,* he thought contentedly, dabbing at beads of sweat on his forehead. *When did it get hot in here?*

"How was everything?" asked Candy, clearing his plate from the table.

"Good." yawned John, ready to sleep where he sat. "Amazing how the body will demand you relax once it's satisfied."

"You betcha," said Candy and turned her attention to one of the others.

"When's it going to be ready?" asked one. Others rumbled their own dissatisfaction at having to wait so long.

It can't always be like this, thought John.

"It's here you ingrates," said Candy, "It's obviously not ready for serving is it."

"Ain't got all day Candy," said a white bearded grizzly in the corner from behind a pair of dark round glasses that helped John figure out where his face started and the hair ended.

"You just sit there, Mole, and hush up. You know Slug makes the best pulled pig and just the rest of y'all," she swept her gaze imperiously across the room, "keep yer tongues in yer heads until its ready. There'll be the normal snacks if you really can't wait."

Must have come in on a special night.

"Would you mind if I rang my," he paused, unsure how to label Peach. She was not really what he could call his girlfriend yet, *we've not even met.* He hoped desperately that she would be more than a friend.

"You got a girl you're visiting?" asked Candy, an expression he couldn't identify crossing her face.

"Kind of. More like a pen pal." He laughed, embarrassed, "I've never even met her. We've spoken a lot on the internet and I thought I should come see her for once."

Candy nodded, almost to herself. "You want to get there tonight hun?"

"I was going to surprise her," he admitted.

"Aww. How sweet."

"I'm so tired now," he said. "If it wasn't that I'd booked the hotel in Spokane I'd be thinking about sleeping in my car."

"There's no need for that," said Candy reassuringly. "Why don't you just relax. It'll all be over soon."

John felt awkward; although Slug had offered him a lift, he realised he had no idea about the who, or the when of the arrangements. He didn't feel he was in a position to ask - it seemed rude to hurry things along when it was entirely someone else's generosity he was relying on.

He laid his head down on the table, the sterile plastic surface was warmer than he'd expected. Somewhere behind him someone said, "Is he there yet?"

I wonder who they're talking about, he thought as he closed his eyes.

***

He was awoken by searing pain, but his mind wouldn't come together. The shock of his body being torn was far away, the immanence of it held at bay by a fog of confusion. He opened his eyes; he could see matt chrome lit by white fluorescence. His mouth was dry, when he parted his lips to scream no noise came. His tongue was swollen, heavy between his teeth.

The pain stretched in a line from the base of his back to the top of his neck. Breathing hurt so he tried not to move his head around too much. Hands pulled at the back of his head, they were huge. Blue twine dropped into his vision before sausage like fingers reached down and pulled it tight against his cheeks and nose. John groaned as the back of his head pressed painfully against a thin hard pole.

A gritty blue surface swung into view. *The floor.* Fear ripped through him, *please...someone help me,* he thought.

"Holy crap he's awake." said a woman's voice. It took John a moment to realise it was Candy. He couldn't turn his head to see even if he wanted to.

"Don't yank my chain," said Slug.

"I told you there wasn't enough in the juice," said Candy.

"There was enough that any normal person would have tasted the difference," said Slug.

"What are you two yakking about?" asked Oink in his New York accent.

"Fella's awake," said Candy.

"No shit," said Oink. No one responded. "You're not kidding?" A pimple scarred face appeared at the periphery of John's vision.

"Help," he croaked, tears spilling from his eyes and dropping to the floor beneath.

"Ha!" Oink laughed, "well I never." His face disappeared from view. "How long before the coal's are ready?"

"They're ready now." answered Slug, "Just got to make sure that the spit is in properly, wouldn't want to tear his skin when we turn him."

"That gravy of yours ready?"

"Will be once we collect the fat off this one. Always better when we add fresh juices."

"Help me," said John, the saliva in his mouth running enough to give him a voice.

"What's that pork chop?" asked Oink.

I know I'm going to die, thought John, *but please let Peach know I was coming for her.* All he managed was "Peach."

"Peach?" asked Oink, sounding surprised.

"Na," said Slug. Something large and hard was pushed deep into John's mouth. "I prefer apples."

The End

Dinner . . . has been served.

Biographies

The Chefs

Stewart Hotston (first & last stories) has been eating since he was born. He's managed to escape repeatedly from places he thought, at the time, were going to feature heavily in an anthology about deaths during dinner. In hindsight he should have kept a journal of these adventures because they might have been exciting to read. While he bitterly reflects on opportunities lost he writes stories and works with pretend money.

Chris Amies was born and grew up in South West London, and lived most of his adult life in Hammersmith (West London). He then returned briefly to Kingston upon Thames, and now lives on top of a hill in Birmingham. A languages graduate, Chris taught English in Greece, then worked for the British Civil Service for many years and now works for a housing association.

He is the author of one published novel, "Dead Ground" which with its sequel "Sea of Stone" is due out from Clarion shortly, and of several stories in anthologies and magazines since the 1990s. His stories have appeared in anthologies such as Music for Another World, Strange Pleasures 3, The Weerde, Eurotemps, and The Mammoth Book of Future Cops.

His writing partakes of horror, science fiction, and dark / urban fantasy. He is a member of the PoW-WoW writers group which meets at the Prince of Wales in Moseley and of the Grey Lodge horror writers group. He is a graduate of Arvon and was tutored there by the much-missed Iain (M) Banks.

Chris is currently working on a strange novel set in Hammersmith, a place he is often drawn to despite having left in 2005, especially its riverside hostelries such as the Blue Anchor. Further up the Thames he is fond of Stein's in Kingston, where he once experienced a perfect moment over beer and sauerkraut as the sun set and swans drifted by on the river. He is often to be seen about Birmingham on a bike.

Jay Wilburn lives with his wife and two sons in the coastal swamps of South Carolina in the southern United States. He left teaching after sixteen years to care for the health needs of his younger son and to pursue full-time writing. He has never looked back except to get material for his horror stories. His novels include Loose Ends with Hazardous Press and Time Eaters with Perpetual Motion Machine Publishing. His most popular collections are Dragonfly and the Siren which he shares with T Fox Dunham and the collection Zombies Believe In You. Follow his many dark thoughts at JayWilburn.com and @ AmongTheZombies on Twitter.

Elaine Pascale has been writing for most of her life. She took a break from fiction in order to give birth to two children and complete a doctoral dissertation. She lives on Cape Cod, MA, with her husband, son and daughter. She teaches a variety of courses at a private university in Boston: from English Composition and Communications to a Vampire Seminar. Her writing has been published in Allegory Magazine, Dark Fire Magazine, and several anthologies. She is the author of *If Nothing Else, Eve, We've Enjoyed the Fruit*, and is also the author of the nonfiction book: *Metamorphosis: Identity Outcomes in International Student Adaptation--A Grounded Theory Study*. Elaine is a vegetarian, yet she has written many stories about cannibalism. Her favourite place to eat is the Lobster Pot in Provincetown, MA.

James Brogden is a part-time Australian who grew up in Tasmania and now lives with his wife and two daughters in Bromsgrove, Worcestershire, where he teaches English. His first published short story, "The Pigeon Bride", won a competition in *The Big Issue* to find a 'modern midlands fable', and since then his urban fantasy fiction has appeared in various anthologies such as the British Fantasy Society's *Dark Horizons,* Anachron Press' *Urban Occult,* Fringeworks' *Weird Trails,* and the Alchemy Press' *Ancient Wonders* and *Urban Mythic.* In 2012 his first novel, the Birmingham-based 'The Narrows' was published by Snowbooks, and he was a winner of Den Of Geek's first talent showcase with his story *The Phantom Limb.* His latest novel, 'Tourmaline' was released in 2013, and he is currently working on a sequel. Blogging occurs at jamesbrogden.blogspot.co.uk, and tweeting at @skippybe.

Lizz-Ayn Shaarawi is a Texan lost in the Oregon wilderness. Her short stories have been featured in numerous anthologies including Fortunes: Lost and Found, Phobias, Ain't No Sanity Clause, and Shadows of the Mind. Her screenplays have been recognized by the Austin Film Festival, The Nicholl Fellowship in Screenwriting, and the International Page Awards. She is always searching for that elusive "next level" of writing and constantly strives to reach it. Though she won't turn her nose up at a good

French restaurant she prefers an old fashioned hole-in-the-wall type greasy spoon where you can get your steak chicken fried and your arteries harden just from reading the menu. You can find her random babblings on Twitter under her username @lizzayn

Richard Freeman is a full time cryptozoologist. He searches for and writes about unknown animals. He have hunted for creatures such as the yeti (a black or brown haired, giant, upright ape in North India), the Mongolian deathworm (a much feared burrowing reptile of the Gobi), the giant anaconda (a monster constricting snake in South America), the ninki-nanka (a dangerous dragon like beast from the swamps of West Africa), the almasty (a relic hominid in the Caucasus of Russia), orang-pendek (an upright walking ape in Indonesia), the naga (a giant, crested serpent in Indo-China) and the Tasmanian wolf (a flesh eating marsupial in Tasmania). He is the Zoological Director at the Centre for Fortean Zoology. This is the world's only full time mystery animal research organization. It is based in North Devon.

He writes mainly non-fiction books about cryptozoology, folklore and monsters including *Dragons: More Than a Myth?* , *Explore Dragons*, *The Great Yokai Encyclopaedia: An A to Z of Japanese Monsters* and *Orang-Pendek: Sumatra's Forgotten Ape*. However he has recently branched out into horror and weird fantasy with *Green Unpleasant Land: 18 Tales of British Horror* and *Hyakumonogatari: Tales of Japanese Horror Book One*. His influences include writers such as E.F Benson, M.R James, William Hope Hodgson, Manley Wade Wellman, H.H

Munro, Edward Lucas White, H.P Lovecraft, Clark Aston Smith, Alan Moore, China Mieville and classic TV horror and SF such as Dr Who, The Prisoner, Quatermass, Ace of Wands, Kolchak the Night Stalker, The Outer Limits and Sapphire and Steel.

Jack Maddox learned to write from old *Tales From the Crypt* episodes. His stories have appeared in *Splatterlands* and *Dark Moon Digest*, and his first novel, *The Dog: Necrophagus*, is available from Necro Publications/ Bedlam Press. He doesn't sleep much.

Stephanie Ellis BA(Hons) is a Southampton-based writer of both poetry and short stories whose favourite eatery is (or was) to be found in the centre of York; an Italian restaurant, it served up not only wonderful pasta but also a highly entertaining floorshow provided by the antics of its Italian waiters. Sadly I cannot remember the name but I really hope it still exists.

Her poetry has received regular publication in magazines, ezines, local and national press and has been shortlisted in a number of competitions. She has started to focus more on her short stories and, to her own surprise, has developed a taste - and some success - for tales with a macabre or sinister twist. This is a route which she is now developing further and her stories, which are being published by *Fringeworks* are the first steps in this. She is widely-read, favouring authors as diverse as Edgar Allan Poe and Terry Pratchett and is slowly returning to Stephen King after making the mistake of reading *It* when alone on a wild and windy night in a creaky old cottage. Her ambition is to write a novel, which she is currently planning, and to continue with her other areas of writing, one aspect of which involves compiling a collection of horror-themed poetry, believing as she does - and to quote a line from her own poem - that '*The darkness is my playground*'.

To support herself and her family whilst trying to achieve these goals, she currently works as teaching assistant in a secondary school. Prior to this she had spent several years as a senior software technical author and project manager for a technical publications company. Her stories and poems can be found on readwave.com and www.rhymeagainstrhyme.weebly.com.

Shenoa Carroll-Bradd lives in Southern California with her brother and dancing dog. She writes whatever catches her fancy, and has just launched a Victorian mystery series on Amazon with "The Widow's Painted Room". Say hello @ShenoaSays or keep up with her progress at www.sbcbfiction.net

Matthew Pegg lives near Leicester and writes fiction and plays. His last play 'Escaping Alice' was produced by York Theatre Royal in 2012. Previous work includes a street theatre show about Nicaragua, a one man adaptation of Twelfth Night and *Ant Farm*, a play for youth theatres set in an ant colony. He is working on his first novel.

Matthew has been an actor, director, graphic designer, and drama teacher. He was head of education in several regional theatres including Leicester Haymarket.

His current day job is running an arts organisation, specialising in street theatre, site specific performances, festivals and events. In 2012 he completed an MA in Creative Writing at Nottingham Trent University.

Matthew learned to cook at school, in the days when schools taught things like baking and how to change a plug. He can still change a plug and enjoys Chinese and Indian cookery. His favourite places to eat include The Woodhouse restaurant in Woodhouse Eaves, The Crown near Tettenhall and the takeaway Indian food van that used to park in Coventry shopping centre.

Matthew lives in a small Leicestershire village and used to foster cats for the RSPCA, many of which refused to be re-homed and stuck around, pestering him to be featured in a short story.

Matthew's website can be found at www.mpegg.co.uk

Sarah Gibbel lives in the United States. She studied English at Western Oregon University. This story was inspired by a conspiracy theory which claimed that a popular fast food chain was serving sacrificed children.

T. T. Trestle lives in Ottawa, Canada, a stone's throw away from the Parliament Buildings, assuming you have the strength of ten men and an exceptionally aerodynamic stone. His stories have appeared in various anthologies and magazines, most recently in *On Spec*. A short film based on "Having A Drink" is scheduled to be released in October 2013 or on the eve of the zombie apocalypse, whichever comes first (hopefully the latter). His favourite restaurant food is Zen Kitchen's somewhat oxymoronically named sesame-crusted local exotic mushrooms, a dish that is definitely not on the menu at Oges Tavern & Eatery. He can be reached at tt@tttrestle.com.

William Holden is an award-winning author of more than sixty short stories, and five books. *A Twist of*

Grimm (Lethe Press), a queer retelling of the Brother's Grimm fairy tales was a finalist for the 2010 Lambda Literary Award for Best Gay Erotica. His collection of horror stories, *Words to Die By* (Bold Strokes Books), received second place in the 2012 Rainbow Book Awards, and was a finalist for the American Library Associations, Foreword Book Award for Best Horror of 2012. *Secret Societies* (Bold Strokes Books), his first novel set in 18th century London during the time of the sodomy trials, was a finalist for the 2012 Lambda Literary Award. *Clothed in Flesh* (Bold Strokes Books), a collection of 18th century horror was released in 2013. As a former personal chef, when he's not writing, he is in the kitchen creating new and exciting recipes, including his own version of carbonara, which has similar effects on people as the version in his story. You can visit him online at www.williamholdenwrites.com

Rebecca Snow is a Virginia writer who shares her life with a variety of creatures, many of them are only found in her mind. She's been known to fashion stories from notes she finds scribbled on the backs of Mellow Mushroom receipts. Her work has been published in a number of small press anthologies. You can find her online at cemeteryflowerblog.wordpress.com and on Twitter @cemeteryflower. On Facebook, look for the bloody handprint.

Jason Norton is a lifelong fan of comic books, science fiction and monster-under-your-bed stories. He is a certified personal trainer and massage therapist. When he's not playing volleyball, he studies wilderness survival skills. Honest. Not even he could make that up. Jason and his wife live in Powhatan, Virginia. He has a son, two cats and two dogs. He prefers the son.

His work has appeared at/in Bewildering Stories,

Fiction Vortex, Gothic City Press, Daylight Dims, e-Horror, The Horror Zine, Inner Sins, Dark Moon Digest and Pro Se Productions. He currently has stories awaiting publication at Nightmare Illustrated, Horrified Press, Pro Se Productions and Angelic Knight Press. He still cries pepperoni-scented tears when he thinks back to glorious evenings spent around a large supreme at Perini's Pizza in Farmville, Virginia.

Daniel Hale is an amateur storyteller living in Massillon, Ohio. He has been published in Beorh Quarterly, Revolt Daily, the "All Hallow's Evil" anthology of Mystery and Horror, LLC., and the "What Has Two Heads, Ten Eyes, and Terrifying Table Manners?" anthology of Mega Thump Publishing.

Lisamarie Lamb started writing in her late teens but it was only with the birth of her daughter that she decided to write more seriously, with the aim of publication. Since that decision almost three years ago, she has had over thirty short stories published in anthologies and magazines.

In November 2012, Dark Hall Press published a collection of her short stories with a twist, entitled Over The Bridge.

Her second short story collection is to be published by J Ellington Ashton Press in November.

She has collaborated on - and edited - a project entitled A Roof Over Their Heads, written by six authors from the Isle of Sheppey about the island where she lives with her husband, daughter, and two cats.

Cover artist Stephen Cooney has been a fan of art for as long as he can remember. Watching fantasy and horror in his youth served as a model of inspiration for his art, as did his dreams of designing heavy metal band album covers. He attended Exeter Art School, but felt it was not a good fit as his teachers didn't fully "get" the dark nature of his artistic inclinations. After years of painting, a tattoo artist fell in love with Stephen's work and hired him to design tattoo flash, which in turn led to him taking up the art of inking clients himself. Since returning to his first love of painting, he has involved himself largely with horror and fantasy projects but welcomes opportunities to move outside of those genres. His influences include Derek Riggs , Ken Kelly, and Edward J. Repka, all artists who design album covers. Stephen and his wife Amanda live in the UK and have two children, Hayley and Steven Junior. Look for his website soon.

The Head Chef

Theresa Derwin has lived in Birmingham since birth and her career has been pretty varied; from Warehouse Packer, then bar work, to being a crap waitress then swiftly into retail, Admin, Professional Student and dosser until finally entering the Civil Service in 1999. She left the Service in 2012 to pursue a career as a writer.

Theresa writes humorous fiction including SF, Urban Fantasy & Horror. She has about seventeen anthology acceptances behind her. She also writes a number of book reviews and at her site www.terror-tree.co.uk

She has loved horror, fantasy and SF all her life, thanks to my father who raised her on 50s Sci-Fi Universal Monsters, tango and popcorn. Her love of the bizarre, (including her Dad) remains constant, to this day. She also owes a great debt to Rog Peyton from the BSFG who introduced her to alternative fiction at the tender the age of 14.

Theresa bought horror imprint KnightWatch Press (www.knightwatchpress.co.uk) on 1st July 14 and intends to take the horror world by storm.

You can follow Theresa on Twitter @BarbarellaFem or find out more about her work at www.theresa-derwin. co.uk.